A Wedding to
REMEMBER

IN CHARLESTON, SOUTH CAROLINA

A Wedding to

REMEMBER

IN CHARLESTON, SOUTH CAROLINA

ANNALISA DAUGHETY

BARBOUR
PUBLISHING

© 2012 by Annalisa Daughety

Print ISBN 978-1-61626-534-2

eBook Editions:
Adobe Digital Edition (.epub) 978-1-60742-780-3
Kindle and MobiPocket Edition (.prc) 978-1-60742-781-0

Scripture taken from the HOLY BIBLE, NEW INTERNATIONAL VERSION®. NIV®. Copyright 1973, 1978, 1984, 2011 by Biblica, Inc.™ Used by permission. All rights reserved worldwide.

This book is a work of fiction. Names, characters, places, and incidents are either products of the author's imagination or used fictitiously. Any similarity to actual people, organizations, and/or events is purely coincidental.

Cover design: Faceout Studio, www.faceoutstudio.com

Published by Barbour Publishing, Inc., P.O. Box 719, Uhrichsville, Ohio 44683, www.barbourbooks.com

Our mission is to publish and distribute inspirational products offering exceptional value and biblical encouragement to the masses.

ecpa Member of the
Evangelical Christian
Publishers Association

Printed in the United States of America.

Dedication

This book is dedicated with love to my grandmother, Ermyl McFadden Pearle. You taught me to roller skate when I was four and you've been teaching me things ever since. Thank you for answering endless questions about gardening and cooking, saving articles that you think I might want to read, and always having time to talk. Knowing that you are praying for me gives me the courage to face any situation. If there ever was a woman who embodied Proverbs 31, it is you. Thanks, Grandma, for being an example of the kind of godly woman I strive to be. I love you.

Acknowledgments

Thanks to all who helped me as I wrote *A Wedding to Remember in Charleston*. Freda Pearle Mixson and Carol Pearle Bates—thank you for your wonderful Southern hospitality and for answering my many questions about life in Charleston. I so enjoyed spending time with the two of you during my visit to South Carolina. Vicky Daughety, Sandy Gaskin, Jan Reynolds, and Lynda Sampson—thanks for reading along as I wrote and for your honest feedback. Megan Reynolds and Kelly Shifflett—thanks for checking on me frequently as I was faced with back-to-back deadlines. I am blessed to have such an amazing support group of people who encourage me and pray for me as I write.
Thanks to the team at Barbour Publishing and to my agent, Sandra Bishop, for the support and encouragement.

He heals the brokenhearted and binds up their wounds.
PSALM 147:3

Chapter 1

Summer Nelson blinked against the bright sunlight that filtered through oak trees older than time, their branches heavy with Spanish moss. She squinted at a tall figure in the distance, solemnly looking down at an ancient headstone. A figure she recognized, even though it had been at least fifteen years since she'd last seen him.

Summer had grown up hearing tales of the many ghosts that inhabited Charleston. She'd scoffed at the idea of homes haunted by long-dead Confederate soldiers, and she'd certainly never given any thought to attending one of the Ghosts of Charleston walks that took place in the historic city almost every night.

But on that random afternoon in late May, she encountered a ghost of her own. Except that Jefferson Boudreaux was the worst kind of ghost. The flesh-and-bone kind that served as a direct link to a past long forgotten. Or at least a past mostly forgotten, except for those sleepless nights of late when she couldn't stop herself from wondering if she'd chosen the right path.

Summer and Jefferson had been the "it" couple of their tightly knit circle since their days in cotillion. Everyone had always expected the two of them to marry and settle into a life of Charleston society. Jefferson would follow in his daddy's footsteps and run for office, and she would host garden parties and raise their perfect children.

Yes, that was the path everyone—particularly Summer's parents—had expected her to take. And Summer herself had been on board with that plan—for the most part.

Right up until the lazy July afternoon when she met Luke Nelson. Sweet Luke, who mowed the yard of her family's enormous South of Broad home—the same home her great-great-granddaddy had somehow persuaded the Yankees to leave alone all those many years ago.

She watched the man in the cemetery for another long moment, not daring to move a muscle. She'd grown so still and cold, she couldn't tell where the stone bench ended and her body began. "Jefferson," she finally whispered, her voice tinged with uncertainty. Maybe the man was a look-alike tourist who just happened to be standing at the Boudreaux family plot. Because the alternative wasn't something she wanted to face.

But as soon as the name escaped her lips, the tall man turned toward her, and his tanned face broke into a smile.

And with a few long strides, Jefferson Boudreaux walked right back into her life.

Luke Nelson chewed on the end of his pencil, a habit he'd had since his school days when yellow number 2 pencils were harbingers of standardized tests. Most of the kids feared taking tests, but Luke lived for those days. He'd always been a good test taker. Inevitably when the scores came back each year, his were the highest in the class. His teachers expected great things from him, but his daddy had sneered at Luke's academic aspirations. "No son of mine is going to spend his days in some stuffy office like he's better than the rest of us," Daddy would say, usually with whiskey on his breath.

Luke had never aspired to follow in his father's footsteps, never been one of those little boys who idolized their dads. Roy Nelson had always been hardest on his oldest son. While Luke's sister and baby brother might have been able to avoid Roy's wrath, Luke hadn't been so lucky.

But the past was the past, and he certainly didn't want to spend time dwelling on it now. He tossed the pencil onto the table and leaned back in his chair. Why was he having so much trouble with this song? The tune had been in his head for weeks, but getting the lyrics right was causing him all kinds of problems.

He stood and paced the length of the living room, decorated with furniture that had been in Summer's family for generations. When they'd first moved into the spacious South of Broad home after they'd gotten married, he'd been a nervous wreck. "What if I spill something?" he'd asked.

Summer had just laughed. "This isn't a museum. It's our home." She'd tipped her glass of sweet tea so a little dribbled onto the tiled kitchen floor. "See?"

Sometimes it was hard for him to believe they'd been husband and wife for nearly seven years. And yet their anniversary was coming up in a few weeks. He had the perfect gift in mind, too. He might not be the world's best husband, but he'd been able to make Summer happy. At least most of the time.

The opening strains of a George Strait song pulled him from his walk down memory lane. He grabbed his phone from the table and punched the button. "Yeah?"

"How do you feel about shooting some pool tonight?" Justin Sanders asked.

Luke exhaled loudly. He didn't want to let down his closest friend and the drummer in his band, but he'd already been out two nights this week and they were playing a gig on Friday evening. Summer hadn't said anything about all his time away from home, but she'd sure given him the cold shoulder this morning. "I don't know."

"Come on, man. Jimmy and Will have permission from their wives for a boys' night out. Don't leave us in a lurch."

He looked at the silver clock on the end table next to the couch. It was already after six. Summer must be working late again. Last night she hadn't gotten home till nearly ten. So maybe she wouldn't care if he made plans. "Yeah, okay. I'll be at your place in half an hour."

"Summer Rutledge." Jefferson Boudreaux grinned down at her. "I don't believe it."

"It's actually Summer Nelson now." She shaded her eyes with her hand. "But I think you know that."

"Things can change." He winked. "Mind if I sit down, Mrs. Nelson?" he asked, his green eyes twinkling.

Summer regarded him for a long moment. "Sure." For a second, she wondered how she looked. Had she aged a lot in the years since they'd seen each other? Just that morning she'd plucked out a gray hair. Granted, she'd looked hard to find it. But today had been the first time she ever wished she were blond instead of brunette, just so the gray hairs wouldn't be as obvious when they really started sprouting.

Jefferson sat down on the bench next to her. "I figured I'd run into you at some point, but the cemetery isn't exactly what I expected." He motioned around the secluded grounds.

She didn't meet his eyes. "It's so peaceful. And you know how I've always loved the old cemeteries around here." Most of the numerous churches in downtown Charleston had a cemetery on their property, some with graves that dated back to the 1600s.

Jefferson gestured at the ancient headstone in front of them. "No one you know then?"

Summer bit her bottom lip. She'd found this grave about six months ago and felt drawn to it. So much so that she'd begun to visit at least weekly, sometimes bringing flowers. "Nope." She patted the edge of the stone bench. "I just like this spot because there's a place to sit."

Jefferson was silent for a long moment. "So how are you? I guess it's been. . ." He trailed off and glanced at her, his eyebrows raised in question.

"Fifteen years," she finished for him. "Graduation night." She and Jefferson hadn't exactly remained friends after she'd dumped him for Luke. The breakup had split their circle of friends in two. But on the night of their high school graduation, they'd all posed together for one last picture, mostly at the prompting of a group of overbearing mothers wielding cameras.

He nodded. "That's right." Jefferson flashed her a gleaming smile. "I think Mom still has a framed picture of all of us from right after the ceremony." He shook his head. "It took her a long time to accept the fact that you and I were no more."

Summer let out a breath. "Yeah. But I'm sure she's over it by now." She glanced at him. Time had certainly been kind to Jefferson. If anything, he was even better looking now than when they'd been eighteen. His shoulders were broader and encased in what looked like a very expensive suit. The hint of crinkles around his eyes when he smiled and a tiny bit of silver mixed in with his dark hair gave him a distinguished look. The difference in the way men and women aged was totally unfair.

Jefferson chuckled. "Clearly you underestimate your power. Every girl I've ever introduced her to has tried and failed to live up to the memory of you."

Her face flamed. "Whatever." She shifted uncomfortably on the stone bench.

"I hear your business is doing well. Mitch keeps me posted on the latest with everyone here."

Summer's younger brother, Mitch, had been one of Jefferson's best friends. "I don't see him very often." She hated saying the words aloud. She and Mitch had been close once. But they'd drifted apart after she left home for college. These days they only saw one another on major holidays, and that was only because their grandmother insisted she show up. And since Gram had always been so good to her, Summer obliged.

Jefferson nodded. "That's what I hear."

Obviously her brother still had as big a mouth as ever. "This is my busiest season," she said, as if that were the reason behind her behavior.

"And how's Luke?" Jefferson's green eyes bored into hers.

"He's great." The less said about Luke, the better. "We're very happy." She hoped her voice didn't give her away. The last person on earth who needed to know that things in her life might be less than perfect was Jefferson. Not only would he probably take personal satisfaction in that knowledge, but he also wouldn't think twice about sharing it with her family.

His eyes searched her face. "I heard about Luke's brother. I'm so sorry. I remember how close they were."

She nodded. "It's been a trying year, but we're making it."

"I'm glad to hear it." He cast one more gaze at the headstone in front of their bench. "Wow. Sad story here, huh? Only a day old." He shook his head and stood to trace his fingers over the cherub that sat on top of the stone.

Summer rose and grabbed her bag from beneath the bench. She suddenly wanted nothing more than to be away from the cemetery and away from Jefferson. "It was nice to see you again. I hope you have a great visit." She turned to go.

"Oh, it's not just a visit," he said quietly.

She turned slowly to look at him.

"I'm back for good."

Chapter 2

Ashley Watson sat on a park bench at the Battery, her face turned upward and warmed by the diminishing sun. When she first moved to Charleston, she called the spot White Point Gardens, like the guidebooks said. But now that she was a local, she knew to refer to it as the Battery. A seagull squawked from its perch on the wooden rail that ran the length of the promenade.

Anytime she regretted packing up and moving hundreds of miles to Charleston, all she had to do was come to the Battery. A few minutes of watching the boats and breathing in the salty sea air, and Ashley knew she'd made the right decision. She'd always heard that the ocean had healing properties. Although after three years of coastal living, her heart was still bruised. Maybe not broken anymore but definitely not whole.

"Thanks for meeting me," a familiar voice called.

Ashley looked up to see Summer leading her huge dog, Milo, down the sidewalk. Or maybe Milo was leading Summer. It was hard to tell. "Hey," she said, rising from the bench. She bent down and scratched Milo behind the ears. "Is it possible that he's even bigger than he was the last time I saw him? And that was only last week."

Summer chuckled. "That's one reason we came out for a walk today. Poor Milo has paid the price of our crazy lives." She knelt down and nuzzled the big chocolate Lab. "He's become a bit lazy and has packed on some extra weight."

Ashley watched her friend adjust the harness around Milo's big midsection. Summer and Luke had rescued Milo from the side of the road when he was a puppy. He'd become like their child. Summer even brought him to work sometimes. "Where are we headed?"

Summer stood and looked out over the water. "I don't care. Let's see where the road takes us."

Ashley raised her eyebrows. Summer had never been one to see where the road took her. Everything she did was planned, usually down to the minute. Something was on her mind, and Ashley had a good idea of what it might be. "Sounds good."

They headed toward South Bay Street. It wasn't even June, and already tourists were out in droves, most of them trying to soak up the remaining sunshine before they'd head to Hymen's Seafood or Slightly North of Broad for dinner.

"Thanks for all your work lately," Summer said after they walked in silence for a few minutes. "I know I've dumped a lot on you, especially with these last couple of weddings."

Ashley smiled. "No problem." She loved working with Summer as an event planner at Summer Weddings. She'd started out answering phones a little over a year ago, but as business had picked up, she'd taken on more responsibility. "I know you've had a lot on your plate over the past few months." Ashley hadn't complained about the added responsibilities, mainly because Summer was her friend. But it had been kind of a burden to carry most of the workload alone. In fact, the long hours she'd been keeping almost made her thankful she was single. There was no way her hectic schedule would allow for a meaningful relationship. Although having a date every now and then might be nice.

"Still though, you've stepped in and kept things going when I could barely get out of bed." Summer shook her head. "I want you to know that it hasn't gone unnoticed."

"I appreciate that." Ashley wondered if this was a good time to approach Summer about her idea of growing the business. Of course, part of the growth she hoped for included becoming a partner and not just an employee. But Summer seemed distracted today, plus she didn't want the request to put a strain on their friendship.

"Mind if we sit for a minute?" Summer motioned toward a bench.

"You and Milo lead the way," Ashley agreed.

They sat in silence for a moment, watching people walk past. Finally, Summer cleared her throat. "Luke's out with the guys again tonight."

So that's what this was about. Luke. "*Again*, you say?" Ashley asked.

Summer didn't talk about her relationship with Luke very much anymore. In fact, some days she didn't mention his name at all. Ashley had been worried they might be headed for trouble but wasn't sure how to broach the topic.

Summer tucked a wayward strand of dark hair behind her ear. "Yeah. Monday night his band played at some little dive bar. Then Tuesday was bowling night. Last night I had that event at the art museum, so I didn't get home until late. And tonight when I got home, he'd left me a note that he was playing pool with the guys." She met Ashley's eyes. "It's like we see each other less and less."

Ashley was in no way qualified to dispense relationship advice. But she considered Summer one of her closest friends. And Luke had always been quick to help her out, especially when she'd moved from an apartment into a house. He'd rounded up his buddies, and they'd moved her stuff in less than a day. "Can you talk to him? Maybe try to carve out time this weekend to go on a date or something? Or cook a nice dinner and have an evening in?"

Summer sighed. "That would all be nice. Except that Luke has some big gig on Friday night. It's the opening of the outdoor deck at some little restaurant on Folly Beach. I think he's hoping it might turn into a regular thing."

"Saturday then?"

"We've been summoned to my parents' house on Saturday for a family barbecue." She rolled her eyes. "Believe me, I don't want to go. Luke doesn't even know about it yet, and I know he's not going to be happy." She absently stroked Milo's head. "But Gram called me on my way home from work and asked me to come." She smiled. "Okay, she *told* me to come, but she said it nicely."

Ashley grinned. Summer's grandmother was the epitome of a Southern belle. Sweet as the tea they serve at Jestine's Kitchen, but not someone to be crossed. She thought for a second. "Tell you what. I don't have anything to do on Friday." Her stomach lurched for a second at the thought of being out on the social scene. She mostly kept to herself. But lately she'd started to worry that she was becoming a sad, lonely old lady. All she needed were a couple of cats and a flowered muumuu and her face could practically be on the Old Maid card. "So what if we surprise Luke? How long has it been since you've seen him play?"

Summer chewed on her bottom lip. "It's been ages. Seriously. He wouldn't know what to think if I showed up to see him." Her face suddenly brightened. "But that's a good idea." She glanced at Ashley. "You sure you don't mind coming with me?"

Ashley forced a smile. "I'd love to." She needed something to get her out of her comfort zone. "Besides, I've never heard his band play. It will be fun."

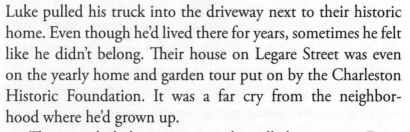

Luke pulled his truck into the driveway next to their historic home. Even though he'd lived there for years, sometimes he felt like he didn't belong. Their house on Legare Street was even on the yearly home and garden tour put on by the Charleston Historic Foundation. It was a far cry from the neighborhood where he'd grown up.

The outside light came on as he rolled to a stop. For a second, he thought it meant Summer was waiting up, but then he remembered the motion sensor they'd had installed a few months ago. There was a time when she'd sleep on the couch until he got home because she said she couldn't stand to be in their king-sized bed without him. But those days were long gone.

He quietly let himself in. The alarm wasn't set, and Milo didn't meet him at the door. That meant Summer was letting the big dog sleep in their bed. Again.

He punched the code and armed the alarm before he went upstairs. Summer forgot to set the alarm more often than not these days. In the old days, he would've teased her for being scatterbrained, but not anymore.

Luke avoided the creaky spot on the next to last step as he reached the top of the stairs. If she was asleep, he didn't want to wake her. He knew how much trouble she had getting to sleep. A glow coming from their bedroom told him that she'd at least left the lamp on so he didn't have to walk in total darkness.

He tiptoed into the master bathroom and closed the door before he flipped on the light. He'd grab a quick shower and save himself a little time in the morning. He worked as a park ranger at Fort Sumter, and his shift started promptly at eight. He'd been late a couple of mornings recently and didn't want his boss to think he was making a habit of it. It might not be his dream job, but he enjoyed it.

Luke opened the linen closet door to grab a towel and noticed the overflowing clothes hamper. He'd asked Summer this morning if she'd be doing laundry tonight and she'd said yes, but clearly that hadn't happened. And he'd worn his last clean ranger uniform today. *How hard is it to remember to do a load of laundry?*

He dug through the hamper and came up with three uniforms. Looked like he was in for an even later night than he'd anticipated. It would easily be after midnight by the time they were dry. He quickly brushed his teeth then grabbed the dirty uniforms. Stepping out into the bedroom, he saw Milo's head raise from *his* pillow. *Some watchdog.*

He walked over to his side of the bed and tugged his pillow from beneath the large dog. It was amazing. On his dog bed, Milo slept curled up in a surprisingly tiny ball considering his size. But whenever he had permission to get in his and Summer's bed, the dog insisted on taking up as much space as his large frame would allow.

He tucked the pillow beneath his arm. He'd sleep downstairs in the guest room tonight. He paused at the door and glanced back inside the bedroom. Summer hadn't stirred through all of the commotion. Either she was sleeping soundly or she had nothing to say to him.

Luke headed to the laundry room downstairs, stifling a yawn.

Tomorrow was going to be a long day.

Chapter 3

Summer waited until she heard Luke's foot hit the squeaky spot on the stairs before she sat up. As soon as he had gone into the bathroom, she remembered his work uniforms needed to be washed. She might be the worst wife ever, but she'd sooner walk across hot coals than admit to him that she'd forgotten. He probably thought she'd done it out of spite over his impromptu boys' night out, and she'd let him think so. Served him right.

She leaned back against the plush pillows and put a hand on Milo. She'd read somewhere that stroking a dog's fur helped to calm people when they were under a lot of stress. She'd certainly put that theory to the test over the past few months. Her stomach knotted as she thought about Saturday's barbecue. It had been weeks since she'd seen her family. And she knew it would be a fight to convince Luke to go with her.

She rolled over and burrowed further underneath the covers. Sometimes she wished she could stay there forever.

The next morning, she grabbed her pink robe and padded downstairs. Milo trailed along behind her, stretching and yawning as he went. "Hey," she said, stepping into the kitchen.

Luke stood at the counter, slapping turkey onto a slice of

bread. He covered it with the heel of the loaf and shook his head. "We're out of bread."

"Good morning to you, too." She grabbed her favorite mug from the cabinet and filled it with coffee. Luke's sweet gesture wasn't lost on her. He didn't drink coffee, so the fresh pot had been made just for her. But she didn't mention his kindness. It made her feel too bad. She couldn't even remember to get bread for his sandwich, yet he'd made her coffee.

"Mornin'." Luke slid his sandwich into a ziplock bag. He leveled his brown eyes on her.

Those brown eyes might have been the reason she fell in love with him in the first place. Summer could still remember the day they met. She'd been sitting in the hammock in the backyard, reading *Pride and Prejudice* and wondering if she'd ever meet a man like Mr. Darcy. She hadn't realized anyone was watching her until he cleared his throat. She looked up to see Luke standing there, a sheepish grin on his handsome face. "Hey," he drawled softly. "I didn't mean to scare you."

She quickly closed the book. Her friends made fun of her for reading too much, especially when they caught her with her nose buried in the classics. "You didn't."

"I'm Luke. Luke Nelson." A shadow crossed his tanned face. "I'm helping my uncle this summer. He owns a landscaping company." He motioned toward the push mower. "Hope it doesn't disturb your reading." He smiled. "That's a great book."

At that moment, Summer looked into Luke's chocolate brown eyes and felt her heart skip a beat.

They were seventeen at that first meeting. At thirty-four it was hard for her to fathom that she'd known Luke for half of her life. And there had been lots of times over the years when Luke's slow smile and beautiful eyes had made her heart skip beats. But that happened less and less these days. Sometimes it seemed like she barely knew him anymore.

"I'm sorry I forgot the bread." She took a sip of coffee and watched him grab a bag of Doritos from the pantry. "I'll go to the store on my way home today so you'll have lunch tomorrow."

He put his sandwich and the chips into his lunch bag. "Don't bother. I'm not working this weekend, so I won't need any." He shrugged. "Until Monday, at least."

"Oh. Right. I guess I'd forgotten today is Friday." *What was wrong with her?*

Luke looked at her for a long moment. "Are you feeling okay? Maybe you should go back to bed. I'm sure Ashley can handle things."

She tensed. "I'm fine. This week has gone by fast, that's all." She noticed the way his hand held on to the counter. It had been forever since they'd held hands. Too long. She stepped toward him, her fingers suddenly itching to touch him.

Luke turned away before she reached him. He opened the refrigerator and pulled out a can of soda. "Don't forget that I'm playing tonight after work. I'll probably go straight there." He motioned at his duffel bag by the door. "I'll change at Justin's. I'm picking him up on the way."

She smiled to herself. He would be so surprised to see her show up. Maybe this would be the first step at getting them back on track. She missed the way things used to be. "Okay. Be careful." She watched as he grabbed his phone and keys then knelt to scratch Milo behind the ears.

Luke stood. "Thanks. Hope you have a good day." He slung his bag over his shoulder. "I'll be in late tonight. Don't wait up."

"Hang on." She walked to the doorway and faced him. "Tomorrow we're supposed to go to a barbecue at my parents' house."

He furrowed his brow. "Why are you just now telling me this?"

She pushed a strand of hair from her face. "Gram didn't call me until yesterday. I haven't gotten to talk to you until now." She reached out and touched his arm, but he shrugged her away.

"Did you tell her we'd come?"

She narrowed her eyes. "Of course. Both of us—so don't think you're getting out of it."

He inhaled deeply and blew out his breath. "Great. Fine. Whatever." He glanced at his watch. "I'm not happy about it, but I'll go." He walked out without giving her another look.

Summer stared at the closed door for a long moment and clutched her coffee mug. There was a time when Luke never would've left without kissing her good-bye. A time when she would've made sure the last words they said to one another were "I love you" and not anything cross. They'd always vowed to have a different marriage than the ones their parents had. But sometimes it seemed like they were two strangers who happened to share a home.

And Summer could pinpoint exactly when the change had happened.

The problem was, unless she could pull a Marty McFly and go back in time, she had no idea what to do about it.

Justin Sanders loved Fridays. Especially every other Friday. But not for the same reason most guys his age did. Sure, he liked to have a good time on the weekend, but every other Friday was special.

He pulled into the driveway at Samantha's townhouse and wondered if she remembered that he was coming today. Two weeks ago, she'd forgotten about his visit and had taken Colton to daycare already.

Justin jumped out of the SUV and walked to the door. It swung open before he could knock.

"I'm so glad you're here," Samantha said. Her bleached blond hair was pulled into a messy bun, and she had dark circles under her eyes. "The baby was up every hour, and then as soon as I got to sleep, Colton woke me up." She managed a smile. "He was so excited that today was his day with you, he couldn't sleep."

Justin's heart warmed. "I'm glad. I'm planning to take him fishing if that's okay with you." He'd bought Colton a Snoopy fishing rod at Walmart the other day. It was identical to the one he'd had when he was a little boy.

"Whatever. That's great." Samantha ushered him inside the tiny townhouse.

"Justy!" Colton exclaimed. The little boy ran toward Justin and grabbed him around the leg.

Justin scooped him up into his arms. "I missed you, little man."

Colton threw his arms around Justin's neck. "I missed you, too."

A cry came from down the hallway. "The baby's awake." Samantha sighed. "Have him back by three, 'kay? He's staying with my mama the rest of the weekend, and I need to get him over there before supper."

"Sure." Although if it were up to Justin, he'd keep Colton forever.

Luke wiped a trickle of sweat from his forehead and slapped his ranger hat back on his head. It wasn't officially summer, but it was as hot as an oven outside. He hated to think of how it would feel in July.

"Excuse me," a woman said from behind him.

He turned and flashed her a polite smile. "Can I help you?"

She held up a cell phone. "Would you mind taking our picture?" She motioned toward a man holding a little girl who couldn't have been more than two. "It's our first vacation as a family," she explained.

He took the phone. "Sure."

The family stood beneath a large flag pole. "Get as much of the fort and the water as you can," the woman called.

Luke grinned. Every tourist wanted the same picture in nearly the same spot. He was such an old pro at this by now he could practically work for Olan Mills. He counted to three and snapped the picture.

"Thanks," the woman said.

Luke handed her the phone. He watched the couple fawn over the little girl. The woman pulled out a bottle of sunblock and rubbed it on the girl's face. The child squealed and wrinkled her nose.

He couldn't help but smile. Part of him wanted to tell the parents to relish those moments. He knew all too well that those happy times could quickly be replaced by sad ones. Life really was a vapor.

"Hey, Luke," his supervisor called from the entrance to the bookstore. "You got a minute?"

He nodded. "Yes sir." He walked toward the older ranger. He'd worked at Fort Sumter for three years now and still had a hard time figuring out if Walter Young liked him or not. Mr. Young was a man of few words, not unlike Luke's daddy.

"With it being the end of the school year, we've got several school groups scheduled for the next couple of weeks," Mr. Young said. "You always have a good rapport with the kids, so I want you to take care of them."

Luke nodded. "Yes sir." Relief washed over him. Every time he was summoned by Mr. Young, he was always afraid he'd messed up somehow. "I'd be glad to."

"You can check the schedule inside. I think there will be six different groups coming. Just do a basic introduction and answer their questions."

Luke knew the drill. "Will do."

Mr. Young turned and went back inside without another word.

Luke sighed. It wasn't even lunchtime yet. This day was dragging on forever. He'd like to chalk it up to the fact that he was looking forward to playing with his band later. But he knew that the main reason the day wasn't going well was because of the way he'd left things with Summer. He didn't know what to say to her anymore.

He watched another couple laughing and walking hand in hand. He wasn't sure if he and Summer would ever get back to that point. And deep down, after everything they'd faced, he wasn't even sure it was possible.

His cell phone vibrated. He pulled the phone from its holster and glanced at the screen.

Rose.

Luke shoved the phone back in the holster. His sister had left two voice mails in the last week, but he hadn't listened to either of them yet. As long as he didn't know what she wanted, he wouldn't feel any obligation toward her.

"Can you tell me how many cannons were here during the battle?" A man asked, startling Luke.

"Sure." Luke went into his canned speech, thankful for the distraction.

Chapter 4

Ashley clicked SEND on an e-mail. From the amount of inquiries they'd had lately from people wanting to hold their weddings in Charleston, it looked like they were in for a busy year. *All the more reason for me to be a real business partner.* She glanced at the clock. Summer must be running late.

Again.

She wished there were someone to share her concerns with. But as far as she knew, Summer didn't have much of a relationship with her family. She'd heard her mention a couple of friends, but even they didn't seem that close. In the years she'd known Summer, it had always been obvious that Luke was her best friend.

And Ashley was pretty sure he was part of the problem in the first place, so talking to him wouldn't help.

Lord, help me figure out how to help her.

The door swung open and Summer walked inside, Milo padding along beside her. She unhooked his leash, and the dog went straight to his familiar spot in front of the large window.

"Sorry I'm late," Summer said. "I didn't sleep well, and then this morning I felt like I was moving in slow motion."

"No problem." Ashley rose from her desk and knelt down to

scratch Milo behind the ear. She watched as Summer thumbed through papers on her desk. Despite her lack of sleep, Summer still managed to look put together. Ashley had always been intimidated by women like that. Women who just seemed to know what went well together and how to pull off accessories without looking like they were trying too hard. Or maybe it was the fact that money wasn't an issue for Summer—Ashley didn't know. She only knew that for Summer, looking classy seemed effortless. The tailored pink jacket and slim-cut black pants showed off her trim figure. Ashley knew there were some days that Summer didn't even stop to eat lunch, and if the weight loss she'd experienced in recent months was any indicator, maybe that was true for supper, too.

"Anything big going on?" Summer asked.

Ashley sat down at the computer. "There was a message on the machine for you." She glanced up at Summer. "It was Rose Drummond. She wanted you to call her back." Ashley shook her head. "She must be a new client, because she's not on our list."

Summer drew her brows together. "Rose is Luke's sister." She shook her head. "I haven't talked to her in a long time." She looked at Ashley. "Anything else?"

Ashley nodded. "I just e-mailed an info packet to a couple from Georgia. They're looking at a destination wedding sometime in August or September and wanted to talk about available dates."

"August or September?" Summer shook her head. "That's not very far off. Why don't people plan in advance these days?"

Ashley didn't mind quick turnarounds, but if it were up to

Summer, every couple would spend at least a year planning for their big day. "You know how it is. They're so excited they just can't wait that long." She chuckled at the grimace on Summer's face. "Surely you remember that feeling."

Summer tucked a strand of dark hair behind her ear. "Not really. I mean, I knew I was going to marry Luke by the time he brought me home on our first real date." She gave a tiny smile. "But we didn't actually get married for several years after that."

Ashley furrowed her brow. She'd never heard the story of Summer and Luke's engagement and wedding. "Why did you wait so long?"

Summer sighed. "I had to finish college. It was part of the agreement with my parents. They would pay for everything, but I had to live in the dorm and all that." She grimaced. "Honestly, I think if it had been anyone but Luke, they would've relented."

"They didn't care for him?"

"It was complicated. I guess you could say that Luke wasn't exactly who they had in mind for me. Adjusting to the idea of him was difficult for them." She chewed on her lip. "And at that time, his only dream was to be in the music industry. So waiting to get married worked out. He went to Nashville for a few years."

"Wow. I had no idea." Ashley had assumed Luke's band was just a hobby. She'd never imagined that he'd actually pursued music.

"It didn't pan out. So he came back and started going to school at night. He worked odd jobs during the day." Summer shrugged. "We got married as soon as I finished my master's."

"I'll bet your wedding was beautiful." Summer's parents would've undoubtedly spared no expense for their oldest daughter's wedding.

Summer laughed. "If you think city hall is beautiful, then yes."

"*You* didn't have a traditional Charleston wedding?" Ashley couldn't hide her shock. Her own wedding back home in Alabama had been full of all the bells and whistles. She'd felt like a princess as she'd floated down the aisle on her daddy's arm. Except that she'd turned out to be a princess without a happily ever after. So maybe a city hall wedding wasn't such a bad idea.

"Nope. Too much trouble. Luke's family was kind of scattered, and mine wasn't very supportive. Except for Gram. She'd been a fan of Luke's from the beginning. But I didn't even tell her."

Ashley sat, stunned. "Were they mad?"

"Let's just say we had some tense holidays after that. But everyone came around." She tapped her fingers on the desk. "Enough about that though. I'm meeting with Sarah Gentry at noon to go over the details for her flowers. We need to let the florist know soon."

Back to business. Summer had been that way since they'd met. It was almost as if she were two people. As soon as she let down her guard and let Ashley in on anything personal, she'd raise the walls back up and flip into business mode. "Okay." Ashley nodded. "And don't forget that I'm getting some quotes for a new web design. I have the components ready, but now I need to find a designer who can put it all together." She grinned. "I can't wait until the site is ready to launch." Ashley took a great deal of pride in the web project. She'd handled it almost single-handedly.

"Awesome. Thanks for your work on that." Summer looked up from her computer screen. "And I don't remember if I mentioned that Luke has a friend who is a web designer. You don't have to use him, but at least add him to the list of people to get a quote from." She leaned back in her chair. "I can't wait to see how the new site impacts business. I think it will make things so much easier, particularly for people from out of state." At least half of their business came from couples who came to Charleston for a destination wedding.

Ashley nodded. Once the site was live, clients would be able to log on and choose from a variety of options to build their own dream wedding. The whole thing would be interactive, so they'd be able to read reviews of venues, watch videos of potential bands, and even see a variety of cakes to choose from. It would be so helpful for brides who wanted a destination wedding in Charleston but were unable to visit ahead of time. "I'm really excited about it." Now would be the perfect time to talk about a promotion. But as usual, the words caught in Ashley's throat.

Would she ever find the courage to speak up for herself?

History and a failed marriage said no.

But Ashley would keep trying to build her confidence. Until then, she'd just keep quiet.

Summer added a few tasks to the to-do list in her planner. Some people preferred to keep track of things on their iPhones or BlackBerries. But she liked the feel of a paper planner. She liked to write down lists and check things off. Planning her days, weeks, and months gave her such satisfaction. Luke accused her of being a control freak. Even when they traveled, she always had a map printed out with the route highlighted. And if he ever tried to go off that highlighted path, as he often did, it filled her with tension.

The unknown scared Summer. Change was not her friend. And time passed so quickly, sometimes she found herself paralyzed with fear that she wouldn't get to accomplish all she planned. Because when it came right down to it, life was short.

She flipped to the monthly calendar where she'd carefully recorded all of her business meetings and civic obligations. If there was a committee, she was on it. She glanced at today's block. The client meeting at noon and then Luke's band tonight at eight were the only things penciled in. "Are you still able to go with me to Folly Beach?" she asked.

Ashley glanced up from her computer. "Sure. I'm looking forward to it." She sighed. "My social life isn't exactly on fire these days."

Summer considered Ashley to be a pretty good friend. But she'd never pried into her personal life. She figured if there were things Ashley wanted to share, she would. She'd hate for anyone to think she was nosy. But she was a little curious. She knew Ashley had been married, but that was about it. "I thought you weren't interested in dating."

Ashley shrugged. "It's not like I'm out perusing the grocery stores or coffee shops for available men. But if I happened to meet a nice one, I wouldn't complain." She shook her head.

"You have no idea how hard it is to meet someone once you're a certain age."

Summer rolled her eyes. "You aren't old."

Ashley stood and came over to lean against Summer's filing cabinet. "Okay, fine. Thirty-six might not be over the hill, but I also know I'm not a spring chicken anymore." She giggled as Summer made a face. "What? At least I'm a realist."

Summer twirled her pen between her fingers. "I'm only two years younger, and I'd bet money that everyone who sees us together thinks you're younger." She gave Ashley the once-over. "You dress a lot cuter than I do."

Ashley laughed. "Translation: sometimes I dress too young for my age." She smoothed her green sundress that was almost the same color as her eyes. "I should probably send half of my wardrobe to my cousin's daughter in Birmingham. And she's sixteen."

"Whatever. You look amazing." With her long, dark blond hair and porcelain skin, Ashley could easily pass for someone in her late twenties.

"Thanks." Ashley looked pleased. "Speaking of clothes, what are you wearing tonight?"

Summer glanced down at her outfit. "This, I guess." She thumbed the jacket collar. "I thought I could take the jacket off and wear the cream-colored shell that's underneath."

Ashley raised her eyebrows and took in Summer's outfit. "Oh. Don't you think that's kind of . . ." She trailed off.

"Uptight?" Summer finished for her. Even when she was a teenager, she'd never been one to follow trends. Her sister, Chloe, had accused her of dressing like Gram on more than one occasion, never meaning it as a compliment. Summer's wardrobe was stylish, but in a classic, refined way. Not trendy and current like Chloe's or Ashley's.

"Actually I was thinking it's kind of businessy. You look more like you're ready for a boardroom than a beachfront restaurant with outdoor seating and a band."

Summer nodded. "I guess." She leaned back in her seat. "Except that my closet is full of stuff like this. I do have a couple of sundresses that I bought last year." She sighed. "I hate shopping. You know that."

Ashley laughed. "Oh, I know. Which is kind of a mystery to me. I adore it."

"Believe me, if you had my mother and sister, you would've grown to hate it, too. It's like their national pastime."

Summer did most of her clothes shopping online now. In fact, she hardly went to the store at all except for groceries. And considering that she'd forgotten to get bread on the last run, maybe she should start doing that online, too. Surely there was some kind of grocery delivery system.

"I was actually going to hit a couple of stores on my lunch break. We could go before your meeting. It'll be fun." Ashley raised her eyebrows in question.

Summer groaned. She'd rather get her teeth cleaned. "I don't want to be late to meet a client."

Ashley chuckled. "Okay, it's not like I'm driving across the country. I'm just going to walk over to King Street."

Summer Weddings was a couple of blocks away from King Street, one of the main shopping districts in downtown Charleston. There were stores for every budget, from discount shops to Louis Vuitton and everything in between. "How about if I give you some cash and you pick me up a new top?" Summer reached for her purse. "Or is that too much of a copout?"

"Hey, it's a start." Ashley shook her head. "You own a pair of dark jeans, right? And strappy heels?"

Summer nodded. "I sure do."

"Okay, I can work with that. Just think of me as your stylist for the night."

"But nothing too flashy. Or revealing." Summer narrowed her eyes. "And no spaghetti straps. Or anything with animal print."

"Is that all?" Ashley smirked.

"Also nothing that looks like something a Kardashian would wear." She smiled. "Other than that, feel free to choose whatever you think is best. But I still have veto power if it doesn't look right on me, so save the receipt."

Ashley laughed all the way to her desk.

Summer turned her attention to the notebook in front of her, filled with possibilities for flower arrangements and bouquets. She tried to keep her mind on the task at hand, but she couldn't help but feel a little excited. Luke had practically been looking through her for months. Maybe tonight if she wore a new outfit, he'd finally focus on her again.

Chapter 5

Justin carefully placed his guitar case in the back of Luke's truck. He'd had such a great day with Colton. Granted, they'd only caught one fish. But those moments were precious. Days like this made him wish he were actually Colton's biological father. At least then he'd have some rights. As it stood, he knew that Samantha could up and move at any moment and he might never see the child again.

"You ready?" Luke asked.

"Yeah. Ready as I'll ever be."

Luke chuckled. "You still have stage fright after all these years?"

Justin nodded. "Little bit." He loved to play, loved to write songs. But actually being on stage in front of people freaked him out. A lot. The other guys made fun of him for it, but Luke never did.

"Look at the bright side," Luke said once they were in the truck and on the way. "At least we don't play for free anymore." He flipped on his turn signal. "I figure that this way even if we're out of tune or if crazy Jimmy falls off the stage again, we'll still make a buck."

"Like you need it," Justin said with a chuckle. "Wish I could find me a girl with old money. Life sure would be a lot easier."

Luke tightened his grip on the steering wheel. "It's not like that, and you know it."

Justin glanced at Luke from the corner of his eye. Maybe he'd been out of line. But he'd been over to their house. Not just anyone could afford to live South of Broad. The taxes alone on those houses were more than most people made in a year. "Sorry. I meant. . ." He sighed. "Just that times are tough."

"Fair enough." Luke relaxed his white-knuckled grip on the wheel. "But for the record, being the poor man in a rich family isn't all it's cracked up to be."

Justin could see where that might be true. But he'd be willing to give it a shot if it meant he could finally buy a house instead of renting and maybe pay off his student loans. "Y'all going anywhere for vacation this year?"

Luke merged onto the James Island Connector. "I wish. It's the busiest time of the year for Summer. I keep telling her that Ashley can handle things for a week or two, but she doesn't seem to be open to that possibility."

Justin knew they'd been through a lot this year. "I'll bet y'all could use a vacation though."

Luke sighed. "Couldn't we all?"

Justin had been friends with Luke long enough to know that he didn't open up very well. No matter the situation, he never showed much emotion. Even at his little brother's funeral last summer, Luke hadn't even flinched. Justin couldn't understand how anyone could stay so strong. Or why anyone would think they had to, for that matter. "I got to hang out with Colton today," he said, feeling a subject change was in order.

"How old is he now? Two? Three?" Luke asked.

"Two and a half," Justin said. "We went fishing. I got him one of those little Snoopy poles." He chuckled. "Of course, he was more interested in playing with the worms than actually fishing. And he was so dirty when I took him home I was afraid Samantha was going to kill me. She actually made me hose him off outside before she'd let him in the house."

"I'll bet." Luke slowed down as they got closer to Folly Beach and the traffic began to thicken. "How's that going?"

Justin sighed. "I know it's weird. It's not like Colton belongs to me. And Samantha and I barely even dated." He shrugged. "But that little boy needs me."

"I'm sure you're right. But be careful." Luke glanced over at him once he'd parked the truck in front of the restaurant. "The more attached you get, the harder it's going to be if Samantha ever moves. Or if she gets married to someone who might not appreciate some other dude hanging around playing daddy to Colton." Luke climbed out of the truck and shut the door, his words lingering behind him.

Justin knew there was truth to what Luke had said. And he also knew that his friend didn't want to see him get hurt.

Even so, the words stung.

Luke would never admit it to Justin, but he still got jittery before going on stage, too. Those years when he'd lived in Nashville, guys like him were a dime a dozen. If he were too nervous to go on, there was always someone waiting in the wings more than willing to take his place.

That was probably one reason why he'd failed. Because honestly, singing lead vocals wasn't his real dream. He'd much rather be behind the scenes, writing the music and lyrics. But somehow that didn't sound nearly as manly as being the lead singer. He'd grown up listening to Chris LeDoux and George Strait. Even his daddy had listened to them and been impressed. No one ever cared about the guy who wrote the song.

"Mr. Nelson?" An older man walked toward him. "I'm Charlie Hamilton."

"Nice to meet you in person," Luke said, shaking the man's outstretched hand.

Charlie smiled kindly. "We enjoyed your demo tape very much. The cover songs sound great, and of course, you're welcome to mix in some original music as well."

That was one reason Luke was so excited about the possibility of this particular gig. A lot of places just wanted a cover band. But the Sand and Suds would allow them to play original songs, too. "Thanks so much for the opportunity. We'll do our best to keep everyone happy."

Charlie chuckled. "Now son, you know that's not possible. It's one of the great lessons in life. You'll never please them all." He pounded Luke on the back. "But if you're taking requests, I'm kind of partial to Kenny Rogers."

Luke nodded. "I'll keep that in mind." He followed Charlie to the stage area where Justin was setting up.

"I'll let you boys get settled. We advertised the music starting at eight, so you've got plenty of time. Just let me know if you need anything." The older man walked back inside the restaurant.

"I just got a text from Jimmy. They're almost here."

Jimmy Baxter played lead guitar, and his brother Will played keyboard and sang backup. They were good guys, always laughing and joking around. By day, Jimmy was an accountant and Will worked as an insurance adjustor. They joked that they only played music for the groupies, but in reality both were happily married with two kids apiece. "Great. You want to grab something to eat? We've still got an hour."

Justin nodded. "Nothing too heavy though." He patted his stomach. "If I get sick in the middle of the set, they'll never hire us for the summer."

Luke chuckled. "True."

They sat down at a table near the stage.

Within a minute, a cute waitress set glasses of water on the table. "What can I get you boys?"

"Just an appetizer platter," Luke said.

Justin smiled at the college-age girl. "We're in the band."

"Well, in that case, I'll have it right out," the waitress said with a wink.

Luke punched Justin in the arm. "We're in the band," he mimicked, laughing.

"Dude. I'm so single it's not even funny. I figure if being in the band gets a girl to notice me, I'd better take advantage."

"Whatever works." Luke shrugged.

"I don't get it. It seems like every time I meet a girl, she ends up dumping me for some jerk." He grimaced. "My brother says I'm too nice."

Luke shook his head. "You just haven't met the right one yet." He certainly wasn't equipped to dispense relationship advice. He used to think he and Summer had a bulletproof relationship. But lately he wasn't so sure. She'd always been a little tightly wound. But now it was like everything put her on edge. And sometimes he heard himself saying things that sounded just like the stuff his dad used to say. Like this morning when he'd given her a hard time about forgetting the bread.

"I guess you're right." Justin let out a sigh. "There's a new girl at church I'm thinking of asking out. She just moved here from somewhere up north. She's pretty cute." He grinned. "Even with that Yankee accent."

Luke tensed. He definitely didn't want to discuss church. He hadn't set foot in a church building since the Sunday before Bobby's accident. Summer had finally given up on asking him to go with her, but he knew it bothered her. "That's nice." He saw the waitress come through the restaurant door. "Looks like our food is here."

"Enjoy," the waitress said, placing a heaping platter on the table. "And let me know if you need anything, okay?" She glanced pointedly at Justin before she walked off.

"Looks good, huh?" Justin asked, reaching for a loaded potato skin.

"You're talking about the food, not the waitress, right?" Luke chuckled.

Before Justin could answer, two women stopped at their table. The taller of the two fluffed her red hair, a broad smile on her face. "Luke?" she asked.

He nodded, trying to place her face. Every now and then

he ran into a tourist who recognized him from a Fort Sumter tour. "Yes."

She slid into the seat next to him, motioning for her friend to sit in the other empty chair. "I'm Jimmy and Will's cousin, Sherry." She reached over and plucked a french fry from the appetizer platter and popped it into her mouth. "This is my friend Maggie." She jerked her chin toward the other woman who was busy batting her fake eyelashes at Justin.

"Hey," Maggie drawled. "We heard y'all play a few weeks ago at that little place on East Bay Street." She leaned closer to Justin. "Y'all should get on one of those reality talent shows or something."

Luke cleared his throat and met Justin's eyes across the table. "Nice to meet you ladies," he said. "Jimmy and Will should be here soon."

"Actually I came to see you," Sherry said. "I heard that you might need my services." She winked. "Jimmy was telling me that you're considering a pretty big purchase for your wife's anniversary gift." She let out a tinkling laugh. "And it just so happens that I can help."

Luke nodded. "Great. Do you have a card or something?" He jerked his chin toward the stage. "It's almost time for us to go on, but I'd love to discuss it sometime next week."

Sherry's full lips turned upward in a smile. "Oh, it would be my pleasure." She reached into her leopard print handbag and pulled out a card with her photo plastered on the front. "Here you go, hon. Call me anytime. I'd be glad to help." She reached over and grasped his forearm. "And if you think about it, could you play some Brad Paisley?" She clutched his arm tighter. "He's my favorite."

Justin tossed his napkin on the table. "Oh, he would *love* to play some Brad Paisley." He smirked in Luke's direction. "Don't you ladies think he looks like Brad?"

Luke's resemblance to Brad Paisley was a running joke with the band. Every time they performed one of his songs, the women in the audience went crazy.

"Oh, he does. We noticed that right off, didn't we, Maggie?"

Maggie nodded, still mesmerized by Justin. "Sure did."

Luke caught Justin's amused expression. "That might be so, but did you ladies know that you're in the presence of one of Charleston's most eligible bachelors?"

The scowl on Justin's face said it all. *If you're going to dish it out, you have to be able to take it.* Luke leaned back and watched the women fawn over his friend.

Chapter 6

"A re you sure I look okay?" Summer asked. She adjusted the red drape-neck top for the tenth time. It was way more flamboyant than her normal style, but she had to admit it flattered her figure.

"You look amazing." Ashley giggled. "I seriously thought that guy in the parking lot was going to get whiplash when we walked past him."

"Whatever. He was totally looking at you." Summer glanced at her friend. Ashley had chosen a turquoise tank top paired with dark denim capri pants and wedge heels. Her chunky coral bracelet and necklace completed the look. Summer never would've paired the colors together, but on Ashley they worked.

"Does Luke know we're coming?" Ashley asked as they walked inside the restaurant.

Summer shook her head. "Nope. He's going to be so surprised." She smiled at the hostess. "We'd like seats out on the patio."

The girl nodded. "Great choice. We actually have a band about to start."

Summer grinned at Ashley. "Perfect."

They followed the hostess through the restaurant and out

another door that led to the outdoor seating area.

"Here you go." The hostess pointed at a table for two that offered a view of the stage and the water. "Your waitress will be with you in a moment."

As Summer sank into her seat, she scanned the deck for Luke. Her eyes landed on a table near the stage. She watched as a woman with hair that was a very unnatural shade of red grabbed Luke's arm and laughed.

"I don't believe it," she whispered. "Look at that. She's all over him."

Ashley followed her gaze. "Man. That's some outfit." She laughed. "And most of the time I'm hard to shock."

Summer swallowed hard. "Do you see how he's laughing with her?" Luke hadn't laughed that way at home in months.

"Hey." Ashley reached over and patted her on the arm. "Don't read into things. Luke is the lead singer for a band. Those are probably just fans."

Even so, Summer's stomach tightened. She watched as the table broke out into another round of laughter. This wasn't how she'd wanted the night to go. She'd hoped to sneak into the crowd once the band started playing and see the pleased expression on Luke's face when he saw her. But now she wished she hadn't come at all. "I think we should leave."

Ashley waved away a smiling waitress. "Give us a minute," she said to the girl. She turned back to Summer. "Don't be silly. Go over there now and surprise him. You'll see that it isn't a big deal."

Summer sighed. "Come with me." She jerked her head toward the table where Luke sat. "I want to introduce you to

Justin anyway. When Luke and his buddies helped you move into your house, Justin was out of town." She stood slowly, keeping her eyes on Luke.

As they made their way to the table, she wished again that she'd stayed home with Milo. She could be watching a movie or going for a run. Or even back at the office answering some e-mails. But no. She was trying to get her husband's attention away from some groupie.

Justin saw them first. "Summer." He jumped up, a smile on his face. Justin was by far the best of all of Luke's friends. She'd seen time and again how tenderhearted he was.

Luke looked up, his eyes wide. "I didn't expect to see you here." The expression on his face seemed more shocked than pleased.

She cut her eyes at the redhead and then back at him. "No, I guess you didn't." She turned her attention back to Justin. "This is Ashley," she said, putting an arm around her friend's waist. "I don't think you guys have met." She turned to Ashley. "Justin is a webmaster by day but a drummer by night," she explained. "He might be a good candidate to redesign our website."

Justin nodded in Ashley's direction. "Nice to meet you."

The redheaded woman stood and held out her hand to Summer. "Hi, I'm Sherry. Jimmy and Will's cousin."

As if that explained everything. "Nice to meet you." She glanced down at Luke who hadn't made a move to get up. He looked uncomfortable. *Serves you right.*

"I guess Maggie and I had better go find a table," Sherry trilled. "We want one with a good view of the stage." She motioned for Maggie to get up then focused her attention back on Luke. "Don't forget what we talked about. And I'll be expecting some Brad Paisley before your set is over." She giggled.

Once the two women were gone, Luke stood. "I can't get over you being here. You never come see me play anymore." He smiled, suddenly looking more like his old self than he had in a long time.

Summer cocked her head. "Ashley's never heard you guys play. She didn't want to come alone." She watched as his face fell and she choked back the truth—that she'd wanted to surprise him. Instead she gestured in the direction Sherry and Maggie had gone. "Friends of yours?"

Luke furrowed his brow. "Nope. Just met them a few minutes ago."

Summer glanced over to see Ashley and Justin sitting at the table, making small talk. "We'll be right back, okay?"

Ashley looked up and nodded.

Summer motioned for Luke to follow her back to her table. "It's like old times having you here. Remember when you used to come hear me play every weekend?"

She kept her face neutral. "Yeah. I remember."

He reached across the table and took her hand.

She instinctively jerked it away. "You looked awfully cozy with that—that. . .Sherry person."

Luke regarded her with wide eyes. "She's Jimmy and Will's cousin, just like she said. I've never seen her before in my life." He shrugged. "Sorry if I didn't send her and her friend away when they sat down. I didn't realize that speaking to fans was off-limits."

Summer realized how ridiculous she was acting. "Sorry. I wanted to surprise you, and then when I saw you sitting with those women and laughing like old friends. . ." She trailed off. "Sorry I overreacted. It was stupid of me." She reached across the table for his hand but was too late.

Luke stood. "Don't worry about it." He jerked his chin toward the stage. "Jimmy and Will are here. And it looks like Mr. Hamilton is ready to introduce the band. I've got to go." He nodded at her. "Hope you and Ashley enjoy the show."

She watched as he walked off and couldn't help but wonder if the sick feeling in her stomach was from her marriage slipping away.

Luke put his old cowboy hat on top of his head and stepped up on stage.

The crowd applauded, and someone in the back let out a wolf whistle.

He grabbed the microphone and peered out at the crowd. "Thanks to the Sand and Suds for the warm welcome and a special thanks to you guys for coming out to support us." He glanced back at Justin and nodded.

Justin tapped his drumsticks together for a four count, and the band started up on cue. Whenever they played at the beach, they always opened with a Jimmy Buffet song. Tonight they'd decided on "Cheeseburger in Paradise."

Luke noticed that Summer and Ashley had moved to a table

closer to the stage. Even if she was only here to accompany Ashley, he was still glad she'd made the effort. And she looked really great tonight, too. He'd seen a couple of guys give her the once-over, and it had made him want to smack them.

He couldn't help but remember the first time she'd heard him play. They were seventeen, and she'd snuck out of her house and met him down at the Battery. They'd sat in the bandstand, and he played his newest song for her.

"It's called 'Summer Girl.' "

"You actually wrote me a song?" She'd tackled him, and his guitar had fallen to the ground with a thud. But Summer in his arms was much better than a guitar, even one he'd saved up six months to buy.

"It's not finished yet though." He'd laughed as she covered his face with kisses.

"That's okay. Just play me whatever you've got."

He strummed the chords and began to sing, loving the way her eyes never left his.

"I love it," she said when he stopped playing. "When will it be finished?"

He'd grinned. "I'm not sure how it ends yet."

Luke held on to the microphone and sang the last line of "Cheeseburger in Paradise," loving the way the audience joined in. His eyes found Summer's as the crowd applauded. All these years and he'd never finished "Summer Girl" for her. Did she even remember it?

The problem was that just like on that balmy August night when they were seventeen, he still wasn't sure how their song would end.

Chapter 7

T hey're really good," Ashley remarked after she'd heard several songs. "Luke has an awesome voice."

Summer nodded. "He's very talented." She turned back to look at the stage. "But his real strength is in his songwriting. He's written several that are catchy enough to be hits."

"Has he ever tried to send them to any record labels?"

Summer shook her head. "It's been years. I think he's resigned himself to playing with a band locally." She shrugged. "It seems to fill the need he has to make music."

"Either way, they sound great." Ashley leaned forward as the band started another song. "So Justin seems nice."

Summer looked at her with an eyebrow raised. "Yes. He's a real sweetheart."

"I set up a meeting with him for next week. It sounds like he'd be easy to work with on the web project." And easy on the eyes too, but Ashley didn't mention that to Summer. He could be married or engaged for all she knew. Which would further solidify her theory that all the good ones were taken.

"Great. I hope that works out." Summer smiled. "But if you think someone else would do a better job, don't feel like we have to go with his company just because he's Luke's friend."

Ashley appreciated the confidence Summer had in her to make the decision. "Thanks." She turned her attention toward the stage. Luke was doing a perfect rendition of a George Strait song. "I can't imagine having the confidence to get up on stage like that."

"He used to break out in hives before he went on. I think being in Nashville broke him of that problem. He told me once that he realized that there was always someone younger and more talented out there. The difference was that he wanted it more." Summer shrugged. "But songwriting is where his heart is. He's an amazing singer, but he has such a way with words."

The last strains of the song ended, and the crowd broke into loud applause.

"Now we're gonna slow it down a little bit and do an original song." Luke grinned from the stage. "This one's going out to all of the lovebirds out there. It doesn't have all the bells and whistles as some of the others we've done tonight, but I think you'll like it." He began to strum on the guitar, and soon his rich voice filled the air.

"Wow. Just him and his guitar," Ashley said. "Have you heard this one before?" When Summer didn't answer, Ashley glanced at her friend.

Tears streamed down Summer's face, and she didn't even bother to wipe them away. She kept her eyes on Luke, never blinking.

Ashley sat back in her seat and averted her eyes. It seemed almost voyeuristic to watch such a personal moment. She had no idea what was going on inside Summer's head, but she could see the emotion pour out. And one thing she knew for sure about Summer, those emotions didn't come out easily or often.

Summer looked around as if suddenly aware that she was in a public place. She pushed back her chair. "I'll be right back," she whispered.

Ashley half rose to go after her but sat back down. Some things you had to face alone, and she had a feeling whatever Summer was dealing with was one of them. She turned her attention back to the band.

Luke sang the closing lines of the song, and the crowd cheered. "We're going to take a little break now," he said. "And if you're interested in purchasing one of our CDs, see Jimmy during the break." He motioned toward the keyboard player.

Jimmy waved and pointed at a table near the stage.

Ashley watched as Luke shook hands with a few people from the audience who'd crowded around him. Mostly women, but at least the redhead from before wasn't one of them.

A few minutes later, Luke made his way to her table. "I saw Summer rush out. Did she get a phone call or something?" he asked, concern etched on his handsome face.

Ashley shook her head. It wasn't her place to tell him that Summer had been crying. "I think she went to the restroom."

"Oh." Luke rubbed his jaw where the faintest hint of a five o'clock shadow was beginning to show.

"I'm sure she'll be back soon though."

Justin walked up to the table. "You enjoying the show?" he asked. With his sun-kissed blond hair and tanned skin, he looked like he spent his days surfing rather than working on websites.

"Y'all are so talented." She smiled.

"Thanks." He turned to Luke and gestured toward the stage. "There are a few people who want autographed CDs. I told Jimmy I'd come get you."

Luke nodded. "Sure." He looked back at Ashley. "Will you remind Summer to set the alarm when she gets home?"

"Of course."

Justin gave her one last glance. "Looking forward to our lunch meeting next week."

Before she could respond, he and Luke headed toward the CD table.

As she watched them go, she couldn't help but wish it were already Tuesday. But at least she had time to prepare. Their meeting might call for a new outfit. Maybe a cute skirt. Definitely some new shoes.

With that happy thought, she set off to find Summer.

Justin sat in the passenger seat of Luke's truck. He was way past ready to get home and into bed. The crowd had stayed pretty thick until nearly midnight, and by the end they were a little rowdier than he'd have liked.

He peered out the window. Luke and the restaurant manager stood talking outside the entrance. Maybe he should've caught a ride with Jimmy and Will.

"Sorry about that. The old man is a talker," Luke said once he'd climbed inside the truck. "The good news is that the job is ours if we want it." He turned the truck toward Charleston.

"That's great." The prospect of every weekend being tied up with a performance wasn't as appealing to Justin as it was to Luke. But the extra money would be nice.

"They liked our original stuff, don't you think?" Luke asked.

"Seemed to." Justin looked over at Luke's profile and wondered again why he hadn't tried harder to work in the music industry. He, Jimmy, and Will were in it for fun. Luke was the real talent. "You know that contest I was telling you about? The songwriter showcase?"

Luke nodded. "Yeah."

"The entry deadline is coming up soon. All you have to do is send in a demo." He'd been trying to get Luke to submit an entry for weeks. "And the final round judges are some big names. People who might actually record your songs if they like your style."

Luke shrugged. "Nah. I wouldn't even know which one to submit." He slowed the truck down as they came to a red light. "I do have a couple of unfinished songs though. I've been thinking about finishing them."

"You should do it, man. I think the deadline is at the beginning of July."

Luke sighed. "I'll think about it."

"So it was great to see Summer tonight." Justin had always liked Summer a lot. She'd gone out of her way to make him feel welcome every time he'd been over to their house. Once when his hot water heater had gone out at his apartment, she'd even insisted he stay in one of their guest bedrooms.

"Yeah. I'm glad to see her get out a little bit. If she's not working, she's off at some committee meeting or something."

He shook his head. "Usually she just wants to stay home and watch some chick flick on TV."

"And I'm glad to finally meet Ashley." Justin had heard about Summer's coworker, but somehow they always missed meeting one another.

"Ashley's great. She's been a real lifesaver. You know how bad things were there for a while. . ." Luke trailed off. "And Ashley stepped up and ran the company on the days when Summer couldn't handle it all." Luke pulled into an empty space in front of Justin's apartment. "You know, I didn't think about it earlier, but I don't think she's dating anyone." He raised his eyebrows at Justin. "I'm not positive, but I can find out."

Justin had wondered about her status. "Cool." He opened the door. "Thanks for the ride. See you next week." He hopped out of the truck. Once he was on the sidewalk, he motioned for Luke to roll down the window. "If you guys want to go with me to church on Sunday, I think we're having potluck."

Luke's jaw tensed. "I think I'll pass." Without so much as a wave, he backed out of the space.

Justin pulled his keys out and unlocked the door. He knew it made Luke mad when he invited him to Sunday services.

That didn't mean he was going to quit asking. He'd just pray about it a little bit harder.

Chapter 8

Luke hated get-togethers with Summer's family. He always felt like such a nobody around them. Granted, her grandmother had always been good to him. Even the house they lived in had been a gift from her, something that hadn't set too well with her other grandchildren. She'd said it was her prerogative and they'd all have to get over it.

He pulled on a faded pair of jeans and an old brown T-shirt he found hanging in the guest bedroom closet where his casual clothes had been relegated to. This might pass muster on stage, but he had a feeling Summer would hit the roof when she saw it. "Too bad," he muttered. "I'm not going to pretend to be somebody I'm not." He looked in the bathroom mirror and raked his fingers through his hair. Not bad.

"You ready?" he called up the stairs to Summer. He hadn't seen her yet this morning. He'd gotten in so late last night that he'd slept in the downstairs guestroom. Summer usually stumbled downstairs first thing for coffee, but one glance in the kitchen told him that the pot he'd made for her hadn't been touched. She must've slept in.

He checked his watch. If they didn't leave within the

next fifteen minutes, they were going to be late. He sighed. "Summer?" he called.

No response.

A sudden panic gripped him, causing his stomach to lurch. He hadn't gone upstairs last night to check on her. The alarm was on when he got home though. And her car was in the driveway. But still. That didn't mean she was home.

Luke took the stairs two at a time, bile rising in his throat. His beating heart pounded against his chest as he threw open their bedroom door.

She was curled up on her side, sound asleep. She held Luke's pillow tightly to her chest.

Milo sat on the floor, staring at her. He cast woeful "I need to go outside" eyes at Luke.

"Summer." Luke said her name sharper than he intended. But during those moments between the kitchen and the bedroom, he'd been so scared something had happened to her. Robbery gone wrong, kidnapping, brain aneurysm—and those were only a few of the scenarios that had played out in his mind. Now, seeing her blissfully unaware filled him with anger. "Summer, wake up." He grabbed her shoulder and shook it.

Milo let out a low growl.

Summer jerked upright. "What? What is it?" She peered at him through sleepy eyes. "What time is it?" She glanced frantically at the clock. "I can't believe I overslept." She jumped up and threw the pillow on the bed. "Why didn't you wake me up?" she asked, glaring. "You know we can't be late." She stomped to her closet. "I don't even have time to shower."

Luke ushered Milo out the door then turned to face his wife. "Simmer down. If we're a few minutes late, it won't be the end of the world."

She scowled. "My whole family will be there, and you know they're always looking for a reason to criticize me." She flung a pair of gray pants on the bed. "I can't believe this."

Luke watched her flip through the vast assortment of tops in the walk-in closet. It had always amused him how she arranged her clothes by color. "You could wear that red top you wore last night." He winked. "It looked nice."

Summer looked at him with wide eyes. "I'm surprised you noticed it."

He shrugged. "Most of the stuff you wear isn't as bright as that. I liked the red."

She yanked a light blue top from a hanger. "Yeah, well it wasn't my style, so it's no wonder you liked it." She stood on her tiptoes and grabbed a shoe box. "Ashley picked it out."

Only he could give a compliment and still manage to say the wrong thing. "I'd better go let Milo out." He paused at the door. "Do you want me to pour you a cup of coffee into a travel mug?"

Her expression softened. "That would be great, thanks."

Luke headed downstairs to tend to Milo. The upside to her oversleeping was that she hadn't had a chance to criticize his choice of clothing.

He figured she wouldn't notice until they were in the car.

And by then it would be too late.

As soon as Luke was gone, Summer sank onto the bed. What an awful way to start the day. A day that would probably contain plenty of trouble all its own without the added stress of running late and fighting with Luke.

And why couldn't she have just been nice when he tried to compliment her on the way she'd looked last night? It was no wonder he'd slept downstairs.

Again.

She hurriedly ran a brush through her medium-length hair, thankful she'd started wearing it wavy. A few drops of texturizing cream, and it looked like it had yesterday when it was freshly washed.

She put on the outfit she'd picked out and grabbed her makeup bag. Thanks to the Saturday beach traffic, it would take at least thirty minutes to get to her parents' house on Isle of Palms. She'd have to do her makeup in the car.

"You ready?" she asked once she made it down the stairs.

Luke glanced up from his favorite spot on the couch. "No." He clicked off the TV and tossed the remote on the couch. "But I guess there's no way out of it."

Summer grabbed the travel mug of coffee that Luke had prepared and knelt to kiss Milo good-bye. "Be a good boy. I'll take you for a long walk when we get back."

Milo yawned and jumped up on the couch. He rested his head on the couch arm and watched her with sad eyes.

"That dog is spoiled rotten." Luke chuckled as they headed out the door. He opened the passenger door on her SUV and motioned for her to get inside.

She brushed past him and climbed in. "He's not too spoiled. He just likes to relax."

Luke glanced at her as he got behind the wheel. "Whatever you say." He started the SUV and slowly backed out of the driveway. "The new crepe myrtle looks good, don't you think?"

Even though his days of working for his uncle's landscaping company were over, Luke insisted on taking care of their yard himself. "It's beautiful." One thing that always cheered her up was their home and garden.

The stucco-over-brick home had been in her family for generations, built right after the American Revolution. Summer's grandmother had lived in the home while Summer was growing up, and her best memories had been made in the lush garden or sitting out on the second-floor piazza listening to stories of Gram's childhood.

Gram's decision to give the home—along with a generous trust for its care—to Summer and Luke as a wedding gift had caused quite a stir in the Rutledge family. Summer's siblings, Mitch and Chloe, had been furious. Her parents hadn't cared too much—until Gram's announcement that she would be moving to a home near theirs on Isle of Palms.

"We have the prettiest house on Legare Street," Summer observed as they drove down the historic street. "And the most gorgeous flowers, too." Most of the homes, including theirs, were in the traditional single style so common in Charleston. What looked like the front door from the sidewalk actually opened to a porch where a second door served as the home's true entrance.

Luke chuckled. "Our neighbors probably think the same thing about their homes." He stopped at the intersection of Legare and Tradd and waited for a throng of tourists to pass before turning left.

She leaned her head against the seat, trying to shake the bad mood she'd woken up with. "You guys sounded great last night." She glanced over at Luke. His profile was perfect. No wonder that redhead had been fawning over him.

"Thanks." He turned onto South Bay Street. "The weekly gig is ours if we want it. The manager liked our style and said he'd heard a lot of compliments."

Summer chewed on her bottom lip. A weekly show was a big commitment. Over the years, she'd gotten used to Luke's band playing shows every few weeks. But weekly seemed like a big step. "What did you tell him?"

Luke merged onto Highway 17. "I told him I'd talk to the guys. Justin is on board, but I have to check with Jimmy and Will. I figure they might need to run it past their wives."

Summer inhaled sharply. Normally she loved the sights from the Arthur Ravenel Bridge that connected Charleston to Mt. Pleasant, but not today. "So Jimmy and Will's wives get a say, but you weren't going to ask me what I thought?" Her voice came out shrill and sounded way too much like her mother for her liking.

Luke wrinkled his nose. "I didn't think you'd mind. You know how much this means to me."

"Yeah." She closed her eyes. "But sometimes you don't

think about what things mean to me."

"So what are you saying? You want me to turn it down?"

Summer flipped through her bag to find her sunglasses. She could feel hot tears welling up in her eyes, and she didn't want to give Luke the satisfaction of seeing her cry. "Of course not." She pulled on the oversized glasses. "But it would've been nice to have been consulted. To feel like my opinion matters." She paused. "For once."

Luke groaned. "You have got to be kidding." He reached over to take her hand, but she pulled it away.

"No, I'm not kidding." She looked out at the water and for a moment wished she were out there in it, swimming toward a deserted island. "It's like I don't count anymore." Her chest was so tight, she wondered if this was what a heart attack felt like. "We never make decisions together. It seems like we live totally separate lives." Despite the pain, she felt a sense of relief at having the statement out in the open. Except that now it hung between them like a haze.

"I can't believe you're doing this just as we're getting to your parents' house," Luke said angrily. "Don't you think you could've saved this conversation for a better time?"

She shook her head. "There isn't a better time. When is the last time you and I talked about anything bigger than who was going to walk Milo or who forgot to take out the trash?"

He slowed down as they got into traffic. "We're both busy, that's all."

She felt his eyes on her but refused to look at him. "We've been busy since we met. But this space between us hasn't always been here." Her voice was barely above a whisper. Saying it out loud was almost as painful as keeping it inside.

And now that the floodgates had opened and the truth was out, she knew they would have to deal with it.

Except that she wasn't sure if either of them was up for that right now.

Chapter 9

Luke silently followed Summer up the steps that led to a huge wraparound porch decorated with white wicker furniture. He'd been to her parents' home plenty of times over the years, but still marveled at what it must've been like to grow up with the beach practically in the backyard.

Every time he came here, he couldn't help but be reminded of the difference in how he and Summer had been raised. His daddy was a shrimper, weathered by the sun and wind. He'd raised his kids with an iron fist, especially after Luke's mama had died. Summer's family, on the other hand, had lived lives full of luxury. Her parents both came from money, and the thought of worrying that there might not be enough food on the table was a foreign concept.

But Summer wasn't snobby like he'd expected. The first day he'd met her in the backyard of the home they now shared, she'd peppered him with questions about the flowers and plants. She'd even invited him to sit with her on the piazza and have a glass of lemonade. His uncle had been furious with him until Summer's grandmother offered them a contract to care for the yard the rest of the year.

Luke met Summer's eyes as they reached the top step.

"Truce?" he asked. "At least until we get back in the car?"

She managed a tiny smile and nodded. "I need you to be on my team while we're here."

"I'm always on your team."

The door swung open, and Vivian Rutledge stood before them. "Summer, Luke. . .come in." Vivian greeted both of them with a kiss on the cheek. Her flowery perfume stung Luke's nose, and he resisted the urge to cough.

"Thanks for having us," he said to Vivian.

His mother-in-law gave him a broad smile. "Everyone else is already here. They're out back by the pool." She raised an eyebrow in Summer's direction. "I was beginning to think y'all weren't going to make it."

Luke stepped in. "It was my fault. I had a late night last night." He grinned, hoping he still had some charm left. "But we're sure looking forward to some delicious barbecue."

Summer caught his eye. "Thanks," she mouthed silently.

He nodded. "No problem," he mouthed back with a wink. He put an arm around her waist and led her to the french doors that opened into the backyard. He wished he could pull her to him and hug her tightly and tell her how worried he'd been that morning. But this wasn't the time or the place, and besides, she'd been so cold toward him lately that he wasn't sure if his affection would be welcome.

"There you are." Gram greeted them with a smile. She hugged Summer and then Luke. "I guess I'm going to have to start dropping by your office if I want to know how my oldest granddaughter is doing."

Summer hung her head. "I'm sorry I haven't been out to see

you lately." She shrugged. "We've been super busy."

Gram raised one drawn-on eyebrow. "Sweetie, when you are too busy for the people you love, you are too busy." She looped her arm through Luke's. "And how is my favorite grandson-in-law?"

He chuckled. "You might not want to say that too loud, considering I'm not your only grandson-in-law."

Gram shot him a mischievous look. "When you've lived as long as I have, you can do as you please." She patted his arm. "Someday you'll know what I mean." She winked.

Summer walked over to them carrying two glasses of sweet tea. "Here you go." She handed one to Luke. "The food looks wonderful."

Luke looked over at the spread of food. "Impressive." He glanced at Gram. "Catered?"

She laughed. "Of course." She shook her head. "I wanted to do the cooking, but Vivian wouldn't hear of it."

"Well, it looks good, but I know your cookin' would taste better," he said with a smile.

Gram's wrinkled face lit up. "Thanks." She motioned toward a table next to the pool. "I'm going to go have a seat. But once you've filled your plates, come sit with me."

Summer nodded. "We will." She turned to Luke. "Guess we should go say hello to Daddy and Mitch."

Luke looked around the expansive backyard. "There sure are a lot of people here. I thought this was just going to be a small family gathering."

"I have no idea what's going on." She motioned toward where her father stood with a group of men. "There they are. Come on."

Luke clutched his sweet tea and followed behind her.

"Hi, Daddy," Summer greeted her father.

Thomas Rutledge bent down to kiss his oldest child on the cheek. "Hey, baby." He nodded in Luke's direction. "Luke."

Luke nodded and shook his father-in-law's outstretched hand. "Thanks for having us, Mr. Rutledge."

"Well, well." Mitch Rutledge stepped from behind his father. "I haven't seen you two in a while."

Summer smiled at her brother. "We've been busy."

"Busy?" Mitch shook his head. "That sounds like a flimsy excuse to me." He pounded Luke on the back. "After y'all skipped out on Christmas with the family, we were all beginning to think we'd done something to offend." He smirked. "I figured it was something Chloe had done, but she denied it."

Luke locked eyes with Summer. Except for Gram, her family had no idea why they hadn't made it to Christmas. "We both were a little under the weather," he explained. It wasn't a lie, exactly. The events before Christmas had made both of them physically ill, but not with an actual sickness.

"Summer *Nelson*. I haven't seen you in fifteen years, and now I see you twice in one week," a deep voice said from behind them.

Luke turned to see a tall, familiar-looking man with his eyes on Summer.

"Hi, Jefferson," she said softly.

Luke fought to keep his face neutral. Jefferson Boudreaux had been Summer's first love. His family and Summer's family had been friends for generations. There were even pictures of Jefferson and Summer playing together as babies. The guy might be rich and good-looking, but as far as Luke was concerned, he was a pompous jerk. "Hi there, Jeff." He knew the nickname would get under Jefferson's skin.

A shadow crossed Jefferson's face. "Luke." He held out a hand. "So good to see you again."

Luke reluctantly shook hands. Back when they were teenagers, Jefferson had done all he could to make Luke look stupid in front of Summer. He'd mocked his clothes, made fun of his vehicle—even accused him of stealing a watch one time. "Good to see you, too." He almost choked on the words. "Hope you enjoy your visit."

Jefferson smirked. "Didn't Summer tell you?" He raised his eyebrows in Summer's direction. "I'm back for good. I'm house hunting now." He pounded Luke on the back. "Maybe we'll wind up neighbors."

Luke would rather walk over hot coals than have Jefferson as a neighbor. "Great." He considered it a minor miracle that he was able to keep from punching that smirk right off Jefferson's face. He turned to Summer. "Babe, let's go get something to eat. I'm starved." He put an arm around Summer's waist and guided her toward the food.

As soon as they were out of earshot, he leaned down to Summer. "Why didn't you tell me that Jefferson was moving back?" he hissed. "And when did you see him?"

She wrinkled her brow. "I ran into him Thursday." She sighed. "And I haven't had many conversations with you since then to tell you." She reached for a plate. "Besides, it's not a big deal."

He sighed. "I don't like for that guy to feel like he's got one over on me."

Summer rolled her eyes. "I know. I almost drowned in all the testosterone over there. Can't you two play nice?" She scooped some potato salad onto her plate. "That was all a long time ago."

Luke grumbled. "He's still a jerk." Maybe he was overreacting. But seeing Jefferson after all this time brought up all the insecurities he thought he'd put behind him. And who wore seersucker anyway? So pretentious.

The sound of silverware clinking against glass rang through the yard.

"Could I have your attention, please?" Mr. Rutledge called.

Vivian walked over to join her husband. "Thanks for joining us today," she said. "We're here to celebrate a special occasion." She smiled broadly.

Luke glanced at Summer, and she shrugged.

"That's right," Thomas said, putting an arm around his wife's shoulders. "We invited you here to tell you that our daughter Chloe has given us some news we've been waiting to hear for a long time."

Luke caught sight of Chloe and her husband, Preston, standing just beyond Thomas and Vivian. Chloe looked like she was about to burst into song.

"What'd they do?" he whispered to Summer. "Cure cancer?"

She elbowed him. "Shh."

"We're pleased to announce that in six months, we're going to have new titles," Vivian said dramatically. "Nana and Poppa." She threw her arms out with excitement.

The crowd burst into applause.

Luke felt Summer stiffen next to him.

She thrust her glass of tea at him, nearly spilling it, and hurried off toward the house.

He froze, unsure of whether he should follow or not.

Gram caught his eye and nodded her head toward the house. She rose and moved as quickly as she could to the french doors.

Luke looked at the abandoned glass of tea in his hand, once again filled with the sense of helplessness that had plagued him for months. Ever since that cold day in early December when he and Summer had learned that she'd suffered a miscarriage.

Even though it had been years since Summer had lived in her parents' home, her bedroom hadn't changed much. The ornate white furniture and pale pink bedding had been fit for a princess. Today, though, they were a painful reminder of all she'd lost.

She sank onto the bed and ran her hand over the soft bedspread. The irony of the situation wasn't lost on her. Her sister, Chloe, had always hated kids. She'd never babysat like Summer had. Never been the one the little kids at church flocked to.

And yet here she was, pregnant.

Not that it should be any surprise. Summer had always heard that when you're trying unsuccessfully to have a child, everyone you know gets pregnant. And that had certainly rung true for her. She couldn't count the number of high school and college friends who'd come out of the woodwork over the past months to share their happy news with the world. It was almost to the point that she hated to log on to Facebook, because she knew she'd be faced with a bevy of new profile photos depicting protruding bellies and ultrasounds.

Maybe things would be different if she'd shared her news with everyone. Then they'd be more sensitive to her feelings. But she and Luke had taken so long to get pregnant, she'd wanted to wait until she was past the first trimester. She'd lost the baby right at the end of the three months, so very few people ever even knew of her loss.

"I had no idea about Chloe, or I would've warned you first," Gram said quietly from the door. Gram had been her lone confidante in the family. She'd promised not to say anything but had urged Summer to tell her parents what she'd gone through.

Summer looked up, tears in her eyes. "I know you would've." She managed a smile. "Maybe I should've listened to you and told them the news months ago." She'd had this great plan to announce her pregnancy at Christmas, thinking it would be such a wonderful surprise for her parents—and had hoped it would be just the thing to bring them close again. But then she'd miscarried just before Christmas and hadn't the heart to tell them. She had seen no reason to share the grief.

Gram came and sat down next to her. "That was your decision to make." She patted Summer on the knee. "And I understand you wanting to protect them. But sometimes there is strength in numbers. You might not be as close with your parents and siblings as you could be, but they would've stood by you as you were grieving. They would've grieved with you."

Summer shrugged. "Maybe. Or maybe Mother would've given me some speech about needing to take better care of myself or about how we should've started trying sooner." She sighed. "But mostly I didn't want them to look at me with pity." She refused to meet Gram's eyes. She knew how ridiculous she must sound. Even though she knew her family loved her, she never felt like she measured up to what they'd expected her to become. And failing to give them a grandchild seemed like one more way her best wasn't good enough.

"You get that streak of pride from your grandfather." Gram shook her head. "He never could admit when he was hurting either." She clasped Summer's hand. "But darling, you might find that if you let people see your weaknesses, it will make you stronger in the long run."

"Maybe." Summer looked down at their entwined hands and felt the strength of the woman next to her. She'd always admired her grandmother so much. At least she had one family member who had always been in her corner no matter what.

Summer stood and walked over to the vanity where she'd gotten ready for so many important events in her early life. She traced her fingers over the smooth top, remembering when she and Chloe had sat in front of the mirror and tried on Mother's lipstick. Her gaze went to an ornate wooden box that she'd kept her treasures in since she was small.

She turned to Gram with a grin. "I can't believe this is still here after all these years. I think the first ring Luke ever gave me is in this box."

Gram looked at her curiously. "The first ring?"

Summer nodded and returned to her spot on the bed. She opened the box and began sifting through old letters, pressed flowers, and trinkets that had once meant the world to her. "Did I ever tell you that Luke proposed to me three times?"

Gram raised her eyebrows but stayed silent.

"The first time we were eighteen. It was the night of my debutante ball." She laughed and pulled out a tiny silver tab from a Coke can. "As soon as he saw me in that white gown, he stuck this on my finger and asked me to marry him." She shook her head at the memory.

She pulled a silver gum wrapper that had been folded and taped and fashioned into a circle. "This one was during my sophomore year of college." She slipped the paper ring onto her finger. "Luke was in Nashville and I was at USC. We missed each other so much." She took the ring off and placed it gently back in the box. "He was home for Christmas, and he begged me to go back with him to Nashville. Said we could get married and get jobs."

Gram patted her arm. "But it all worked out. And the third time was the proverbial charm."

Summer nodded and put the lid on the box that held so many mementos of her past.

Gram cleared her throat. "I may as well tell you that there's something I've been worrying about." She peered at Summer with those crystal blue eyes that didn't miss anything. "I try not to worry—try to give my troubles over to the Lord." She sighed. "I don't mean to pry too much into your personal life, but I have this awful feeling that something is. . .off between you and Luke."

Summer had always heard that the first step to recovery was admitting there was a problem. And while she might be ready to finally admit to herself that something was amiss between them, she certainly didn't want Gram worrying about it. "We'll be fine." Now it was her turn to pat Gram's hand reassuringly rather than the other way around. "Dealing with Bobby's accident and then losing the baby have made the past year difficult. But Luke and I are fine." She managed a smile. "Really, we are."

Gram raised an eyebrow but didn't press the issue. "Well, just know that if you want to talk to me about anything, I'm here to listen."

"I know." Summer gave her a smile that she hoped was convincing.

"And I'll be praying for you both."

Summer's eyes filled with unexpected tears.

Prayer might be the only thing that could help them now.

Chapter 10

Luke stood in the grand foyer of the Rutledge home. It looked like no one else from the party had noticed Summer's abrupt exit. That was best for everyone. The last thing she needed was for a fuss to be made.

"Everything okay?" Jefferson asked from the doorway. "I noticed Summer rush off. I hope she's feeling okay."

Luke eyed him suspiciously. Surely Summer hadn't confided the truth in Jefferson when they'd seen each other earlier in the week. Gossip spread within Charleston society faster than the Confederate Jasmine that crept up the wrought iron gate leading to their house. If Jefferson knew about her miscarriage, Summer's family would, too. "She's fine." He took a sip of tea. "It's awfully hot out there today. I think she needed to come inside for a few minutes to cool down."

Jefferson raised an eyebrow but didn't comment on the feeble excuse. "Did she mention that I've moved back to town?"

Luke held his tongue. Somehow, even after all these years, Jefferson managed to bring out the worst in him. "We didn't really talk much about you." *Because you don't matter to us anymore, you arrogant man.*

"I'll admit, Summer choosing you over me was a huge

part of the reason I left Charleston in the first place," Jefferson said. "But now that I've been around the world and had some wonderful experiences of my own, I figured it was time to come back home. I missed my family too much to let such an insignificant thing keep me away."

Luke's jaw tensed. Jefferson was clearly trying to bait him into some kind of argument. But why? "Well, I'm sure the welcome wagon will be wheeled out for you before long."

Jefferson laughed. "You still don't like me very much do you?"

Luke leveled his gaze on his old nemesis. "I don't give you much thought anymore."

"Well, maybe you should try this on for size: you may have thought you won back then, but really there was no competition." Jefferson's lips turned upward in a menacing smile. "Oh, I know you thought there was. And sure, I played along because you were so much fun to mess with. But if I'd have really wanted her, I would've had her." He shrugged. "It's that simple."

Luke took a step toward Jefferson. The other man might be taller, but Luke had broken up enough bar fights to know how to throw a punch. And there was nothing he'd like more than to wipe that smug expression off of Jefferson's face.

"How's it going in here?" Thomas Rutledge asked, coming into the room and looking from Luke to Jefferson. "The party seems to have moved inside. Is the heat too much for you boys?" The worry etched on his face belied his casual tone.

Jefferson chuckled. "No sir. I had to make a phone call, and Luke here was checking on his wife." He gestured upstairs. "I think she's in her room."

Thomas clasped Jefferson on the back. "Mitch is looking for you." He jerked his chin toward the french doors. "I think he wants to challenge you to a game of horseshoes."

"I'm never one to back down from a challenge." Jefferson shot a parting look at Luke and walked out of the room.

Luke raked his fingers through his hair, suddenly uncomfortable at being left alone with his father-in-law. "Thanks for having us over," he said finally.

Thomas looked at him with eyes that looked remarkably like his daughter's. "I wish you and Summer would visit more often."

Luke stood silently. In the months since Bobby's accident, Summer's dad had reached out to him numerous times. And each time, he'd rebuffed. Those memories from when he and Summer had first met, and how her parents had disapproved of him, stung too much. If he hadn't been good enough then, he wasn't good enough now. "We stay pretty busy. Summer's business really picks up about this time of year, and it's hard for her to find a free weekend."

Thomas took a sip of his drink. "Well, you're welcome even if she can't make it. I'm always looking for a fishing partner."

A laugh caught in Luke's throat. All these years, and Thomas wanted to be friends now? Too little too late. Same as his own dad. "I appreciate the offer. Maybe we'll do that one of these days."

The words seemed to placate Thomas. "Is Summer not feeling well? I saw Mother go after her." He frowned. "That woman has a sixth sense when it comes to one of her children or grandchildren being sick."

So her exit hadn't been as unnoticed as he'd hoped. "I think she's just hot. And tired." He shook his head. "And she hasn't eaten anything yet." He forced a smile. "Bad combo."

Thomas nodded. "She needs to take better care of herself." He sighed. "Well, remember my offer. You have my number. If you ever have a free Saturday, I'd love to hit the water."

"I'll keep that in mind." *Not a chance.*

An hour later, Luke had made small talk with several of Summer's relatives and family friends.

Alone.

He hated this kind of thing, but he forced a smile and turned on the charm.

"Please drag my sister away from work one night, and let's all go out to dinner," Summer's younger sister, Chloe, trilled. "Preston and I love Fig. We go there all the time, and I always say, 'We should ask Summer and Luke to meet us here,' because, you know, it isn't far from where you live." She paused for a breath. "And I'm thinking of getting Summer to help plan my baby shower. The big one, you know, the main one. Like the one that will be more of an event. Not just a tea or something, but a real sit-down dinner and celebration of our good news."

Luke watched her mouth, wondering how such a tiny person could use so many words in such a short time. Listening to her exhausted him. He glanced over at her husband, Preston. The man watched her adoringly and hung on to her every word. *It takes all kinds.* "I'm pretty sure that Summer is booked for a while." The last thing his wife needed was to have to plan her sister's baby shower. Not now.

Preston put an arm around Chloe. "We'll make sure you have the biggest, most fantastic baby shower this city has ever seen." He pulled her close and planted a kiss on her cheek. "Anything for my girl."

Chloe giggled like a teenager on her first date.

Luke fought to keep from rolling his eyes. "Great to see you guys." He jerked his chin toward the house. "I'm going to see if Summer's ready to go."

Thirty minutes later, he and Summer finally climbed into their SUV. She leaned her head against the seat. "Man. What a day." She glanced at him. "Sorry I left you to navigate the party alone." She reached over and patted his knee.

He pulled onto the main road. "No problem." He sighed. "Your dad invited me to go fishing with him. And I had a run-in with Jefferson. And Chloe and Preston."

She removed her hand from his knee. "Sorry."

They rode in silence for a few minutes. Luke wanted nothing more than to get home. He needed to mow the yard, and one of the flower beds could use some mulching. Sometimes it seemed like he could never get everything done.

He flipped on the radio and turned it to an '80s station. The sound of U2 filled the vehicle, and Luke felt the tension begin to leave his body. Until he felt Summer's eyes on him. He finally turned the volume down and glanced at her from the corner of his eye. "What? Is it too loud?"

"You don't think we should talk about things?"

He sighed. "I know we argued earlier, but can't we put that behind us?"

"You want to put everything behind us. Pretend like nothing has happened." She sniffed. "It doesn't work like that."

"I don't know what you mean."

"Don't you? Because if you're serious, then you really are the world's worst communicator." She crossed her arms. "You didn't want to talk about Bobby's accident. You didn't want to talk about our baby." Her voice shook with emotion. "But maybe *I* need to talk about those things."

Luke shook his head. He knew her well enough to know that when her voice took that tone there was no reasoning with her. "You're upset about Chloe's pregnancy. You can take it out on me if you want to. I'm used to being the scapegoat."

"You're wrong. I'm not upset about Chloe. I'm *happy* for her. It was a shock, that's all. I wish I'd had some warning. Learning about it in such a public place was hard." She sighed. "You know how much I looked forward to making our own announcement."

He'd looked forward to it, too. He'd had this image of himself passing out those pink or blue bubblegum cigars to all the guys at work. He'd seen that once on some TV show, and it had stuck with him. But he could never tell Summer that. There was no reason to make her any sadder than she already was. "I know. And I'm glad you're happy for Chloe. Me, too." Maybe not, but he would be by the time the baby arrived. It's not like they saw her that much anyway.

Summer sighed. "I don't want to fight anymore. It's been such a long day."

"You want to go out to dinner tonight?" He glanced over at her. "We could go to Magnolia's." Her favorite restaurant was bound to lift her spirits. "I'll even spring for fried green tomatoes." He hated fried green tomatoes, but Summer had always loved them.

"Yeah. That sounds great." She reached over and turned up the radio.

The familiar strains of Bon Jovi's "Never Say Goodbye" filled the vehicle.

"No way." Luke chuckled. "Do you remember this?"

"Of course I do," she said. "How could I forget the first time you told me you loved me?"

Luke reached over and took her hand.

"What a night that was," he said. "And just think. . .if I'd have had my way, you would've married me as soon as we could get to a justice of the peace."

She looked down at their intertwined hands. She'd held on to his hand through so much. The first time he'd told her he loved her had been such a magical night.

"You were the most beautiful debutante I'd ever seen." Luke squeezed her hand. "And I still say that you could've passed for a bride in that white dress."

Summer's mouth turned upward in a smile. "I must've looked like some kind of crazy person sneaking out of Gram's house in that dress. But I wanted you to see it. When I got ready that night, it was you I wanted to impress." After the ball, she'd climbed down a ladder from the second floor piazza and hurried to the Battery to meet Luke.

"Have you been waiting long?" Summer hurried up the steps to the bandstand.

Luke let out a low whistle. *"I'd wait on you forever."* He grabbed her around the waist and pulled her close. *"Don't you know that?"* He leaned in and kissed her on the lips until they were both breathless.

"Sorry that it took me so long to get here. My parents kept questioning why I wanted to stay at Gram's tonight." She grinned. *"Sometimes I think Gram knows that when I stay with her I sneak out and meet you, but she hasn't said anything about it yet."*

Luke laced his fingers with hers. *"I'm glad I have at least one fan in your family."*

"You have two." She reached up and traced her fingers over his smooth face. *"I'm your biggest fan. I always will be."*

He raised his eyebrows. *"You sure you wouldn't rather be with Jeff?"*

She rolled her eyes. *"Jefferson doesn't hold a candle to you. How many times do I have to tell you that?"*

Luke knelt down and flipped on a tiny radio, and a Bon Jovi ballad filled the night air. *"May I have this dance?"* He pulled her close, and they swayed to the music. *"There's something I need to tell you,"* he murmured against her hair.

She pulled back so she could see his face. *"You're really a mirage?"* she asked.

He laughed softly. *"No. I'm totally real. And I love you, Summer Rutledge. With all of my heart."* He kissed her gently on the mouth. *"I always will."*

Luke squeezed her hand. "You okay? I don't think you've

heard a word I said."

Summer glanced over at him. "Sorry. I was just thinking about that night. We were so young—"

"And so in love." He slowed down as they reached their street.

Summer nodded. *So in love.*

She wondered if Luke would've done anything differently if he had it to do all over. Would he have given up on his dreams to move back to Charleston to be with her? Would he have married her despite her family's misgivings?

She wondered those things, but she didn't have the guts to ask.

Chapter 11

Ashley poured herself a second cup of coffee. The phone at Summer Weddings had been ringing nonstop all morning. And with Summer out meeting a client, Ashley was manning the office by herself. She'd already had to talk a very grumpy bride off of a ledge. The young lady wanted to change her wedding colors at the last minute and hadn't been happy to hear the cost involved.

Adding to her stress was the fact that Justin was supposed to meet her for lunch today. She knew it wasn't a date. It was just business. But nevertheless, she'd taken great pains to look nice. Her bright pink wrap dress clung to her figure in all the right spots. With her hair pulled back into a smooth ponytail and her strappy black sandals, she'd felt pretty confident when she left the house this morning. She might be on the back side of thirty, but she could still pass for younger.

But as the lunch hour neared, her confidence waned. Friday night she'd felt cute and sassy and had even flirted with Justin. But she'd learned a long time ago that there was something about a warm Friday night, listening to music and laughing with friends, that made her feel light and free. Now, in the light of day and the middle of the workweek, she only felt foolish for even thinking a nice guy like Justin could be interested in being more than just her web designer.

She took a deep breath. Going through a divorce was hard for anyone. But when you had to sit by and watch as your husband chose another woman over you, it stripped away all of your self-confidence. It made you feel worthless and unlovable. Ashley had fought with those feelings of unworthiness for years. She'd thought she was over them. But today they were back with a vengeance.

The ringing phone jolted her from her walk down memory lane. "Summer Weddings, this is Ashley," she said into the receiver.

"Ashley," a male voice said. "It's Justin. Justin Sanders. We're supposed to meet today."

Her heart pounded so hard, she was sure he could hear it over the phone. She was so out of practice at this. "Y–yes. How are you, Justin?"

He laughed, a warm, rich sound that reminded her of summertime and lemonade and all the things she'd loved from childhood. "I'm just dandy." He cleared his throat. "Actually, somethin' has come up at the last minute. I was wondering if we could reschedule."

Disappointment washed over her. "Oh sure." She tried to tell herself it had nothing to do with him not wanting to spend time with her. He was a busy man. Something probably had come up.

"Well, I was thinking. . .maybe we might get together tonight?" Justin asked.

"Sure. I can stay late if you want to come by. I usually leave around five, but I can stay until six or so if that works for you." She wasn't crazy about staying late but would if she had to. Especially if it meant getting to know Justin a little better.

Justin laughed. "No. That's not what I meant. I was thinking more like maybe I could come pick you up at your place. Take you out to a nice dinner. How's seven?"

Was he asking her on a date? Because that sounded awfully datelike. "Um. . .sure. That could work. Seven is fine." She gave him directions to her house and hung up.

Ashley was still staring at the phone when Summer walked into the store.

"You okay?" Summer asked, a concerned expression on her face.

"What? Oh yeah. I'm fine." She filled Summer in on the development with Justin.

Summer's eyes widened. "That's awesome. You'll have a great time. Justin is the sweetest, nicest guy, but he's always been painfully shy. I'm surprised he was so brazen as to suggest coming to your house. He's not making any effort to hide that he wants to get to know you on a personal level."

"I wouldn't normally give my address to some guy I only met once. But since you and Luke know him so well, it should be okay. Right?"

Summer grinned. "Definitely okay. He's the most respectful guy you'll ever meet."

Ashley couldn't hide her excitement. She was finally ready to move on with her life.

And Justin sounded like exactly the kind of guy she'd been looking for.

Summer was happy for Ashley, but she didn't envy her. The thought of dating at this stage in life didn't sound like much fun. "I'm going to run out and grab some lunch." She walked over to Ashley's desk. "Do you want to go? Or do you want me to pick something up for you?"

Ashley shook her head. "Thanks. But I think I'll just heat up a Lean Cuisine."

"Suit yourself." Summer grabbed her bag and headed out the door. She wouldn't have minded if Ashley had come with her, but since she was alone, she'd be able to stop by the cemetery. Ever since Chloe's announcement at the barbeque, Summer had felt the need to go and spend some time at the grave of the little baby who'd passed away so many years ago.

She slipped her sunglasses on and walked down King Street. Several shoppers milled around, their hands full of bags. She passed by a frozen yogurt shop full of college students from the nearby College of Charleston.

Summer peeked into the window of an antique shop. She'd always loved antiquing, even though Luke preferred brand-new things. Their home was decorated with an eclectic mix of pieces that had been in her family for generations and new purchases she and Luke had bought together. She kept going, enjoying the warm breeze. Charleston could be unbearably hot in the summer, but late May was perfect.

She reached the entrance to the church cemetery and

walked through the iron gates. The shade made the temperature drop immediately. She inhaled, and the sticky-sweet smell of honeysuckle took her back to a childhood spent playing amid the gardens of Gram's friends.

She settled onto the stone bench and read the headstone for what had to be the hundredth time. A tiny life, only on this earth for a day. She wondered again about the child's mother. How had she survived the loss? Had her will to live died along with her baby? If she could find the energy, she could probably locate the story in the archives. But she knew it would be a story of sadness. Even if the woman had gone on to have ten children, that didn't diminish the loss of this one.

"I thought I might find you here."

She turned at the sound of Jefferson's voice. "Were you looking for me?" She hadn't spoken to him much at the barbecue, but Luke had confessed over dinner Saturday night that he and Jefferson had gotten into it a bit. No surprise there.

His face broke into a grin. "Yes and no." He nodded toward the bench where she sat. "Do you mind?"

She shrugged. "I guess not."

"I didn't set out to look for you, but I happened to be walking by and thought I'd pop in to see if you were here." He stretched his legs out in front of him. "My office is right down the street. It's amazing how things have stayed the same. There are more tourists though." He raked his fingers through his hair. "I was going to go grab lunch, and there are lines outside most of the restaurants."

She laughed. "Hey, tourism is good for my business, so I don't mind."

"I guess." He was quiet for a moment. "I want you to know how nice it is to see you again. I know I've done things in the past, things I'm not proud of." He peered at her. "But I've turned over a new leaf."

She raised her eyebrows. Jefferson had never been a bad guy, just a spoiled one. The kind of guy who was used to getting what he wanted and never knew how to handle himself when he was rebuffed. "I'm glad to hear that. Although I imagine it's just that you've grown up." She pushed a stray hair from her face. "We knew each other as kids. Not adults. We're both different now."

He shook his head. "Not that different. The same things that drew me to you back then draw me to you now."

Summer ducked her head. "Don't be silly."

"I don't mean to make you uncomfortable. At all." He shook his head. "But I do want to be your friend. We have a history that dates back to us in a playpen." He chuckled. "I don't want to throw away that kind of history just because we didn't work out as a couple."

Friends. With Jefferson. A part of her said it would be improper. But another part was happy to see him. Jefferson reminded her of being seven years old and learning to ride a bike. Of suffering through manners classes at the insistence of their mothers. And of going Christmas caroling in the sixth grade. She nodded. "I'd like to be friends."

He looked her in the eyes. "I'm glad. I wanted to talk to you at the barbecue. I was worried about you. The way you ran off like that."

"I wasn't feeling well." Even to her own ears, the excuse sounded flimsy.

He nodded. "That's what Luke said. But I could tell he was concerned." Jefferson rose from the bench and smoothed his gray suit jacket. "Just know that if you ever need an old friend to talk to, I'm right down the road."

"Thanks," she murmured.

With a wave, Jefferson headed toward the gate.

Summer let out a sigh and turned her attention back to the headstone in front of her. She should've brought flowers.

Maybe next week.

She walked slowly out of the cemetery and headed toward her office.

Chapter 12

Justin pulled up in front of Ashley's house in his brother's car. A fancy red sports car. He was going to put forth his best effort here. He hopped out of the car and hurried up the sidewalk.

The car wasn't the only thing borrowed for this date. He'd left behind his normal uniform of T-shirt and jeans and allowed his sister-in-law to choose his clothes for the night. Thankfully he and his brother were the same size. He tried to block the thought that the clothes he wore tonight probably cost more than the money he brought home in a month.

He rapped on the door and waited for Ashley to answer it. He hoped that the borrowed car and clothes would help him shed his normal self. Justin was tired of being the perpetual friend. The one girls told their problems to before they proceeded to settle for some jerk. Nope. That was the old Justin. The new Justin was going to be a different kind of guy.

The door swung open, and Ashley stood before him with a grin on her pretty face. She wore a pink dress that clung to her figure in all the right places.

"Wow." He smiled. "You look amazing." Her blond hair was pulled back into a ponytail, and her makeup was minimal.

Which he appreciated. There was nothing worse than a woman who hid behind a lot of makeup.

She blushed. "Thanks." She motioned into the house. "Do you want to come in for a minute?"

He shrugged. "Sure." He glanced at his watch. "But we have reservations, so we need to leave soon."

"Reservations?" Her green eyes were wide. "It isn't a fancy place is it? Maybe I should change."

He shook his head. "Not too fancy. And you look fine."

She wrinkled her forehead. "Okay. Well, let's go then." She grabbed a black purse and ushered him to the door.

Once they were outside, he hit the unlock button on the key fob. His own vehicle, an old pickup truck, didn't have one of those. Even the windows had to be rolled down manually. Daniel's car was much better suited for dating.

Ashley paused at the passenger door for a moment. He knew she was giving him the chance to open the door for her. Normally, he would've been all over that. He was nothing if not a Southern gentleman. But he'd seen the way it worked. Women always fell for jerks.

So tonight he intended on being one.

Ashley settled into the low leather seat of the sports car and buckled her seat belt. For some reason, she'd pegged Justin as a truck guy. The flashy red car surprised her.

But one thing she'd learned was that people weren't

always what they seemed.

Justin hopped in the car and started the engine. He flashed her a smile. "Hope you're hungry. Our reservation is at the Peninsula Grill."

Ashley raised her eyebrows. She'd never been there but had heard good things about the place. It was a little more upscale and romantic than she was used to. And definitely not what she'd had in mind for a first date. "Sounds great."

He merged onto the interstate going south, cutting off another vehicle in the process.

Ashley cringed as he maneuvered the little red car through traffic like they were in a life-sized game of Frogger. She gripped the seat belt and prayed they'd make it safely.

"Not going too fast for you, am I, babe?" he asked, adjusting his sunglasses.

She furrowed her brow. Babe? "Um. Actually you *are* going a little fast. I didn't realize we were in some kind of race."

He chuckled. "Life's one big rat race, didn't you know?" But he slowed down some. "So tell me about yourself."

Ashley took a deep breath. She was really doing this— dating. Moving on. Getting to know someone new. It felt scary, but the good kind of scary. Like when she'd gone paragliding that time in Switzerland. "I'm originally from a small town in Alabama. I graduated from Auburn with a degree in business and lived in Birmingham for a while." She shrugged. "And I moved to Charleston three years ago."

Justin reached over and patted her on the leg. "I'm so glad you did."

She froze. It was way too early for any kind of physical

contact. She wasn't a prude, but she did think the hand on the knee should wait until they at least knew each others' birthdays. She shifted in the seat, hoping he'd get the hint. "Yeah, it's been a good move. I enjoy working with Summer, and I've found a church I like." There. Surely a mention of church would shame him into taking his hand off of her.

"That's great." He squeezed her knee again.

She jerked her leg out of his reach. "Please don't do that."

He pulled his hand away. "Sorry. You just look so good in that dress."

"Thanks." Relief washed over her as they got to the restaurant.

Justin pulled the car into a space and hopped out.

Ashley sat for a long moment, but he didn't open her door. How strange. . .and rude. He'd seemed so normal the other night. But now. . .he was another person. She got out of the car and walked over to where he stood on the sidewalk. "I'm starved."

"I'm glad to hear it. Most of the girls I go out with only eat salads." He looked her up and down. "But you look like you enjoy a real meal every now and then. Not like those stick-straight, skinny girls."

She widened her eyes in horror. She'd always been curvy, but she wasn't overweight. But to hear a guy she barely knew comment on her shape threw her for a loop. Still reeling, she followed Justin up the sidewalk.

They entered the restaurant, and Justin sauntered up to the hostess. "We have a reservation." He grinned. "For Sanders."

The girl returned his smile and scanned the list. She

looked up with a puzzled expression. "I don't see that name on the list."

Justin leaned forward. "Can you check again? S-a-n-d-e-r-s."

The flustered hostess shook her head. "I'm sorry. It's not on here." She glanced at Ashley. "I'm really sorry about that."

"You're *sorry* about it? How exactly does that help us?" Justin sneered.

The hostess glanced down at the list. "We're not too busy tonight. If y'all don't mind waiting a little while, we'll be able to seat you even without a reservation." She looked at them hopefully.

Ashley gave her an encouraging smile. She'd worked her way through college as a hostess and knew all too well what it was like to deal with rude people.

"How long will the wait be?" Justin asked.

The hostess checked the list again. "Probably about thirty minutes. Maybe forty-five."

"That's not acceptable," Justin said. "It isn't our fault that you messed up our reservation. Is there a manager I can speak with?"

Ashley couldn't take it any longer. She placed a hand on Justin's arm. "Actually, if it's okay with you, I'd like for you to take me home."

He whipped around and stared at her with wide eyes. "Take you home? But we haven't eaten."

She would've liked nothing more than to tell him exactly what she thought of him. But she wanted to make it home in one piece. "I'm not feeling that great. I'd appreciate it if you'd take me home now."

Ashley didn't even try to make small talk in the car on the way back to her house. There was no point. She wanted to get home and change into her comfy clothes and forget that this disaster of a night ever happened.

Chapter 13

What is wrong with you, man?" Luke asked. "Why would you ever think that was a good idea?"

"I'm a complete idiot." Justin put his head in his hands. He'd been so distraught, he'd asked Luke to meet him for lunch. Except that after last night's disaster, Justin had completely lost his appetite.

Luke shook his head. "Not usually. But this time, yeah, you were."

Justin cut his eyes at Luke. "Thanks for the brutal honesty."

Luke held his hands up. "I'm sorry, but pretending to be someone you're not is kind of idiotic."

"Yeah, she wasn't much of a fan. In fact, she asked me to take her home after the fiasco with our reservations." He made a face. "I should've come clean right then, but I knew how dumb it would sound."

Luke nodded. "It does sound pretty dumb."

"Cut me some slack, okay?" Justin asked. "You know my track record. I date women who end up leaving me for guys who treat them like dirt. It's a never-ending cycle." He took a sip of his Coke. "Look at Samantha. She'd rather exchange letters with a guy in prison than date me."

Luke almost spit out his drink. "I'm not sure, but I think the problem might be them. Not you." He shook his head. "I'm only going to tell you this because you've clearly gone off into the deep end here." He met Justin's gaze. "But I think part of the problem is the women you choose. I've watched you go through them. And Justin, these ladies have problems. Problems too big for you to fix."

Justin nodded. He did have a habit of getting involved with women whose lives were in shambles. "I like to feel useful."

Luke snorted. "Okay. So find a nice, normal girl who needs help mowing her yard. Or changing a tire. Not raising a child or bailing her mama out of jail."

Justin managed a smile. He had definitely gone out with some colorful characters. "Ashley seems like she's got it together."

"She does. At least as far as I know." Luke took a sip of his drink. "I'm thinking you might want to give that one another shot. Only without your alter ego."

"You think she'll speak to me again?" Justin asked.

"I have no idea. But there's only one way to find out." Luke glanced at his watch. "I have to run. I have a meeting." He pounded Justin on the back. "But good luck."

Summer paced the length of her office. "I'm really sorry. That doesn't sound at all like Justin." She couldn't believe the story Ashley had told her. "If I'd had any idea he would act like that, I never would've encouraged you."

"It's not your fault." Ashley looked up from her computer. "I thought I'd become a pretty good judge of character, but clearly I was way off the mark with this one."

"Well, if it makes you feel any better, I never would've thought he would act like that." Summer sat down at her desk and crossed her legs. "But then I've never been on a date with him." She was glad to see a smile finally brighten Ashley's face.

"Maybe it's me. I'm some kind of magnet for bad boy behavior. Clearly I can turn even the nicest guy into a world-class jerk." She shook her head.

"Don't say that."

"Seriously. My ex-husband had everyone snowed. Me especially. I didn't know what I'd gotten into until I was legally bound. And now with Justin. . ." Ashley trailed off. "I know I'd only met him once, but I thought he was one of the good guys."

Summer smiled. "Think of it this way—you're slowly but surely weeding out the guys who aren't right for you."

Ashley sighed. "I guess."

"Don't give Justin another thought." Summer locked eyes with Ashley. "Put him out of your mind. At least you didn't invest more than one night, right?"

"Right." Ashley brightened. "You're exactly right. I'll forget him and move on."

Summer motioned toward the door. "Now I'm going to run and grab some coffee from City Lights. You want me to bring you a muffin or something?" City Lights Coffee on Market Street was one of Summer's favorite spots. She adored local places where the barista knew her name and the coffee was served in a real porcelain mug.

Ashley shook her head. "No. Thanks though. I think I'll go out to lunch to cheer myself up." She managed a smile. "Maybe splurge and get a cupcake or something."

"A girl needs a cupcake every now and then." Summer grinned. She shoved her sunglasses on top of her head and hurried outside. Just as she was about to cross Meeting Street, she saw Luke standing outside of Toast. The restaurant was one of their favorites. If she'd known he was going to be around at this time of day, she would've offered to meet him for lunch.

"Lu—" The word caught in her throat as she watched him wave to a familiar redhead.

Sherry. The girl from the Sand and Suds.

Summer watched in horror as Luke held the door open for Sherry. She froze on the sidewalk, causing a woman to run into her.

"Sorry," the woman said. "I didn't see you stop." She shot an irritated look in Summer's direction as she passed by.

Summer struggled to keep breathing. She leaned against the brick building she was in front of, hoping her legs were steady enough to get her back to the office. Her knees wobbled, nearly buckling underneath her.

"Ma'am," a college-aged guy said. "Are you okay? Can I help you?"

"I–I'm not feeling well," she said weakly.

He peered at her through kind brown eyes. "You're white as a ghost." He jerked his chin toward a bench. "Let me help you sit down." He grasped her by the elbow and led her to the bench.

"Let me run inside there and get you a Coke." He pointed at the Subway restaurant across the street. "I'll be right back, ma'am. Just sit tight."

Summer had never been more thankful for well-brought-up Southern boys. Although she could've done without the "ma'ams." She took a deep breath and wondered what she should do next. Confront Luke? March right inside the restaurant and act surprised to see him?

"Here you go." The young man walked up clutching a fountain drink. "Maybe your blood sugar was low."

"Yes. . .maybe." She took the drink and smiled at him. "Thank you so much for your help." She dug through her purse and came up with a five-dollar bill. "Here you go—this should cover the drink."

He shook his head. "Don't worry about it. You can be my good deed for the day." With a wave, he was gone.

Her blood pumped so quickly, it thundered inside her head and drowned out the street sounds around her. The thought of Luke with another woman made her physically ill. Sure, they'd been going through a rough patch, but she'd never dreamed he might turn to someone else.

Summer kept her eyes glued to the door of Toast.

After what seemed like an eternity, Luke and Sherry exited the restaurant. They stood on the sidewalk, talking and laughing.

Sherry reached up and gave Luke a hug and hurried off down the street.

Summer stood. Had they made another date? She quickly

crossed the street and stopped in front of her husband. "Fancy meeting you here."

She watched as Luke's eyes grew wide. And couldn't help but see the flicker of guilt flash across his face.

Chapter 14

Luke couldn't believe his luck. He must be cursed or something.

"Hi there, honey."

Summer narrowed her eyes. "Don't 'honey' me. Do you have lunch with groupies often? Or is the redhead special?"

He groaned, wondering if he could talk his way out of this disaster. "No. I ran into her, and we were both headed to the same place." He shrugged. "No big deal." He looked closely at Summer's face to see if she believed his fib. Clearly she did not.

"I saw you meet up with her on the sidewalk. It was a planned meeting. Don't lie to me, Luke. We've been through too much for that."

He swallowed. Maybe it was time to come clean. "I'm parked in the lot on Queen Street. Come with me, and I'll explain."

He put his hand on the small of her back to guide her, but she sidestepped away from him.

"I don't want to go anywhere with you." She looked at her watch. "Besides, I should be getting back to work."

Luke sighed. Her life revolved around work. "Ashley can

cover for another hour." He faced her and put his hands on her shoulders. "Please. Trust me. There's something I want to show you."

She didn't speak for a long moment. "Fine. But I need to be back to the office in an hour." She locked eyes with him. "Promise?"

He nodded. "Come on."

They walked silently to his truck. It took all his restraint not to let his anger out. The idea that he was the kind of man who'd sneak around on the sly and meet up with random women really annoyed him. Summer had been the absolute center of his universe since he was barely seventeen. Seeing the accusation on her face and hearing it in her voice ran all over him.

"Where are we going?" she asked once they were in the truck.

He shook his head. "Nope. Just be patient." He cast a sideways glance at her. "Please?" This wasn't how he'd wanted to do it. He'd expected to have more time to plan. But he'd learned a long time ago to roll with the punches.

Twenty minutes later he slowed down and pulled into a parking lot.

"The marina?" Summer looked at him with narrowed eyes. "What are we doing here?"

He couldn't hide his smile. "You never were very good at patience, were you?"

"Might not be my best virtue, but I'm good at other stuff."

Luke chuckled and brought the truck to a stop. He walked around and opened the passenger door and held out a hand.

Summer accepted it and stepped daintily to the ground. "This had better be good. Because I haven't forgotten about you and that *woman*."

Luke shut his eyes. If he were still in the habit of praying, he would've prayed that the Lord would give him strength to tolerate her barbs without snapping. But instead, he'd just wish for it. "I have a surprise for you, actually. And that's what my meeting with Sherry was about." He reached over and grabbed her hand, hoping she wouldn't jerk away.

She didn't.

"Honestly. I wasn't having some covert affair with Jimmy's cousin." He shook his head. "I would hope you know me better than that by now."

Summer gripped his hand. "Sometimes I don't feel like I know you at all anymore," she said quietly.

The words pierced his heart. His only hope was that the anniversary gift he'd gotten her would help bring them closer together. "Sure you do. I'm still the same old Luke." He pulled her into an embrace. "I'm the same boy you fell in love with. And the same man you married seven years ago." He'd missed having her in his arms. They fit together perfectly. "I wanted to give you this gift on our actual anniversary, but since you caught me finalizing the deal, I'm going to go ahead and give it to you today."

He led her down to the water where a line of boats sat in a row.

They stopped at the third boat. "See that?"

She looked at him with a puzzled expression. "Yeah."

"Look at the name of the boat."

She took a step closer and peered at the side of the boat. "No way," she said.

"The *Summer Girl*," Luke said. "I hope you love it."

Summer smiled. "I can't believe you did this." She shot him a sideways glance. "We've always said we were going to buy one."

"And spend our weekends out on the water, just the two of us." He returned her smile. "I even got a life vest for Milo so he can come, too." He chuckled. "Although he might have to lose a couple of pounds first."

She joined in his laughter. "We'll have so much fun."

Fun. They hadn't had much fun together over the past year. It seemed like it had been one thing after another. Luke had hoped that purchasing the boat would bring them closer together again. "I'm glad you like it."

She threw her arms around his neck then pulled back. "But how does the redhead figure into things?"

Luke laughed. "She paints names and scenes on boats. It's part of her business." He rubbed Summer's back. "I mentioned to the guys several weeks ago that I'd bought the boat, and Jimmy told me about his cousin." He shrugged. "She's had some hard times and could use the business, so I hired her. I didn't want to have lunch with her at all. I'd just planned to drop off a check. But then she begged me to sit with her, said she hated to eat alone. So I did." He tipped Summer's chin. "Nothing more to it."

She at least had the decency to look sheepish. "Sorry." She drew her brows together. "But how did you manage to make a purchase this large without me knowing?" Summer kept the books for their accounts because she loved the satisfaction of seeing all the numbers balance.

He'd hoped she wouldn't ask. "Oh. That." He cleared his throat. "Well, I knew there was one account you wouldn't monitor."

Realization dawned on her, and the color drained from her face. "You didn't."

He swallowed. "It's not a big deal." He'd thought he'd have time to fix this before she found out.

"Not a big deal? Not a big deal?" Her voice rose with each word. "You used the money from the baby account, didn't you?" she hissed.

He nodded. He'd known she might be a little upset but hadn't counted on the venom he saw in her eyes. "Don't get so worked up. It was just sitting there, and I thought that would be the best way to keep it a surprise."

Tears rolled down her face. "I knew you didn't want to keep trying to have a baby. But I never thought you'd do something like this."

Luke paced in front of her. "We can replenish it." He reached out to brush a tear away, but she stepped back. "It's not a big deal."

"Quit saying that. It *is* a big deal. At least to me." She wiped her eyes and took another step backward. "You didn't even consider how this would make me feel, did you?"

"I thought I was doing something that would make you happy."

She shook her head. "You haven't made me happy in months. You tried to pretend that our baby never existed." Her tears started falling again, and this time she let them fall. "You wouldn't talk about it, wouldn't grieve with me." She sobbed in earnest now. "And I didn't have the energy to fight then. Not even when you emptied out the nursery and took all the baby stuff to the dump."

"I was trying to help."

She fished around in her purse for a tissue and wiped her face. "I'm done."

He sighed. "Do you want me to take you home instead of the office?"

Summer shook her head. "No. I'm done. Here." She pointed from her to him. "Us. I'm done."

Luke furrowed his brow. "I know you're mad, but don't you think you're overreacting?"

She leveled a steely gaze at him. "Maybe. But I don't care right now. You like this boat so much? Then why don't you plan on staying on it for a while?" She turned and started walking toward the road.

Luke ran after her. "Summer, come on. Get in the truck."

"No. I'm too tired. Tired of pretending everything is okay. Tired of pretending like we aren't broken. I need some time alone."

Something in her voice stopped him in his tracks. "You want me to leave you here?"

She lifted her chin defiantly. "I'll call Ashley. She'll come pick me up."

He watched her walk toward the main road. There was no use in going after her.

If space was what she wanted, space was what she'd get.

Summer climbed into Ashley's Honda Accord. "Thanks for coming to pick me up."

Ashley looked at her with concern. "Are you okay?"

Summer shook her head. "No." She put her head in her hands. "Can you take me home?"

"Of course." Ashley turned the car toward downtown.

Summer tried to process everything, but her brain felt too foggy. "I'm sorry," she whispered. "I know I've been out of the office most of the day."

Ashley let out a sigh. "Don't you think you should focus on something besides work right now?" She slowed down for a red light. "Something has obviously happened, something bad." She looked at Summer. "Do you want to tell me what?"

Summer let out a shaky breath. She knew it seemed crazy to most people for her to be so focused on work, but that was what she'd clung to these past months. When everything else spun out of control, she could at least make sure her business ran smoothly. "Luke and I got into a fight. A big one." She filled Ashley in on what had transpired at the marina. "And the awful part is that he probably thinks it's about the money. It isn't." She shook her head. "He can buy all the boats he wants to buy. But that account was special."

"I knew things between you guys had been strained, but I didn't realize you were at the end of your rope like that." Ashley pulled into the driveway at Summer and Luke's house.

For the first time in a long time, Summer didn't admire the home she loved so much. Today it seemed more like a mockery than anything else. From the outside it looked like the kind of home a happy family inhabited. But inside it felt as lonely as a tomb. "I know he thinks I'm crazy for reacting like that." She shook her head. "I realize he was trying to give me a gift and do something nice for me."

Ashley nodded. "It sounds that way."

"But he's been so distant. First with Bobby's accident and then when I lost the baby." Ashley was one of the few people besides Gram who had known about Summer's pregnancy. "After I miscarried, he told me that he didn't want to keep trying. He said he didn't want to do the fertility treatments anymore. That maybe it would happen naturally, even though my doctor didn't think so." She shook her head. "So by using that money, money I'd set aside specifically for my child, it's the same as him saying that we will never have a baby of our own."

"And you're not ready to give up on that dream."

Summer shook her head. "We'd only done one round of treatments when I got pregnant. The doctor said there was no reason I couldn't carry a child to term, even after the miscarriage. But Luke wouldn't even discuss it."

Ashley sighed. "I don't know what to say. I had no idea what you'd been dealing with."

"Luke has slipped further and further away from me over the past months. It's to the point where I have no idea what to say to him most of the time. He doesn't listen to me, doesn't want to hear me talk about my day. And it seems like he finds reasons not to be home at night."

"But you love him."

Summer let out a bitter laugh. "Of course I love him." She met Ashley's eyes. "But for the first time, I wonder if love is enough."

Ashley didn't respond.

"Thanks for the ride. I'll walk Milo over to the office later and pick up my car."

"You're welcome. And if there's anything I can do for you, please let me know."

Summer paused. "Just pray. That's what I need the most."

She watched as Ashley backed out of the driveway and for a split second wished she could have her friend's life. It seemed so uncomplicated. No family around, no husband to argue with. That sounded perfect right about now.

She stumbled into the house and greeted Milo.

"Go outside, sweet boy." She opened the door and watched him run a loop around the yard, sniffing and marking his territory. In a minute, he was back. "Let's go to bed early, what do you say?"

Milo followed her up the stairs. With each step, her feet felt heavier and heavier, almost as if she'd accidentally stepped in wet cement. She made it into the large bathroom with its giant tub and expensive tile. She'd always thought of this as her sanctuary, but today it did nothing to calm her.

She sank onto the floor, and the tears began to fall in earnest.

Milo sat next to her and rested his head on her leg.

The gentleness of the big dog only made her cry harder.

"Lord, why are You letting this happen?" she asked. "What am I supposed to learn from this?" She didn't bother to wipe the tears. "I'm not the one who turned my back on You. Even when I lost my baby, I kept my faith." It had been Luke who'd lost his faith. Luke who'd refused to set foot in a church building after Bobby's accident. Luke who wouldn't pray with her after she lost their baby.

"Please. Please take my pain away," she whispered, hoping God was listening.

And there, huddled on the cold tile floor, Summer hoped she'd finally hit rock bottom. Because if things got worse, she wasn't sure how she would survive.

Chapter 15

Ashley walked into her house and promptly collapsed on the couch.

Work had kept her busy right up until nearly six. She'd taken care of several things that Summer had left behind. It seemed like the least she could do.

Although, the more Summer got distracted, the more Ashley felt entitled to a partnership in the business. Except that with the state Summer was in, it still didn't seem the right time to ask. But maybe there would never be a time that felt right. Maybe she would have to put aside her fears and go for it.

And as much as she hated to admit it, she took some satisfaction with the knowledge that if Summer turned her request down and she resigned, the business would take a hit. Summer didn't have time to find someone else who knew the ins and outs of their upcoming events, and despite all that was going on in her personal life, she would never let her business suffer.

Which gave Ashley leverage.

With that thought in mind, Ashley pulled on an old pair of yoga pants and a T-shirt from a long-ago 5K. She scrubbed the day's makeup from her face and twisted her long hair into a messy bun.

Tonight she would veg. Her DVR contained the entire last season of *The Bachelor*, and she had leftover pizza in the fridge. Perfect combo.

Ashley popped a couple of slices of pizza on a plate and was about to put them in the microwave when the doorbell rang.

She groaned. Probably someone wanting to sell her something. Or a church group wanting to invite her to an upcoming revival. Not that either of those things was bad, but there were times she wished she lived in one of those big gated homes where no one could get to her door unless she wanted them there. Like a princess in a tower.

She peeked through the blinds and saw an unfamiliar pickup truck in her driveway. For the hundredth time, she wished she had a dog. It might give her a little security when there was a stranger at the door. Although she'd probably end up with a dog like Milo, who was more likely to lick someone than bark at them.

She pushed a wayward strand of hair behind her ear and gingerly opened the door.

Justin stood on the porch, holding a bag in one hand and a bouquet of flowers in the other.

You have got to be kidding me. "Justin." She forced a smile. "What brings you here?"

A sheepish expression washed over his boyish face. "I came to apologize."

She shook her head. "That isn't necessary. I appreciate you coming all the way out here though." Her North Charleston home was convenient to lots of shopping and dining, but getting here from downtown meant fighting traffic.

He hung his head. "I knew you'd probably say that, but I also knew that I'd always kick myself if I at least didn't try to explain my behavior."

She regarded him silently for a moment. "Go on," she said finally.

He gestured toward the old pickup. "That's my truck. It's my only vehicle. I've had it since I was in college. My daddy and I built it with parts we got from a scrap yard, but it runs just fine." He gave her a feeble grin. "It's not fancy, but I love it."

She opened her mouth to speak, but he cut her off. "And what I have on right now is the kind of thing I wear pretty much every day." He glanced down at his faded Gamecocks T-shirt and khaki shorts. "Unless I'm meeting a client, and even then I don't dress up much. I can't remember the last time I wore a tie, and I hated that suit I wore the other night." He met her gaze. "It was my brother's."

She smiled at his obvious sincerity. "Then what was that all about? The car, the suit. . .the attitude?"

He handed her the bouquet of flowers. "Can I come in and explain?" He held up a white bag. "I brought something to eat. Burgers from my favorite place."

She waved him inside. Even if she didn't plan to give him another chance, she could still hear him out. Besides, those burgers smelled yummy.

"This is a nice place. I didn't tell you that when I came to pick you up, but I thought it." He followed her into the kitchen and watched as she pulled two plates down from the cabinet.

"Thank you. It took a lot of years, but I was finally able to buy my own place." She'd been proud of the purchase. Living on a single income wasn't always easy. But she'd scrimped and saved after the divorce and finally had enough for a down payment. It might not be South of Broad like Summer and Luke's home, but it was perfect as far as she was concerned. Three bedrooms, two baths, and enough space in the backyard for a flower garden.

"I'm not quite there yet," he said. "I live in an apartment near downtown. It works for now, but I'm kind of at the point where I'm ready to have more room."

She held up bottled water and a soft drink from the fridge and looked at him with raised eyebrows.

"Water, please."

Ashley handed him a bottle and motioned for him to follow her back into the living room. "We can eat in there if that's okay." She paused. "If you're sure you don't mind something casual."

He chuckled. "That's more than okay with me. I'm just thankful you're giving me the chance to explain."

They settled on the couch, and he pulled out a burger from the bag and handed it to her. "I wasn't sure what you'd want— or even if you'd let me past the door—so both of them are the same. Mayo, lettuce, and tomato." He unwrapped his burger. "That's how I always get them."

"Sounds delicious." That was exactly how she liked her burgers, too, but she didn't see any reason to share that information.

Justin handed her a basket of fries. "Hope you like fries."

Ashley smiled broadly. "I'm a huge fan."

He cleared his throat. "Mind if I say a blessing before we eat?"

Wonders never cease. "Please."

He thanked God for their many blessings and asked Him to watch over them.

Ashley met Justin's gaze after he said Amen. "Thanks for praying."

"I know I probably gave you the wrong impression the other night." He shook his head. "None of the stuff that came out of my mouth was stuff I'd ever say or think." He gave her a sideways grin. "Except the part where I said you looked nice."

"Well played." She returned his smile.

He chuckled. "I'm not playing. This isn't a game, I promise. I'm honestly sorry. It's just. . ." He trailed off and put his head in his hands.

Ashley might not have always been the best judge of character, but she knew in her gut that Justin was remorseful for the way he'd acted. "It's okay." She sighed. "But how about you tell me why you did it?" Nothing about his actions the other night added up.

He raised his head and met her gaze. "I'm the perpetual friend. The nice guy." He shrugged. "Since I was in high school, I've been the one women call when they need help or want a shoulder to cry on."

"That all sounds nice to me."

"Well, it's been a world of hurt for me. Because inevitably I'll get close to the girl, and then once her heart is all healed from whatever wound she carries, she moves on to another jerk."

Ashley gave him a tiny smile. "I've seen that kind of thing happen before. I've even been one of those girls actually."

"Yeah?"

She nodded. "And you know what? Those are always the guys I look back on and wish I'd have given a real shot." She'd learned a long time ago that playing "what if" only led to trouble. But there had certainly been some nice guys she'd let slip away, and sometimes she couldn't help but wonder how her life might be different if she'd made better choices.

"I guess I was tired of being that guy. My brother advised me to be someone else this time. So I did." He shook his head. "I could see the repulsion on your face at the restaurant when I was giving that poor girl a hard time. I almost came clean then but wasn't sure how you'd react."

"I admit, I was shocked. And Summer was so surprised when I told her what had happened. She'd told me that you were this wonderful, sweet, respectful guy."

"And then I acted the exact opposite."

She dipped a fry into ketchup. "Pretty much."

"I apologize. And I'd like it if you'd consider giving me another chance."

Ashley sat back on the couch and regarded him for a long moment. She felt certain he was telling the truth. But still, doubt lingered. "I appreciate you coming to explain things to me. Your little act the other night didn't do a lot to restore my faith in men." She met his curious gaze. "Because you're not the only one who has been hurt in the past."

Justin hadn't been sure dropping in unannounced was a good idea, but he felt certain it had been the only way to explain himself. And now, sitting on Ashley's couch, he knew he'd made the right choice. "I think a certain amount of past hurt is to be expected. Otherwise, you haven't really lived." He glanced over at her. "Right?"

She nibbled on her burger, lost in thought. "I guess." She gave him a slow smile.

"So what's your story then? What happened to diminish your faith in men?"

Ashley cocked her head and gave him a sideways look.

He had the feeling she was still sizing him up, still deciding if he could be trusted. That was fine. He'd be happy to prove that he was one of the good guys, no matter how he'd acted on their date.

"I'm divorced. It's been a little over three years since it was final." She sighed. "No kids. Sometimes I see that as a blessing, because I know how difficult it is to watch your parents get divorced. And sometimes I see it as a curse, because I'm afraid that was my chance at being a mom and I didn't take it."

Justin couldn't help but think how beautiful she was right now. He was pretty sure this was more real than any date they could have gone on. There was something intimate about a conversation over burgers in her living room that was better than any loud, fancy restaurant could ever be. "I can't imagine dealing with a failed marriage. That must've been tough."

She nodded. "And my family sided with my ex, at least for the most part. That's what brought me here. I needed to start over and reinvent myself."

Her family sided with her ex? Justin hoped he hid his shock at that statement and resisted the desire to ask why they would do such a thing. Might be best to leave the topic for another time. "Well, Charleston is a great place to live, so you made a good choice. I grew up here and don't plan on ever leaving."

"Yeah. I've been happy here. I love what I do." She gestured around. "I found a home that suits me." She shrugged. "That's my story. Now how about you?"

Justin shook his head. "I told you most of it already. I guess I have this habit of choosing women who have problems." He grinned. "Luke gives me a hard time about it." He glanced at her. "That's one of the things I liked about you. You seem to have it all together. Even Luke says what a help you are to Summer's business. That's not exactly what I'm used to." Even his own mama got on his case about the women he chose to date. Samantha had been the one who'd caused his family the most grief though. They'd been friends in college, even though they didn't have much in common. She'd always been fun to hang out with. And when they'd reconnected a couple of years ago, she'd been pregnant with Colton. She said she didn't know who the father was, and Justin could tell she was terrified at the thought of raising a child alone. She'd considered putting the baby up for adoption but had changed her mind at the last minute.

Justin would readily admit that the two of them were more

friends than sweethearts, but he'd chosen to stick beside her as she adjusted to motherhood. She'd been totally overwhelmed. Then he'd fallen in love with the baby and had stayed a part of Samantha's life so he could have a relationship with Colton. These days Samantha had moved on, even had another child, but Justin had remained her friend.

He wondered how Ashley would react to his relationship with Colton. The guys gave him a hard time about being a pseudo daddy to the child. But he figured he was still on shaky ground with Ashley, so this was no time to bring it up.

"I haven't always had it together. But over the past couple of years, I've worked hard to simplify my life. I enjoy work, have a few close friends, and am involved with my church." She grinned. "I think I've finally found that ever-elusive balance."

Justin appreciated her outlook. "That's great. I think so many people search for that their whole lives. They put work in front of their family and in front of their spiritual life. And really, without those things, how do they enjoy their success?"

Ashley looked at him with surprise. "Exactly."

"So. . ." He trailed off with a grin. "Any chance you'd be able to put the other night behind us and consider going with me to a movie or something this weekend?"

"I'd love to. As long as you leave your race car driving skills at home."

"It's a deal."

Chapter 16

Luke sat on the boat and stared out at the water. He'd been expecting his phone to ring and to hear Summer's voice on the other end, asking him to come home.

But his phone had been silent all night. Not even a text.

He knew he'd done a lot of things wrong in his life. And the past year had been one of the toughest he'd ever endured. It ranked right up there with the year he was ten and his mama died.

Grief did funny things to a person. Luke learned that lesson more than twenty years ago. After Mama died, his dad had turned to the bottle, and it had almost been as if he'd died, too. Rose had started staying at their aunt's house most of the time, and Luke and Bobby had been left to fend for themselves. *"I've always got your back, little brother."* How many times had he said that to Bobby? He'd covered for his brother through the years, taking the blame for everything from breaking a lamp to forgetting to mow the yard. He'd protected Bobby from as much pain as he could.

But he hadn't been able to protect him from the semi whose driver had fallen asleep at the wheel and drifted into the wrong lane.

People kept saying the pain would go away in time.

Luke felt certain those people had never experienced sudden loss, never received that phone call that blares out in the middle of the night, and before you even answer it, you know bad news is on the line.

Mama's death had been expected. Still hard. Still life-changing. But expected. She'd fought her cancer like a warrior, but in the end she'd been too tired to fight anymore. Knowing she was finally at peace gave him some comfort, though he was only a child.

But Bobby's accident had blindsided him like a bullet from a sniper's gun. There'd been no preparation. No last good-byes or final words. His brother was there one day and gone the next. Luke had called Bobby's phone out of habit many times over the past few months. As soon as it would ring, he'd remember. Bobby would never answer his calls again.

Luke had been tough his whole life. But putting his brother in the ground had been the hardest thing he'd ever done.

The cell phone rang beside him, and the light from the screen lit up the darkness.

"Hello," he said, not even bothering to check who was on the other end. He was ready to go home to his wife.

"Luke," Rose said. "I can't believe I actually connected with you. I've been trying for weeks. Don't you ever check your voice mails?"

He sighed. "Sorry. Things have been a little crazy. How are Dave and the kids?"

"They're great. Of course, you would know that if you ever came for a visit. Katie Beth asks me all the time why her uncle

Luke doesn't come see her anymore."

He had all but lost contact with his sister and her family after Bobby's accident. It made him too sad to be around them. "Sorry." He sighed.

"Well, I need you to come out to the house soon." Rose's voice sounded identical to Mama's. She'd even acquired that tone that told him there was no declining her request.

"I'm not sure when I can make it out there."

"Find the time. You know we've moved into the house. Not that you offered to help us, but we finally got all moved in. And I've got to get rid of some of the stuff that's here. I don't think Daddy ever threw anything away."

"Why do you want me to come out there?" Luke asked. He'd avoided his childhood home for years.

"Bobby's stuff is here. If you want anything of his, you need to come look through it."

"Can't you just store it somewhere?"

"I've been storing it," Rose said sharply. "It's been almost a year. I've got to do something with it." She let out a loud sigh. "It's been hard on all of us, Luke. But we've got to deal with his belongings."

"I can pay for a storage building."

"You don't get to throw money at this and make it go away," Rose said quietly. "Come out here and look through it. Besides, there's still a ton of your old things here anyway. I don't want to toss it all without you at least seeing it."

He knew it was time to man up. "Okay. I'll come out Saturday if that's okay."

"Perfect. I'll cook lunch, and you can stay for a visit. I hope

Summer can come, too."

Luke let out a breath. "She's probably busy, but thanks." His sister would hit the roof if she thought there was trouble between him and Summer. She'd often told him over the years that Summer was the best thing that had ever happened to him.

And she was right.

"See you Saturday. The kids will be thrilled."

They said their good-byes and hung up. He looked at the clock on his phone. It was after ten. If Summer had planned to call him, she would've done it by now.

Guess it was time to see if the living quarters in the boat were as nice as the salesman had promised.

Summer peeled herself off the tile floor and looked at the clock. She couldn't believe she'd slept there most of the night.

"Come on, boy," she said to Milo.

The big dog opened one eye and rolled over.

Summer went into the bedroom where she'd dropped her purse and phone yesterday. She picked up her phone. No missed calls.

She sank onto the bed, wide awake. Even though she'd never been angrier at Luke, she couldn't help but worry about him. Had he slept on the boat? Checked into a hotel?

She considered calling Justin to see if he'd stayed there but thought better of it. There was no reason to involve anyone else in their problems. She already regretted telling Ashley what had happened yesterday.

She'd always been a private person and had never liked people to know when she had problems. Even in high school when she'd struggled with math, she'd hired a tutor from a different school so none of her friends would ever know.

Today she felt better though. More at peace. She'd woken up a couple of times and each time had prayed that God would see her through. Today's peace was undoubtedly a result of those prayers. She still had a lot to deal with and knew that she and Luke had problems to face—but she didn't feel alone anymore.

She got up and quickly got ready for work. She and Milo would walk to the office, hopefully before Luke came to the house. She knew he'd have to come home to get a uniform. And she didn't plan on being there when he did.

An hour later, she and Milo walked through the deserted downtown streets. She'd forgotten how peaceful it could be. At this hour, the tourists were still sleeping, tucked away in their historic bed and breakfasts. The residents were just beginning to wake.

And she and Milo had the city all to themselves.

Chapter 17

"You sure do yawn a lot," a little boy said, peering at Luke from his spot next to a cannon.

Luke gave him a smile. He'd just delivered what might be the worst ranger talk in park service history. It was a good thing none of his coworkers had listened to him stumble through. "I didn't get much sleep last night."

The child looked at him with wide eyes. "My bedtime is eight. Maybe your bedtime should be eight, too."

Luke chuckled despite himself. "I'll keep that in mind."

"Sorry," the boy's mother said, walking over and putting an arm around her son. "Tommy has never met a stranger."

"Not a problem." Luke smiled at the boy again. "Hope you enjoy the rest of your tour." He watched them walk off, hand in hand. Kids sure kept you on your toes. A pang of sadness hit him hard. Not a day went by that he didn't think of the child he and Summer had lost.

He reached into his wallet and pulled out a tattered black and white ultrasound picture. The edges had become frayed, but the picture was clear. That tiny speck of life frozen in time on the page had once given him such happiness. He couldn't count the times he'd stared at the photo, wishing things had turned out differently. When Summer miscarried, they'd been close to finding out if it was a boy or a girl. Luke would've been happy with either but had secretly longed for a son of his own.

"Everything okay?" Walter Young asked.

Luke jumped at the sound of his boss's voice. "Yes sir." He hurriedly stuffed the photo back in his wallet, but not before Mr. Young had seen it.

The older man peered at him. "Are congratulations in order?" he asked. "The idea of becoming a father for the first time is certainly enough to distract a man."

Luke frowned. "No sir. Summer's not. . .she's not pregnant anymore."

His boss clasped him on the back. "I'm sorry to hear of your loss." He motioned toward the museum. "Listen, if you need to take some time off, say the word."

Mr. Young's obvious concern touched him. "Thanks. I don't need time off, at least not right now." Would time off give him the chance to fix his crumbling life? Probably not. "But thank you."

Mr. Young nodded. "We like you here, Luke. You do a good job. The visitors enjoy your programs." He furrowed his brow. "But I've noticed that these past weeks you've been struggling." He gestured toward the wallet in Luke's hand. "And I think this is probably why."

Luke didn't say anything. He'd thought his emotions were pretty well in check. But maybe not well enough. Embarrassment washed over him. He hated the thought of his coworkers thinking he wasn't doing a good job. "I'm sorry, sir."

Mr. Young drew his brows together. "Don't be sorry, son.

Dealing with real-life stuff happens. We don't expect you to be a robot." He smiled. "Actually, now that I know what's going on, I feel better about the opportunity that's about to come your way."

"What's that?"

"Well, it's clear that you have a talent dealing with the school groups who come through here. I'd like for you to consider tacking that onto your job responsibilities permanently. I know it's something we normally share between rangers, but I think we might be better suited if you take sole responsibility." Mr. Young peered at him over round glasses. "And there'd be a pay grade increase to go with it."

Luke couldn't hide his surprise. "Really?"

Mr. Young chuckled. "Think about it for a few days and let me know. You may not want more responsibility." He glanced at his watch. "Nearly quitting time. I'll let you get back to work."

Luke nodded. He'd never been readier for the day to be over. Summer may have been able to avoid him this morning by leaving early, but she would have to face him tonight.

Two hours later, he pulled into the driveway. It looked like she wasn't home yet. That was fine. He could wait.

He went upstairs and pulled a duffel bag from the closet. He threw in a few changes of clothing and some toiletries. He opened the linen closet and grabbed a couple of towels and the extra-soft blanket someone had given them as a wedding gift years ago.

That should just about do it. Luke zipped the bag and grabbed the pillow from his side of the bed. He cast one last look around their bedroom and headed downstairs. As he reached the bottom step, the front door swung open.

Milo bounded inside and jumped onto the couch.

Luke set down his bags and steeled himself for what he knew would come next.

The workday had been a struggle for Summer. She'd wanted to call Luke so many times but had decided against it. She was still angry, but she felt like she owed him an apology for telling him to stay on the boat last night. And that apology needed to be made in person. They weren't the kind of couple who gave up when things got tough.

She knew he was probably furious with her, but seeing his truck in the driveway had been a huge relief. She followed Milo inside the house, trying to figure out what her first words should be.

Luke stood in the entryway at the bottom of the stairs.

As soon as she saw him, her eyes filled with tears. "Luke." She dropped her purse and planner inside the door and walked toward him.

Then she saw his duffel bag and pillow sitting next to his guitar case.

She stopped in her tracks. "What's that?" she whispered, already knowing the answer.

Luke sighed. "I can't very well stay on the boat without some of my things. I don't want to have to drive over here every morning before work."

She locked eyes with him. "You don't have to do that. I don't expect you to stay there."

He raked his hands through his hair. The dark circles under his eyes told the tale of a sleepless night. "Let's talk." He motioned toward the living room.

She felt her heart drop to her stomach. This couldn't be happening. This wasn't what she meant to happen. "Okay," she whispered. She perched gingerly on the couch next to a sprawled out Milo.

Luke sat down next to her but didn't touch her. "I didn't sleep last night. Not a wink. I've had a lot of time to think."

She nodded but didn't say anything. She was afraid if she said a word, she might burst into tears.

"You were right to leave me there yesterday." He gave her a sideways look. "I don't understand how it's come to this. But I know that I don't want to be this guy. I don't want to hurt you any more than I already have."

She focused on her breathing. "What are you saying, exactly?"

"I hear the things that come out of my mouth." He shook his head in disgust. "That's not who I am. Or at least, who I want to be."

Summer let out a hot breath. "Luke. Just spit it out, okay? What's going on?"

"I need some time to get myself together. I'm not the guy you married. You didn't sign up for this." He shrugged. "Me not realizing how upset you'd get about that money was the icing on the cake. I've felt for a long time like we were headed down the wrong path. And it hit me last night. You've been walking on eggshells around me. Haven't you?" He peered at her, his brown eyes serious.

"Yeah, maybe. I mean, I know how tough things have been for you. I shouldn't expect you to bounce right back from two awful tragedies."

Luke shook his head. "I'm so sorry. Really. But I can't do this to you anymore. I remember what it was like to live in a house where you had to walk on eggshells. I don't want that to be your life. So I think it would be best if I stayed on the boat for a little while." He refused to meet her eyes.

She sat in shock. She hadn't anticipated this ever happening to her. "So that's it? You're just walking out?"

He furrowed his brow. "You told me to stay on the boat. You told me you needed some space."

"Yeah, for a few hours. I didn't think you'd—I didn't think you'd. . ." She looked at him in horror. "So you're done? Is that what you're saying?"

"No." He leaned back and rested his palms on his forehead for a second, then sat up and faced her. "I'm saying I think you were right. We do need some space. I need to get it together. You don't deserve what I've been putting you through."

"What about counseling? The church has a counselor on staff. I could make an appointment."

He glared at her. "I don't want counseling from someone at your church. I want time to work things out on my own." He stood.

She stayed frozen to the spot. Her mouth felt dry, like cotton. She put a hand to her forehead. Did she have a fever?

"Summer?"

She looked up at her husband. Her husband who was moving out.

"Okay," she whispered. "Will I see you ever?"

"Yeah. I want to take care of the yard. And see Milo." He shrugged. "If you're here, I'd like to see you, too. But if you'd rather me come when you're gone, that's fine."

She nodded.

Luke bent down and nuzzled Milo. He was rewarded with a lick on the face. "Bye, boy." He locked eyes with Summer. "Maybe I can take him sometime? The boat's not that big, but it would be nice to have him as company."

"You're not taking him on the boat. He belongs here."

Luke held his hands up in defeat. "Sorry. Just asking." He slung his bag over his shoulder and picked up his guitar. "Take care."

She watched her husband walk out the door without a backward glance.

Chapter 18

Ashley put the finishing touches on an itinerary for an upcoming wedding at the Mills House Hotel. From what she could tell, this one would be spectacular. She loved working with brides who had similar taste as her. It always made it a little more fun.

Summer came through the door, a stoic expression on her face.

"Mornin'," Ashley said. "I just made a fresh pot of coffee."

Summer gave her a tiny smile. "Thank you."

"Everything okay?" Ashley asked. Ever since the day she'd picked Summer up from the marina, she'd been worried about the couple. She hoped their fight had been resolved.

Summer poured herself a cup of coffee and sat in the ornate chair in front of Ashley's desk. "Since we work together, I may as well tell you. Luke and I have separated."

Ashley set her coffee cup down and walked over to Summer. She knelt down next to the chair. "I'm so sorry. Is there anything I can do?"

Summer closed her eyes. "There's nothing anyone can do. This is all my fault." She looked up, her eyes brimming with tears. "I practically pushed him out."

Ashley sat in the chair next to Summer's. "There is no point in assigning blame. Just focus on what you can do to fix things."

She listened as Summer filled her in on all that had transpired.

"And he wanted to take Milo. Like share him." Summer wiped a tear away. "He won't even consider counseling. Says he wants to work things out on his own." She shook her head. "How does he think he can fix this on his own?"

Ashley frowned. "How are you dealing with it?"

Summer shrugged. "That's the thing. I'm not angry. I'm mainly numb. I don't feel anything." She took a sip of coffee. "It's kind of weird, actually. Last night after he left, I watched TV. Like nothing had happened. I ordered a pizza and took a bath."

Ashley narrowed her eyes. That didn't sound like Summer at all. "Really?"

Summer rose from the chair and walked over to her desk. "What was I supposed to do? It's not like there's a book called *How to Act When Your Husband Leaves* or something." She flashed a feeble smile. "So I'm going to do the best I can and trust that this will all work out somehow."

Ashley remembered saying the same thing back before she and Brian split up. Although, in some ways it had worked out. She was much better off without him. But she hoped and prayed Summer and Luke could work it out. "I'm sure it will."

Summer sat down at her desk. "It has to."

Justin paced the length of the sidewalk in front of his

apartment. They were going to be late for the show if Luke didn't hurry up. He knew he should've driven separately. Although without a lead singer, it's not like the band could do much. Jimmy was pretty good at backup vocals, but he wasn't a front man.

Luke's truck finally pulled into the parking lot.

Justin jogged over and hopped inside. "We're going to be pushing it to make it on time."

"I know. Sorry." Luke pulled onto the road and headed toward Folly Beach. He flipped up the volume on the radio.

Justin glanced over at him from the corner of his eye. He'd hoped to fill Luke in on his upcoming date with Ashley. But the strain on Luke's face was evident.

"Any change to the set list?" he finally asked after several minutes of silence.

Luke shook his head. "Nope. I figure we should stick with what we know, especially since we didn't practice this week." He'd called and canceled their midweek practice, saying that something had come up.

"Sounds good."

Luke pulled into the parking lot and killed the engine. "Right on time." He jerked his head toward the restaurant. "Let's go."

Justin followed his friend up the stairs that led to the Sand and Suds. Something was off. He wasn't sure what had happened, but Luke wasn't acting like himself.

Jimmy and Will were already there, getting things set up.

"Thanks for showing up, guys," Jimmy said. "I was starting to think I was gonna hafta put on my Garth hat and put on a show."

Justin chuckled.

"Sherry wanted us to find out if your wife was happy with her artwork," Will said to Luke. "She said it was the prettiest palm tree she'd ever painted."

Luke nodded. "Yeah. She loved it."

"I forgot about the boat. So you've already given Summer the present? I didn't think your anniversary was until later in the summer."

Luke scowled but didn't say anything.

"Man, I don't blame him for giving it to her early," Jimmy said. "It's a sweet boat. This way they can start enjoying it now."

The night passed in a blur for Justin. Even though he still wasn't completely comfortable on stage, he'd at least gotten to the point where he enjoyed himself. They sounded pretty good tonight, too. At least for the most part.

"Thanks guys," the restaurant manager said after they were through with their final set. "The crowd loves your music."

Jimmy and Will loaded their equipment into Jimmy's SUV.

"We're having a cookout on Monday for Memorial Day if y'all are interested," Jimmy said. "I have a new grill, and the pool is ready." He nodded at Luke. "And Martha told me to make sure you told Summer not to worry about bringing anything."

"Thanks," Luke said. "But I don't think we can make it. Maybe another time."

Jimmy glanced at Justin. "How about you? You already have plans?"

Justin hoped to have plans with Ashley, depending on how

tomorrow night's movie went. "My family is cooking out, so I'll probably head over there."

"You might be the two biggest party poopers in the state of South Carolina," Jimmy said. "But that's okay. Every party has to have one." He chuckled and climbed into the vehicle.

Justin followed Luke over to his truck. "So what do you and Summer have planned for the long weekend?" he asked. "Are y'all going to take the new boat out?"

Luke sighed. "No. At least not together." He climbed into the cab of the truck and started the engine.

Justin followed suit. "Does she have a wedding?"

"No. But we're kind of going through a rough patch right now."

"Oh." Justin glanced over at Luke's profile. He'd figured something must be wrong. "That why you forgot the words to three songs tonight, including one that you wrote yourself?"

"Yeah. My heart wasn't in it tonight." Luke let out a sigh.

Justin hated to see his friend hurting but had no idea how to help. "Y'all have been through a lot. You think maybe a weekend away or something would help?"

"I think we're past that." Luke gripped the steering wheel. "I moved out. I'm staying on the boat for a little while."

Justin let out a breath. He'd had no idea things might be that rocky. "Sorry, man." He shook his head. "Listen, if you need to sleep on my couch for a few days, you're welcome to it."

"Thanks. But the time alone is giving me some time to work through things. Summer shouldn't have to put up with my moods. I don't want to put her through more than I already have."

"I'll be praying that it all works out."

Luke's jaw tightened, but he didn't say anything.

Chapter 19

After a few nights of sleeping on the boat, Luke's entire body felt like one big knot. He'd been sure some time apart from Summer was the right thing, but it seemed like it might be at the expense of his health. He rubbed a kink out of his neck and climbed into the truck.

If he didn't show up today, Rose would send out a search party. He didn't know why she was so insistent that he look through Bobby's stuff.

He headed toward North Charleston and couldn't stop his thoughts from turning to Summer. They'd been a permanent, daily fixture in each others' lives for so many years, it seemed like part of him was actually missing. Like his arm was gone. He reached for his cell phone but drew his hand back. What would he say? It wasn't as if he'd thought about anything else. Talking to her would probably only bring him down more. There was a time when they'd had a routine on Saturday mornings. If Summer didn't have a wedding, the two of them would sleep in and then laze around in their pajamas until noon. They'd talk and laugh and argue over whose turn it was to choose that night's restaurant. And then Milo would jump right in between them until they'd finally get up and take him for a walk down to the Battery.

Luke sighed. Those were some great times. But they hadn't had one of those Saturdays in months.

He slowed the truck as he neared the neighborhood where he'd grown up. A few of the houses were more rundown than he remembered, but for the most part the place looked the same. He drove past a group of kids playing in a sprinkler in their front yard, a little boy on a bike on the sidewalk, and an old man out mowing his yard. It was nice to know the area hadn't gone downhill.

Luke pulled into the driveway and found himself flooded with memories. Mama had taught him to roller-skate right there on the pavement. He couldn't have been more than four, but still he could clearly remember holding her hand and sliding his feet back and forth in his skates.

"Uncle Luke," Katie Beth called from the doorsteps. She ran out to his truck, and he scooped her up into his arms.

"I can't believe you're all grown up," he said, groaning like she was too heavy to lift.

She giggled. "I'm five now. That's not a grown-up, silly."

Luke set her on her feet, and she took his hand.

"Come on. Dale is probably up from his nap now."

Luke let his niece lead him into his childhood home.

Rose met them at the door. "Hey, Bubba." She leaned in and kissed him on the cheek. "How are you?"

He glanced around the living room. Not much had changed. The same pictures still lined the walls that were covered with the same flower-printed wallpaper. Daddy hadn't changed anything in the years he'd lived in the house alone. "I'm okay."

She cocked her head and locked eyes with him. "No, you're not. But you can tell me what's wrong later on." She motioned toward Katie Beth. "Sweetie, why don't you go see if Dale is up?"

Katie Beth nodded and ran toward her brother's room.

"Dale's in your old room," she said. "We've barely moved in, so your old stuff is still in there all over the walls."

He wrinkled his forehead. "Still? I figured Daddy would've cleaned that out a long time ago." When he left home after high school, he hadn't taken much with him. Just the clothes he could fit into his old duffel bag.

Rose grinned. "It's all there. From your honor society certificate to your Bon Jovi poster."

Katie Beth and Dale ran into the room giggling.

"Hey, little man." Luke knelt down to see his nephew face-to-face. The child was the spitting image of Bobby at that age. He held out his hand for a high five, and Dale slapped it.

"Kids, do y'all want to watch Dora?" she asked. "I need to talk to your uncle Luke."

Katie Beth nodded and grabbed her little brother's hand. "Come on, let's go." They went into the den where the TV had always been.

"They're growing up so fast," Luke said.

Rose nodded. "I know." She motioned toward the kitchen. "You want some coffee or something?"

He wrinkled his nose. Coffee had never been his morning beverage of choice. He started his day out with a tall glass of milk. Summer used to always tell him how cute it was. "Do you have any milk?"

She chuckled. "Of course. I could put that in a sippy cup for you if you'd like."

He laughed. "A regular glass will be fine. I promise not to spill." He followed her into the kitchen and propped on a stool while she poured milk for him and coffee for her.

They settled at the old kitchen table that had been in the same spot since Luke could remember. He traced his fingers over the yellow Formica top. The corner of the table was cracked and peeling, just as it had been when Luke sat at the table as a boy.

Rose met his eyes over her coffee cup. She looked so much like Mama. Quick math told him she was about the same age Mama had been when she'd been taken from them.

"Dave had to work today but said to tell you hello," she said finally. "He said y'all need to go fishing sometime soon."

Luke nodded. He'd always liked Dave. He and Rose had been sweethearts practically since they were in elementary school. "Tell him hi."

"I'm glad you came out here today. I sort of expected you to bail at the last minute." She sighed. "I didn't want to be solely responsible for getting rid of Bobby's stuff."

His jaw tensed. "I'll look through it, but I have no idea what I would want that was his."

She shrugged. "There are lots of T-shirts, books, CDs. . . you know, stuff like that."

"Yeah, okay. I'll go through it. And then what? You're giving it away?" Luke hated the thought of Bobby's stuff loaded into bags and tossed in the Goodwill bin.

Rose sighed. "We don't have the room for it here. Daddy's

and Mama's stuff is here, too. And there are four of us. We need all the space we can get."

Luke finished his milk and set the glass on the table. "I don't understand why you'd want to live here anyway."

"Things were tight in the apartment. This house has been a huge blessing to us." She frowned. "I know you have bad memories of the place, but this is a great neighborhood for the kids to grow up in."

"I guess."

She raised an eyebrow. "Besides. The nursing home isn't far from here. Just down the street. Something you would know if you ever bothered to visit."

He sighed. He should've known she'd shame him about that. Their daddy had been in the nursing home since Bobby's accident.

And Luke hadn't stepped a foot in the door to check on him.

Summer pulled her dark hair into a ponytail and leaned closer to the mirror. Her eyes still looked puffy. She'd never been a pretty crier, never been one of those girls who cried dainty tears and then looked perfect. Her face turned red, her eyes swelled, and her nose ran for hours. Super attractive.

"Come on, Milo." She headed downstairs, the big dog padding along behind her. "Let's go for a good long walk."

Milo shook with excitement as she clipped the leash onto his collar.

They set out down the street, Milo pausing to sniff every few steps.

She loved the way things slowed down on Saturdays. Even the breeze coming from the water seemed to waft by slower, as if it knew it was the weekend. She and Milo walked down Legare Street and headed toward the Battery. The park there allowed dogs off leash. She wasn't sure if she wanted to try to handle Milo alone, but she might give it a try if there weren't too many other dogs around. Luke always let Milo off leash with no problem, but it made her a little nervous.

"Summer?" a voice called from the other side of the street.

She flipped her sunglasses to the top of her head and glanced over to see Jefferson waving.

He jogged over to where she and Milo stood. "Hey there, Sunshine."

His old nickname for her might've been cute when they were sixteen, but now it seemed silly. "Please don't call me that." She watched as Milo sniffed around the gate where they stood. "What are you doing over here anyway?"

Jefferson's eyes twinkled. "Just moved in." He pointed to a home across the street. "I'm actually renting a carriage house right now. I don't want to buy until I've had time to look around." He shrugged. "And I haven't decided if I want to be here or somewhere like James Island."

She nodded. "I don't blame you for wanting to look around. Plus you've been away for so long, it's probably best to kind of get your bearings before you put down roots."

"You and I always have thought alike." He walked closer to Milo. "And who is this handsome fellow?"

"Milo. Luke and I rescued him off the highway when he was a puppy."

"I'd love to get a dog, but right now isn't the time." He absently scratched Milo on top of the head. "So where are you headed?"

"The Battery." She suddenly remembered her puffy eyes and put her sunglasses back on.

Jefferson shook his head. "Too late. I already saw those red eyes. And I'm pretty sure it's not an allergy." He raised his eyebrows but didn't question her tears. "Come on. Let me walk with you to the Battery. I haven't been down there since I got back."

They walked toward the park, Summer feeling more unsure with each step. The last thing she needed right now was an old friend who could get her to let her guard down. Because no one could know that Luke had moved out. Word would spread like kudzu. "I'll bet your mama is glad to have you back in town."

"Sure is. We're already gearing up for the annual Boudreaux family beach vacation. We still go to Kiawah Island every year." He glanced over at her. "But you probably remember. I think you came with us a couple of times."

"I know I went the year you'd gotten your driver's license. Because my parents were so worried about me riding in your convertible."

He chuckled. "I remember. I drove over to pick you up, and I thought your daddy was going to have a fit. But that was a fun trip."

She'd forgotten about those lazy beach days. She didn't

make it to the beach much anymore. She and Luke went every now and then, but they'd been so busy last summer. At the thought of Luke, she grew somber.

"You okay?" Jefferson asked as they walked into the park.

Her eyes landed on the bandstand where she and Luke used to meet. "Yeah, fine." She pulled a dummy out of her pocket. "Look what I have, Milo."

The dog let out an excited bark and sat so she could take his leash off.

"Now, you'd better mind me." She unclipped the leash and tossed the dummy.

Milo bounded after it and scooped it up.

"Bring it here," she called. She glanced at Jefferson. "I don't usually let him off leash. That's Luke's department. But Milo needs some exercise."

"He definitely shops in the husky dog department."

Milo ran toward where she and Jefferson stood but veered off course. He dropped the dummy and charged full speed after a squirrel.

"Milo, no!" Summer ran after the big, brown dog. A busy street surrounded the park, and she wasn't sure if he'd stop before he got to the road. "Milo!"

The squirrel darted around the bandstand and past a trash can then crossed South Bay Street.

Milo followed behind.

"Milo, stop right now," she called as she ran.

The dog ran into the road, oblivious to traffic.

Summer's heart pounded. She gasped for breath and said a silent prayer for the dog's safety.

An SUV screeched to a stop, nearly hitting Milo.

She waved at the driver and reached the sidewalk where a startled Milo now sat. She sank to her knees and buried her face in the dog's fur. Her quiet sobs racked her body.

"He's fine now," Jefferson said, putting a hand on her shoulder.

She stroked Milo's coat, trying to stop her tears from falling.

Jefferson knelt down next to them. "Hey," he said in a low voice. "Do you want me to call Luke to come pick you up?"

Summer shook her head and wiped her eyes. "No," she whispered. "Luke's not at home."

Jefferson furrowed his brow. "Is he working?"

"No. I don't know. It doesn't matter." She searched her pocket for a tissue and came up empty-handed.

Jefferson held out a handkerchief. "Take this."

She managed a smile. Jefferson might be the only guy she knew who actually carried handkerchiefs. "Thanks."

"Now fix your face and tell me what's wrong." He took the leash from her hand and clipped it onto Milo's collar. "Come on, boy."

They walked toward Legare Street, the silence punctuated by Summer's sniffles.

"Well?" Jefferson said finally. "Spit it out. I may not have seen you in fifteen years, but I still know you well enough to know when something is wrong."

"It's nothing I want to talk about." As soon as she said the words, she realized they weren't true.

"Is it your business? Is it in trouble?"

She shook her head. "Nothing like that. Business is

booming." If only her problem were business related. It would be much easier to rebuild a business than a marriage.

"Then what? Luke?" Jefferson peered at her closely.

She fought to keep her face neutral. "It's nothing."

"Sunshine, I know when you're lying." Jefferson directed Milo around a tree. "Your secret is safe with me."

"Whatever. You'll tell Mitch, and he is the mouth of the South. My parents will be at my front door before I can even blink."

"That's not true. If you want to unload on me, I'll keep it to myself. Promise."

Her eyes filled with tears. She was becoming one of those weepy girls she'd always hated. "There's a lot to the story, and it's very complicated. I don't want to get into it right now. But Luke and I have some things to work through. He's staying on our boat for a few days."

Jefferson drew his brows together. "I'm sorry." He raked his fingers through his hair. "I mean that. I am sorry that you're going through any pain."

"Thanks. I think it's been hard for him to bounce back after Bobby's accident." She didn't mention the miscarriage. But she knew in her heart that it had been both things together that had been too much for Luke to handle.

"That's tough." Jefferson shook his head. "I'm sure he'll get things worked out though." He glanced at her. "And I know he doesn't mean for you to be hurt in the process."

She widened her eyes. She'd expected Jefferson to rip Luke apart, not defend him. "Yeah. I know you're right. I just hate this unsteady feeling."

They stopped in front of her house.

"Thanks for your help." Summer reached over and took Milo's leash from Jefferson. "And for your handkerchief."

He chuckled. "You're welcome. And you can hang on to that handkerchief."

She managed a tiny smile. "What, you don't want it back?"

"Consider it my gift to you." Jefferson grinned. "I hope things get better soon. And I'd be glad to lend an ear if you need to talk."

"Thanks." Summer and Milo went through the gate that led to the house. She waved to Jefferson over her shoulder and went inside.

Jefferson might not be her first choice for advice, but at least he seemed to think things for her and Luke would be back to normal soon. And that was oddly comforting.

Chapter 20

The ringing phone blasted Justin out of a very sound sleep. "Hello," he mumbled.

"I need your help," Samantha said, her voice barely audible. "I think I'm getting strep throat, and the baby has the stomach virus. Mom's coming to get Allison, but she can't handle her and Colton both."

"You need me to come get him?"

"Please. Can he stay with you for a few days? I don't want him to catch this."

Justin sat up. "Sure. Of course." He held the phone back to see what time it was. Not even ten. After the late night, he hadn't bothered to set an alarm. "I'll have to run over to my parents' and switch cars with my mom." He felt safer putting Colton's car seat in Mom's Taurus than in his old pickup. "I'll be there in an hour."

He clicked off the phone and hopped out of bed. He didn't have groceries suitable for Colton. He'd have to swing by the store and pick up some stuff. Colton had spent the night before, but never multiple nights.

Thirty minutes later, he had showered and called his mom to tell her about Samantha. He headed toward his parents' house to switch cars. Just as he flipped on his blinker to turn into their subdivision, an awful thought hit him.

Tonight he was supposed to have his first official date with Ashley.

After the way he acted last week, he was afraid canceling would be the death of any potential relationship. But he hadn't told her how involved he was in Colton's life.

He pulled into his parents' driveway and turned off the engine.

Mom met him at the door with her keys in her hands. "Hey, hon." She gave him a kiss on the cheek. "Does this mean we'll have a little one at the cookout on Monday?" she asked.

Justin nodded. "Probably. Hope that's okay."

"Of course. I might have your dad pick up one of those little pools for Colton to play in."

His parents were past ready to become grandparents. But Justin's brother and sister-in-law were focused on their careers right now, and he hadn't met the right girl yet. "That sounds great. I know he'd love it."

"I guess this means you'll get to bring him with you to church," Mom said.

He nodded. "Yeah. I'm excited about that. I've thought about seeing if she'd mind if I pick him up every Sunday, but I'm afraid of overstepping my boundaries."

Mom put an arm around him. "You have to do what you think is best. It seems to me that she'd probably be happy for you to take him off of her hands."

"Maybe." He was never sure. Sometimes he honestly thought Samantha would give Colton to him if he asked.

But the child needed a mother, even one who wasn't totally involved in his life. Right?

"Either way, we'll be happy to see the two of you tomorrow at church and at the cookout on Monday. I'm proud of you, son. Colton isn't your responsibility, yet you step up and care for him when he needs you. Not a lot of guys your age would do that."

He blushed. Her kind words made him feel awful considering what he was about to ask. "Thanks. I'd do anything for the little guy. He needs a man in his life." He raked his fingers through his hair. "But is there any way you and Dad could keep him for a few hours tonight? I already had plans, and hate to cancel."

Mom raised her eyebrows. "Your dad and I already have plans to have dinner with a couple from church. Why? Do you have a date?" Her voice rose at least an octave as she asked the question.

He groaned. His mother worried nonstop about his love life. "Yes. I do. A date that I've already gotten off on the wrong foot with. I'm pretty sure canceling because I have to babysit an old girlfriend's son isn't going to win me any points."

"Is she a nice girl?" His mom sounded so hopeful.

He chuckled. "Yes. Very nice." Ashley was the kind of woman he'd always hoped to find. But he'd hoped to get to know her better before springing his relationship with Colton on her.

"Well, then she should understand." His mom smiled and held out her keys. "Now go pick that sweet boy up before he gets sick."

He kissed his mom and got into the older model white Taurus. He pulled his cell phone out of his pocket. May as well get this over with. He scrolled to Ashley's name and hit the button to call her before he lost his nerve. He hit the SPEAKER button as he backed out of the driveway.

"Hello," Ashley said on the other end.

"Hey, Ashley, it's Justin." He took a deep breath. Would this end things for good? Only one way to find out.

"I've got some bad news." He forced the words out. He'd disappointed her with the way he'd acted last week. And now he was disappointing her by canceling.

Justin felt certain he would never regain her trust after this.

Ashley furrowed her brow. "What's wrong?" She set down her coffee cup and waited for the bomb to drop. Getting a "bad news" call from a guy on date night never ended well.

"I'm not going to be able to make it tonight," Justin said. "Something's come up."

Ashley waited for him to explain, but he didn't. "What do you mean? Do you guys have a show tonight or something?"

"No, nothing like that. It's a favor I have to do for someone."

She could hear noise in the background. He must be in the truck. "A favor?" She knew she sounded like a parrot. But what was the deal with this guy? First he acted like a jerk. Then he apologized and she totally bought his explanation. And now he was canceling because of some kind of vague favor? Something didn't feel right about this.

"I'm so sorry. I hope you'll let me make it up to you. Maybe one night next week?"

She furrowed her brow. "Next week? I'm free tomorrow night after church. And off work on Monday for the holiday." She hated this position. If she gave him a hard time for canceling, she would come across as unreasonable. But if she let him get away with it, it would set the wrong tone for any future relationship that might happen.

"Oh, well. . ." He trailed off. "I'm actually going to be busy for a few days."

Right. Busy. "You know what, Justin? Maybe we should forget it. If you can't give me a reasonable explanation for canceling, then I'm not sure we should bother rescheduling." As soon as the words left her mouth, she felt proud of herself. The old Ashley would've let him get away with canceling and treating her badly. But not anymore. It was time to find a backbone. No more doormat.

Justin sighed. "Okay. Tell you what. I'll be there tonight. But there will be something we have to take care of. I'll need you to have an open mind."

She had to admit she was curious. "Fine. See you at six?"

"We'd better make it an earlier night if that's okay. Can you be ready at four?"

Four? What had she gotten herself into? "Yeah, I can do that." She clicked off the phone and wondered what Justin had up his sleeve.

He was clearly up to something.

Chapter 21

So how is Daddy anyway?" Luke asked.

Rose pinched the bridge of her nose and closed her eyes. Finally, she looked up. "Not well. Not well at all." She sighed. "He couldn't recover from Bobby's accident."

Luke at least could identify with that. "So his memory is. . .gone? Like he doesn't know you at all?"

She shrugged a shoulder. "Not exactly. Alzheimer's is a tricky thing." She tucked a strand of blond hair behind her ear. "He's best in the morning. Sometimes he will know who I am then, and we can have lucid conversations. But there are days he doesn't know, days he thinks I'm Mama."

"Really?" He knew the resemblance was strong. It made sense that Daddy would think that.

"I let him hold my hand and talk to me. He talks about us and Bobby. And sometimes work." She smiled. "I used to try to correct him and explain who I am. But it seemed to make it worse. This way he stays calm."

"How often do you visit?"

She met his eyes across the table. "Daily. And quite frankly, you should be ashamed. I know you haven't been there even one time, because there's a guest book in his room."

He leaned back and rested his head in his hands. He and Daddy hadn't gotten along when the old man was lucid. Why should it be any different now? "I'd probably only upset him."

Rose narrowed her eyes. "He's our daddy, Luke. He provided for us for all those years. I don't care that you didn't have the best relationship with him. He's still the only daddy you're ever gonna have."

Luke nodded. Summer had said much the same thing to him in February when he turned down Rose's invitation to Daddy's birthday celebration. "I know. But he wouldn't want to see me anyway."

Rose shook her head. "He talks about you. And it isn't anything bad either. I think you should go."

"Maybe."

"Well, I need you to change that 'maybe' to an 'I promise,' because I need to be out of town for a few days."

He raised his eyebrows. "Where to?"

Rose smiled. "We're taking the kids to Disney World in Florida. They're so excited. At Christmas this year, we gave them little Mickey Mouse ears with their names on them. Katie Beth knew immediately."

"That will be awesome." Luke had always envisioned that kind of family vacation. But they hadn't had the funds when he was growing up, and now he and Summer didn't have a family and probably never would. "When do you leave?"

"It hinges on your promise." She reached out and gripped his hand. "I can't leave town for five days without knowing you'll go visit him."

"So you are saying that if I don't go visit Daddy while

you're gone, you're gonna disappoint your kids?"

She nodded. "Yep. And I'm going to tell them it's because Uncle Luke is so selfish."

He scowled. "Sis, I think you might be a little evil. You know I don't want to be the reason your kids don't meet Mickey."

"Then you'll do it? Just an hour or so a day?"

"Fine. But some of it will have to be after work."

She jumped up and came around the table to throw her arms around his neck. "Thank you so much."

He laughed. It had always been impossible to stay mad at Rose. "When do you leave?"

"Two weeks from today." She jerked her head toward the living room. "Now why don't you go on in Bobby's room and look through his stuff while I get lunch fixed?"

He set his milk glass in the sink and made his way toward his brother's room, not sure he wanted to look through Bobby's things.

Somehow divvying up his stuff made everything feel too final. It was time to let his little brother go, and Luke still wasn't ready to do that.

He walked into the room and sat on the bed, remembering when it had been decked out with a Star Wars comforter.

Unexpected tears filled his eyes, and he angrily batted them away. He hadn't cried. Not when the call came. Not at the funeral.

Summer had tried and tried to get him to talk about his feelings, and each time he'd pushed her away.

But today, in the silence of Bobby's room, he wished she were there holding his hand.

Summer sank onto the leather couch and flipped through the DVR to see what she had saved to watch. It was hard to believe there was a time when the DVR was the source of most of the fights between her and Luke. He'd store as many shows as they had memory for, but she liked to keep the list pared down. Especially old sporting events. What was the point of having an old football game saved? He knew the outcome. When he'd find out she'd deleted some old game, he'd get so upset.

Most of their fights had ended in laughter and kisses. Not like now. But she didn't feel like they were fighting as much as they were simply no longer connecting. Ever since she told Jefferson about their temporary separation, she'd been wondering if it was really temporary.

They'd promised to stay together until death parted them. And she'd always thought those vows were serious. But maybe they weren't as binding as she'd expected.

She took off her wedding ring and looked at it. She still wore the same ring Luke had given her nearly seven years ago. Even though he'd offered numerous times to buy her a bigger ring, she refused. This one was her. Was them.

She wondered if Luke was still wearing his ring. It had been days now since they'd talked. She'd expected him to call by now.

But her phone stayed silent.

She clicked off the TV and went upstairs. When she got to the top of the stairs, she turned right instead of going to her bedroom. She opened the only closed door down the hallway.

The room that was to have been the nursery.

A wooden rocking chair was the lone piece of furniture in the room. Luke had gotten rid of everything from the nursery except for the rocker. It had been the one his own mother had rocked him in.

She sat in the chair and slowly rocked back and forth, just as she'd always imagined rocking their baby. Even though they'd never found out if she'd carried a boy or a girl, she'd always thought the baby was a boy. She never told Luke though. When he'd ask, she'd smile and say they'd have to wait and see.

But she'd known how much he wanted a son, and she felt in her heart that a son was what they'd lost.

And even though they hadn't had a real memorial service, there wasn't a day that Summer didn't remember her baby. Even if Luke tried to pretend it never happened, Summer knew better. She'd carried that tiny life inside of her, and that was something she could never forget.

Chapter 22

Y ou okay?" Rose asked from the door of Bobby's room.

Luke looked up from the papers and books he was sifting through. "Yeah. I found a couple of mementos. One of his high school yearbooks and a tattered copy of *The Old Man and the Sea*."

Rose smiled. "You want any of his old T-shirts?"

Luke shook his head. "No. I wouldn't wear them. And then they'd be in my closet staring at me, reminding me that he's not here anymore." He met her gaze. "Not that I need reminding."

She sat next to him on the bed. "You've had a tough time with it. Tougher than the rest of us, I think."

"I still wish we would've fought harder for a prosecution."

She sighed. "It was an accident. That other driver was so upset, he didn't know what to do." She patted Luke's back. "You know that."

He let out a breath. No one else had seen it like him. Not even Summer. He'd pushed everyone to go after the other driver, certain the guy had been doing something wrong. But everyone had tried to get him to drop it.

Summer had even mentioned him seeing a grief counselor. They'd had a huge argument about it. She'd thought it would do him a world of good, but he couldn't stomach sitting in a room with some stranger and sharing his feelings.

"You sure that's all you want?" Rose asked, motioning toward his paltry stack.

He nodded. "Yeah." He didn't need material things to help him remember Bobby. He'd remember him when he saw a Ford Mustang drive past or when he heard a Kenny Chesney song or when he saw two little boys with their fishing poles at Folly Beach. Memories like that were worth more than material possessions anyway.

Rose walked over to Bobby's dresser. "There's something I'd like for you to have."

"What's that?"

She opened a drawer and pulled something out. She walked over and handed him a tattered blue leather book. "His Bible. He had the same one since he was thirteen and got baptized."

He recoiled then accepted the Bible from her. Bobby's full name was engraved in gold down in the right-hand corner: ROBERT JAMES NELSON. Luke ran his fingers over his brother's name. He hadn't cracked his own Bible open in nearly a year. "Thanks." He refused to meet Rose's gaze.

"Luke, some people let a tragedy tear their whole life apart. Grief is one thing. But letting it eat you up is another. Do you think Bobby would want that?"

"How do we know what Bobby would want? He's not here to tell us, and we sure shouldn't answer for him."

Rose sighed. "I can answer for him. So can you. We knew him. We knew what he was all about. Bobby was fun and love and laughs. Do you think he'd like it if he knew the brother he adored, the guy who practically raised him, was sitting here looking like a shell of himself?"

Her words stung. He didn't want to think about what Bobby would think or say. That only made him miss his brother more. "I'm fine. I don't know why everyone keeps thinking otherwise."

Rose raised an eyebrow. "So Summer agrees with me?"

He dropped his head in his hands. "I moved out." Saying the words out loud pierced his heart, but he knew Rose wasn't going to let up before she got it out of him.

She sat beside him on the bed. "Tell me. Tell me everything."

Ashley paced the length of her living room. It was nearly time for Justin to be there, and her nerves were starting to get the best of her.

The other night over burgers, she'd felt like they had a connection. It seemed like he was truly remorseful for his bad judgment on their first date.

But now, she wasn't sure what to expect.

A knock sounded at the door.

Showtime.

Ashley pasted on a smile and flung the door open.

Justin stood on the steps with a big grin on his face, a tiny blond-haired boy at his side. He held on to the child's hand. "Hi, Ashley." He nudged the little boy. "Like we practiced," he whispered.

"Hi, Miss Ashley." The child's face lit up with a smile.

Ashley shot Justin a puzzled look and knelt down to see the little boy. "What's your name?"

"Colton," he said. "I'm this many." He held up three fingers.

She couldn't help but laugh. "Nice to meet you, Colton." She stood and motioned toward the living room. "Come on in."

Justin pulled a truck out of his pocket and handed it to Colton. "Sit right here at the coffee table and play with your truck while I talk to Miss Ashley, okay?"

"'Kay." Colton sat down and started running the truck along the length of the coffee table.

Justin motioned for Ashley to step into the kitchen. "I'm sorry. His mom and little sister are sick. He didn't have anywhere to go, so he's spending the weekend with me."

"Are you his. . .dad?" she asked. It seemed like Justin would've mentioned being a father.

He shook his head. "Nope. His mom, Samantha, and I only went out a couple of times. We knew each other from college. But we stayed friends. And when she had Colton, I sort of stepped in to help care for him." He shrugged. "Strange, I know. But that kid has a piece of my heart. His situation isn't his fault, and I want to make sure he has a man in his life."

She felt her heart melt right then and there. "You should've told me. I would've understood."

"I wasn't sure how to bring it up. And then I was afraid it would sound like an excuse not to see you." He touched her arm. "And I did want to see you. But I hope that a date night with both me and Colton is okay."

"It's more than okay. It sounds perfect." She returned his smile and felt a flutter in her stomach she hadn't felt in a long time. "So what do you have in mind?"

"Is someplace kid friendly good with you? And then maybe we'll drive out to the beach and walk around or something."

"My kind of day." She glanced down at her denim capris, red tank top, and flip-flops. She'd had a feeling it would be a casual date and hadn't been wrong.

"Let's go, little man." Justin scooped Colton into his arms, and the little boy giggled.

Ashley couldn't tear her eyes away. Was there a sight cuter than a man and a child sharing a bond? If her biological clock ticked any louder, everyone would hear it. She followed them outside and locked the door. "Third time you've been here, and third car you've driven." She laughed.

Justin smiled. "When I have Colton with me, I borrow my mom's car. I don't feel safe otherwise." He lifted Colton into the car seat and buckled him in then opened the passenger door for her.

"Wow. So that was part of your act the other night too then?"

He flinched. "Yeah. Sorry. It just about killed me to not open the doors for you." He climbed inside the Taurus and glanced back at Colton. "Are you hungry?"

"Yes!" Colton exclaimed.

Justin turned to Ashley. "Is Chick-fil-A okay with you? I think there's one not too far from here."

She nodded. "Sounds perfect."

He started the car, and the music blared a children's tune.

Justin turned down the volume. "Sorry."

She burst out laughing. "I didn't peg you for a 'Wheels on the Bus' kind of guy, but I like it."

He backed the car out of the driveway and headed toward the restaurant.

Ashley listened to Colton's sweet voice singing along and couldn't help but smile. She'd never gone on a date quite like this one.

But she was having the time of her life.

Chapter 23

I don't want to talk about it." Luke stood up from where he'd been sitting on Bobby's bed and walked over to the chair in the corner. He sat down and crossed his arms, wishing he hadn't told his sister that he'd moved out.

"For someone so smart, you can be really dumb sometimes," Rose said. "Just tell me what's happened. Maybe I can help."

He shook his head. "No one can." He filled her in on the fiasco with the boat.

She furrowed her brow. "But why does the account matter so much to her? You guys have plenty."

He'd hoped to avoid telling Rose. "The money was what we'd set aside for the baby."

Rose's brown eyes lit up. "Is she pregnant? That's such wonderful news. The last time I saw her, she mentioned that you guys were hopeful it would happen soon."

Luke scowled. "No. She's not." He sighed. "But she was."

Rose came over and put a hand on his shoulder. "Oh Luke. I'm so sorry. You should've told me."

He scratched his head. "Nah. We'd planned on announcing it to everyone at Christmas. But she didn't quite make it that far."

"I could've helped her."

He drew his brows together. "How?"

She sat down on the end of the bed, facing him. "I've been through it. Before we had Dale, we lost a little girl. Susanna Elyse."

"You named her after Mama?"

Rose nodded. "That was the name I had picked out all along. We'd just learned that we were having a girl when it happened. It was the lowest point in my life."

He met her eyes. "How'd you get over it?"

She shrugged. "Just by grieving. We talked about her a lot. Still do, actually. It always gave me comfort to think that she was with Mama. But that didn't stop the hurting."

Luke shook his head. "Summer always wants to talk about our child. She wanted to guess what he or she would've grown up to be and who the baby would've looked most like." He frowned. "But I didn't think talking about it was a good idea."

"That was her baby, Luke. She carried that baby inside her body. Of course she's not going to forget about her child. She probably felt really guilty, too. When something like that happens and you're so powerless. . .all you can do is wonder if you somehow did something wrong."

He wondered if that's how Summer had felt. He hoped not. She was certainly not to blame. She'd been so cautious, following all the rules the doctor gave her. She always followed the rules. "I know that she isn't going to forget the baby. But I wasn't sure if talking about the loss was healthy for her."

"You sound like a chip off the old block. Daddy's never

been able to talk about his feelings either."

Luke hated to be compared to his father. "I thought it would be best for everyone if we moved on from what happened."

"Best for everyone or best for you?" Rose asked.

He let her words soak in for a minute. "Everyone."

She shook her head. "Well, you're welcome to look at Susanna's memorial stone. It's in the front of the house in the flower bed." She patted him on the leg. "Sometimes remembering what we've lost is comforting."

"Mama," Katie Beth said from the doorway, "Dale needs to go potty."

Rose glanced at Luke. "I'll be right back."

Luke picked up Bobby's things and stood. "Don't worry about it. I should go anyway." He kissed her on the cheek. "It's been great to see you."

She clutched his arm. "And I can count on you to check on Daddy? Because you know I'm going to expect you to let me know how he's doing."

He nodded. "You can count on me." He headed out the front door and stopped at the sidewalk. There amid the flowers was a stone with Susanna's name on it.

"She's our angel, you know," Katie Beth said, coming up behind him.

He jumped at her voice. He hadn't realized she'd followed him outside. "Yeah."

"Just like Mommy's Mommy. They're in heaven together watching over us. And now Uncle Bobby is with them. Like a family reunion except without the Kentucky Fried Chicken."

He smiled down at her. "When did you get to be so smart?"

She shrugged. "Kindergarten, I guess." She grinned, revealing a missing front tooth. "Are you sad, Uncle Luke?"

"Why would you say that?"

Katie Beth grabbed his hand. "Because Aunt Summer couldn't come with you today."

He knelt down in front of her. "Aunt Summer would've loved to have seen you. She loves you a lot."

"And Dale, too?"

"Yes. Dale, too."

Katie Beth tugged on his hand. "Next time can you bring Aunt Summer and Milo with you? I think he would like to see us, too."

He couldn't help but smile. Last year right before Bobby's accident, they'd all gotten together, and Milo had been a huge hit with Katie Beth. By the end of the day, they'd been best buddies. "He'd like to see you, too."

"But not Dale, because he pulled his tail last time."

Luke chuckled. "Milo is pretty forgiving, so I think he'd be happy to see both of you. Now I'd best get going."

Katie Beth flung her arms around his neck and gave him a kiss on the cheek. "Bye."

He kissed her on the cheek. She smelled like cherry Kool-Aid and sunscreen. "Bye." He climbed into his truck and tossed Bobby's things in the passenger seat.

Luke headed toward the marina, realizing it wasn't even five. The long weekend stretched out ahead of him, and for the first time since he could remember, he didn't have any responsibilities.

The logical side of him said that should make him happy.

That's what he'd wanted, after all. Peace and quiet to sort out his thoughts without anyone making any demands on his time.

So why was it that the weekend felt more like a prison than like the freedom he'd expected?

Memorial Day dawned bright and clear. Summer had to admit she felt pretty proud of herself. She'd finally remembered to set the timer on the coffeepot last night.

She hadn't realized how much she depended on Luke to brew her coffee. The first couple of mornings after he left, she'd stumbled down the stairs and stared bleary-eyed at the empty coffeemaker, saying words unbecoming of a lady.

But today she sipped her coffee at the table as Milo snored at her feet. Even though she still felt like she was on rocky ground, that simple act of independence gave her a sense of control.

Control.

Luke, Ashley, and pretty much everyone who'd ever met her had accused her at one time or another of being a control freak. She didn't see it that way though. Summer appreciated it when things made sense. And order made sense to her. Her books were alphabetized on their shelf and sorted by paperback and hardback. She arranged her closet by color. Her filing system at work was so pristine, anyone could come in and find a file even if they'd never opened her file cabinet before.

Order made sense. And when things made sense, she didn't

feel as tense as she did when things felt out of control.

She'd always figured it was one of the reasons she and Luke worked so well together. He dreamed the dreams, and she put the foundations underneath them. Without him, she'd be completely without imagination. And without her, he'd drift aimlessly.

At least that's what she'd always thought.

But he must be getting along okay, because he hadn't called her.

And she might not be doing okay, but at least she'd remembered to make the coffee. Baby steps. That was all she could ask of herself.

Today, though, would be a test. Her parents' annual Memorial Day get together had always been her family's way to kick off the summer. She and Luke went every year.

Going solo to the party could be dangerous. There would be landmines everywhere. Well-meaning relatives jumping out of the azaleas to ask where Luke was or when she was planning to start a family. Chloe would be there with her pregnancy glow to make Summer feel like a complete failure. Gram would take one look at her and know something was wrong.

Not to mention the usual dealings with her mother, who would be oblivious to her pain and probably want to talk about planning an upcoming shopping trip.

Yes, the landmines would be impossible to dodge. But she couldn't hide from them forever.

Thirty minutes later, she turned her SUV toward Isle of Palms. She rolled the windows down and turned the radio up.

The blue sky and bright sunshine made it a perfect Chamber of Commerce day. It looked like the brochures they sent out to tourists to entice them into visiting.

Except that Summer knew what was in store for her. Each mile brought her another twinge of anxiety.

She parked in her parents' driveway and walked up the steps that led to the porch. She took a deep breath. These people were her family. They had her back no matter what. Or at least that was how it was supposed to work.

She opened the door. The foyer was empty. Everyone must be outside. She walked into the living room and tucked her purse underneath a chair.

"I wondered if you'd make it today," Jefferson said from behind her.

She jumped at the sound of his voice. "Sneak up much?" she asked, turning to face him.

"Sorry." He grinned sheepishly. "Everyone's outside. Even my parents."

"Thanks again for helping with Milo the other day."

She followed him into the kitchen and let him open the door for her to go outside.

"No problem." He leaned down. "And your secret is safe with me," he said softly.

Summer nodded. "It had better be." She waved to her dad, who stood next to the grill. He must've talked Mom into letting him do the cooking today.

"Hey baby doll," Dad said, kissing her cheek. "Where's that son-in-law of mine?"

"Sorry he couldn't make it," she said. "You know how

crazy things can get."

"Did he have to work?" Dad asked.

Before she could answer, Jefferson jumped in. "That smells delicious. I think you could get a job at Five Guys if you tried."

Dad laughed. "Thanks, but I believe I'd prefer to keep my amateur status."

Summer shot Jefferson a silent thanks. "I'd better go say hi to Gram." She hurried toward her grandmother, leaving Jefferson to talk to her dad.

She bent down and hugged Gram's neck. "Hi there."

Gram smiled and patted the seat next to her at the patio table. "Have a seat, hon."

"It's a beautiful day for this, isn't it?" Summer glanced around the spacious backyard.

Gram raised an eyebrow. "Don't you try to make small talk with me. Where is your husband, and why did it look like you came out here with Jefferson?"

Summer felt the heat rise up her face. She'd known Gram wouldn't miss anything but hadn't bargained on her broaching the subject so soon. "Jefferson and I ran into each other in the foyer."

"He must've been waiting on you then, because this is the first I've seen of him."

Summer shook her head. "I'm sure it was a coincidence. He probably arrived right before I did."

"And Luke?"

Summer couldn't lie to her grandmother. Besides, knowing Gram was praying about the situation would give her a lot of comfort. She quickly filled Gram in on what was going on.

"No one else in the family needs to know though. I feel sure we'll get everything all worked out in no time."

Gram gripped her hand. "I'm sorry to hear this, honey. Do you know how Luke is holding up?"

Summer furrowed her brow. "This was his decision. He's the one who felt the need to pack a bag and go."

"But honey, I know how much he loves you. You've practically been his whole world since he was a teenager. Being without you must be killing him."

Summer scowled. "I'm sure he's fine. If not, I would've heard from him by now." Gram's words made her feel guilty. As if this were her fault. She'd certainly not wanted this to happen.

"Okay. Well, keep me posted. I'll be praying for a quick reconciliation."

Summer leaned over and kissed her grandmother on the cheek. "Thanks," she whispered.

"Anyone over here up for a little volleyball?" Mitch asked, walking over to the table where Summer and Gram sat. "How 'bout it, Gram? You in?" He displayed a dimple that had been making girls swoon since he was in junior high.

Gram chuckled. "I believe I'll sit this one out. Maybe next time."

Summer joined in her laughter. "I'm in." She followed Mitch out to the section of beach behind the house.

Jefferson waved as she walked up. "Well, well. I didn't think Mitch could talk you into playing."

She slipped her sandals off and grimaced at him. "I happen to be a stellar athlete. I could practically be on the Olympic team."

Mitch tossed her the ball. "I forgot how competitive you were." He shook his head. "Or maybe it's more like I blocked it out."

"You're just mad that your sister used to beat you at everything," Jefferson taunted.

Summer cocked her head. "Not everything. Mitch always beat me at Ping-Pong."

"Of course. Because Ping-Pong requires such athleticism."

Mitch glared at Jefferson. "I don't remember you being crowned Athlete of the Year in high school either."

Summer threw the ball at Mitch. "Okay, you two. Enough. I think we've established that *I* was the sportiest one of the three of us. Tell me again. . .how did y'all feel about always getting beat by a girl?"

"That was years ago. Everything's different now." Jefferson winked. "Besides, if I remember correctly, you are a little older than us. So let's see if you can still keep up."

She wrinkled her nose. "I'm only a month older than you. I doubt that gives you much of an advantage."

Preston and two of the neighbors walked up.

"Let's do this," Preston said.

They quickly divided into teams.

She took her place in front of the net. Every year for as long as she could remember, they'd all played beach volleyball at her parents' cookout. She and Luke always made sure to be on the same team. She blinked back unexpected tears. What was Luke doing today? Did he miss being here with her?

She looked up to see Jefferson's eyes on her from his spot directly across the net.

"You okay?" he mouthed.

She nodded and quickly wiped her eyes. She turned to look at Preston who stood ready to serve the ball. "Let's go." She clapped her hands and got into position.

Nothing like a little fake enthusiasm to chase the blues away.

Chapter 24

Ashley pulled into Justin's parents' driveway and put the car in PARK. She had butterflies the size of eagles in her stomach. She knew it was probably way too soon for a "meet the parents" situation, but when Justin had asked her over for a cookout, she hadn't been able to resist.

Their date on Saturday night had been perfect. She'd enjoyed Colton's antics and had especially liked watching how Justin interacted with the child. After dinner they'd gone to Folly Beach and collected shells.

Ashley didn't allow herself to dream about the future anymore, but Saturday night had given her a glimpse of what a life with Justin might be like. And it would be a good life.

But it was way too early to be thinking long term. She knew she needed to slow down. After her divorce, she'd been certain she'd never have feelings for anyone ever again. And even though she and Justin had gotten off to a rocky start, she knew he had all the qualities she'd been looking for.

"Hey there," Justin said, walking out to meet her in the driveway. "I thought you were just gonna sit in your car all day."

"Sorry."

"Nervous?" He raised his eyebrows.

She shrugged. "A little bit. What if your parents hate me?"

He shook his head. "No way. But don't worry. I told them we've only just met. No one is going to ask you any tough questions." He grinned mischievously. "They'll save that until the second time you come out."

"Second time? What makes you think there'll be a second time?" she asked teasingly.

He put a hand on the small of her back and guided her through the front door. "Wishful thinking," he said softly.

A shiver of excitement ran up her spine. He was a keeper—she just knew it.

Justin nodded his head at the patio door. "They're out back."

She followed him outside and glanced around. A small crowd stood around the grill and another group around a swimming pool where Colton was splashing around, clad in green swim trunks and a baseball cap. His pudgy little belly was so cute, it was all Ashley could do not to go lift him out of the pool and blow raspberries on it until he laughed.

"Everyone, this is Ashley." Justin slung an arm around her shoulder. "Ashley, this is everyone."

Once she had made the rounds and met his relatives, she settled into a chair near the pool. Justin's family didn't make a big fuss over her. Instead, they made her feel right at home. After three years of barely seeing her own family, it was nice to be around what was obviously a tightly knit group.

"Are you enjoying yourself?" Justin's mom asked, taking the seat next to her.

She smiled. "Yes, ma'am. Thank you for having me over."

"We're glad to have you," Mrs. Sanders said. "Justin never brings girls to the house. I think he's afraid we'll embarrass him."

Ashley chuckled. It felt good to hear that she wasn't one of many. Maybe it meant he thought she was special if he'd been willing to risk embarrassment for her.

Colton squealed as Justin sprayed him with the water hose. He bent down and splashed water at Justin.

Justin grabbed a towel and scooped the laughing child up in it.

"They love each other to pieces," Mrs. Sanders remarked. "Justin would raise Colton as his own if he could."

Ashley found the situation puzzling to say the least. From what Justin had told her Saturday night, Colton's mom wasn't neglectful, but she wasn't very engaged in the child's life either. Still, Colton seemed pretty well adjusted. "I know. He'd make a great dad." As soon as the words escaped her lips, she wished she could take them back. *Scary girl who only just met you wants to have babies with your son.*

But Mrs. Sanders smiled. "He sure will."

"Hey, you two," Justin called to them. "You'd better not be talking about me."

His mom stood. "Don't flatter yourself. We have far more interesting things to talk about." She gave Ashley a wink. "I'd better go see if Jim needs help with the grill."

An hour later the food was almost all gone. "It was delicious," Ashley said to Justin's dad as she tossed her paper plate in the garbage.

"Glad you liked it," he said.

Justin lifted his empty glass. "I'm going to get more Coke. Do you want anything?"

Ashley shook her head. "Nope. I'm fine."

He looked her up and down. "You sure are."

She felt the blush rise up her face. "Shh. They'll hear."

"Sorry. I just call it like I see it."

It had been so long since a guy she liked gave her a compliment. She loved Justin's obvious appreciation for the way she looked. "Thanks."

"Why don't y'all get out of here for a little while?" Justin's mom asked. "Colton is down for his nap, and we'll be glad to watch him if he wakes up."

Justin raised his eyebrows at Ashley. "Sound good to you?"

She nodded. "Sure."

"Thanks, Mom." Justin kissed Mrs. Sanders on the cheek. "We'll be back soon." He put a hand on the small of Ashley's back and led her inside the house.

"So where are we going to go?" she asked.

He thought for a second. "How about I show you a piece of my childhood? You mind walking?"

"I could certainly use some exercise after that meal." She chuckled.

"Whatever. I think you're perfect."

She beamed. "Thanks." She followed Justin out the front door. Once they got to the end of the driveway, he took her hand.

"This okay?" he asked. "Or are you not a hand holder?"

She laughed. "It's more than okay." And it was. The way her

hand felt in his was so comforting, so normal. It was almost as if they'd been doing it their whole lives.

They walked in silence for a few moments.

"Thanks for being so understanding about Colton," Justin said finally. "I was a little nervous that you'd be weirded out about it."

She squeezed his hand. "I think it's fantastic. Honestly. I can't imagine many guys so willing to rearrange their lives for a kid who isn't even theirs."

"You make me sound like some kind of saint. I'm certainly not."

"So tell me your flaws."

Justin took a deep breath and blew it out. "You really want to know? I don't want to chase you off so soon."

She giggled. "Try me."

"I forget to put the top on the toothpaste. I eat a lot of takeout because I'm a terrible cook. I never ask for directions. And I have kind of a tender heart."

"How's that one a flaw?"

He bumped his shoulder against hers. "I cry at stuff. I know it's not manly. Weddings. Movies. Even big sporting events. Some girls hate that. And my friends make fun."

"A sensitive man. I didn't know those existed except for in books and movies." She grinned. "I won't hold any of that against you, I promise."

"Good to know." He motioned toward a park. "Here we are." Justin led her through the gate and onto a sidewalk that wound around the park. "I can't tell you how many hours I spent here growing up."

"Looks like paradise." The giant trees scattered along the perimeter of the park were heavy with Spanish moss. The lush, green grass conjured up images of running barefoot and picnics and all the things that made summertime special.

Justin tugged on her hand. "Come on." They walked past a water fountain to a set of bleachers in front of a deserted baseball field. "After you," he said.

She climbed the bleachers and sat down.

"I learned to hit a baseball right there," Justin said, sitting down next to her and pointing at home plate. "My dad coached my T-ball and Little League team. This is where we practiced and played."

"I'll bet you were adorable in your little uniform."

He blushed. "My mom thought so." He chuckled. "She came out here every day with a cooler of cherry Kool-Aid and those little paper cups." He pointed at an old wooden dugout. "She'd set it up in there, and by the time we got finished, we'd all have red Kool-Aid mustaches."

"Sounds like a perfect childhood." Ashley's own parents had split up when she was in kindergarten. Her dad hadn't been in the picture, and her mom had always been too busy searching for her own "happily ever after" to worry too much about her only child.

"Some people might think my parents were too involved in my life, but I realize now how blessed I was. And still am."

She tilted her head and admired his blue eyes. "Is that why Colton's so important to you?"

Justin nodded. "I've always wanted a family of my own. Since I was a kid. Most guys are looking for freedom and making conquests. I've always prayed that God would lead me to the kind of woman who would make a good partner and who wanted a family as much as me."

Her heart fluttered. She'd looked for that same thing. Prayed for the same thing. But had settled for Brian. She'd been terrified that he was her only shot at marriage and family. And when it didn't work out, she'd assumed that real happiness wasn't in the cards for her. "That's an amazing dream. Most guys are so worried about being successful, they don't give much thought to their family life." She squeezed his hand. "At least the guys I've met, up until now."

Justin locked eyes with her. He reached out and traced the back of his hand along her face. "I'm going to kiss you now. And it's going to mean something."

She gave him a tiny smile and leaned forward to meet his lips. The kiss was soft at first. Tentative. It grew deeper, more passionate, and by the time she pulled back, they were both breathless.

"Well then," Justin murmured. "That was. . ." He trailed off.

"Nice?" she asked.

He burst out laughing. "I guess that's one way to put it. I was hoping for something a little more enthusiastic."

She wanted to keep her enthusiasm to herself, at least for the time being. The last guy she'd kissed had been her husband. And there'd been a time she thought those kisses were pretty great.

But they didn't compare to kissing Justin.

"How about amazing?"

He nodded. "Amazing will do."

"Well, how would you describe it?"

He took her hand. "I'd say that was the best kiss I've had in all of my twenty-nine years on earth."

Ashley almost fell off of the bleachers. Twenty-nine? He was only twenty-nine? Her heart—that had been so full of hope for their budding romance—dropped.

She knew herself. And at thirty-six, she knew there was no way she could date someone who hadn't even reached the thirty milestone yet.

No way.

Even if she'd never been kissed quite like that before.

Luke pulled into the driveway at his house. Disappointment washed over him at the sight of Summer's empty parking space. He'd hoped she'd be home by now.

Her parents' traditional Memorial Day party must've run long, because usually Summer was aching to get away from their house. Although maybe she wasn't looking forward to coming home to an empty house. Just like he hated going to the quiet loneliness of the boat.

He let himself into the house and turned off the alarm. At least she'd started remembering to set it.

Milo looked up from his spot on the couch. The big dog rose and stretched. He padded over to Luke and looked up at him.

Luke knelt down and gave Milo a pat. "Hey, boy.

Have you missed me?"

Milo sank lower onto the floor and rolled onto his back.

Luke scratched Milo's stomach, and the dog wriggled with happiness. "Let's go outside and take care of the yard."

Mowing the yard made him think of meeting Summer for the first time. He couldn't help but grin to himself. His buddies had told him that someone like her would never go for a guy like him, but he'd been smitten from the first time he saw her.

They'd started out as friends. He'd looked forward to the weekly visit to her grandmother's house, because after a few weeks, Summer was always there. She'd bring him something cold to drink, and after he'd finished working, they'd sit on the porch and talk about books and music and what they wanted to do with their lives.

"Someday you're going to hear my songs on the radio," Luke told her.

Summer gave him a slow smile. "I'd be your biggest fan."

"Yeah, well when that happens, maybe your daddy won't mind if I ask you out." Luke's ego still stung from learning that Summer's dad wouldn't hear of letting her go out with him.

She shook her head. "What he doesn't know won't hurt him."

Luke had asked her out to a movie, but she'd balked at the thought of him picking her up in his old truck and said her daddy wouldn't let her go with someone whose family he didn't know.

"So you'll meet me then? Even though you might get in trouble?"

Summer tossed her dark ponytail. "I'm staying at Gram's tonight. I'll tell her I'm meeting a friend for a movie." She grinned. "Which is totally true."

"Awesome. Meet me at the bandstand at the Battery at seven."

She nodded. "I'll be there." She stood. "I'd better go inside."

He grabbed her hand and felt a twinge of excitement. "I'll see you tonight."

At the time, it had seemed like it was them against the world. Luke had tried to make a good impression on her dad when they'd finally met, but Mr. Rutledge had always been cool toward him.

His own family had loved Summer from the beginning. She'd even broken through his dad's gruff exterior. The elder Nelson had told his son that hanging on to Summer was the smartest thing he'd ever done.

And if he remembered correctly, Daddy had also warned him not to mess it up.

As he finished mowing the yard, he wondered if he'd messed up bad enough that they couldn't come back from it. Nothing irreversible had happened. He'd just packed a duffel bag and spent a few nights away.

He sat on the porch steps and took a swig of water. He'd wait for her to get home. Give her an apology. She was the most important person in his life. And she deserved to be treated better.

He leaned back and stretched his legs out in front of him. Just those few days apart and he'd realized that he needed to do whatever it took to get them back to where they used to be.

And if that meant going to counseling with some guy at Summer's church, then he would have to man up and do it. The talk he'd had with Rose had made him realize a lot of things. Number one being that he'd crumbled under the grief of losing Bobby and the baby, and Summer had been the one to suffer because of it. He would have to figure out a way to make it up to her.

Milo barked at the gate.

Luke looked up to see Summer's SUV pulling slowly up the driveway, Mitch's red Porsche following behind her.

Summer climbed out of the vehicle and walked over to the porch. "I didn't expect to see you here." She looked good. Her khaki shorts and green polo shirt showed off her trim figure.

He stood. "I wanted to get the yard done and see Milo." He met her gaze. "And you."

Hope flickered across her face. "Yeah?"

Luke wanted nothing more than to run to her and take her in his arms. Kiss her until she couldn't think straight and then carry her up the stairs to their room. But he knew they had a lot of talking to do first. "Yeah."

"Luke, we missed you at the cookout," Mitch said.

He looked up in surprise. He'd been so happy to see Summer, he'd forgotten that Mitch had followed her into the driveway. Much to his chagrin, Jefferson stood next to Mitch, an amused expression on his face. "Yeah, sorry I missed it."

"Your wife put us to shame on the volleyball court," Jefferson said. "That's why we're here. We promised to take her out to dinner tonight if her team won two out of three."

"And they won three out of three," Mitch grumbled. "So here we are."

Summer locked eyes with him. "Why don't you come with us? I think we're headed to California Dreaming. You know how I love their crab cakes."

He shook his head. "I'd better not. But you go on."

She climbed the porch steps and stood next to him.

His hands ached to touch her. But he didn't.

"I'll go get changed. Be right back." Summer brushed past him and went into the house, Milo at her heels.

The three men stood in silence for a long moment.

Mitch cleared his throat. "Well, this is a tension convention. I'm gonna go in and grab a bottle of water. You boys play nice." He trotted up the stairs and into the house.

Luke eyed Jefferson. "So have you settled in yet?"

"I'm renting a carriage house a few houses down from here." He raised an eyebrow. "That should make you feel better, knowing that if Summer needs anything, I can be over here in a few minutes. Especially now that she's living all alone."

So he knew Luke was staying on the boat. She'd told Jefferson of all people. Luke would've rather been sucker punched than betrayed by his own wife. "Yeah. It makes me feel loads better."

Jefferson chuckled. "Now, now. It sounded to me like you brought all this on yourself."

"Have I mentioned how happy I am that you're back in town?" Luke asked. "Just gives me a warm, fuzzy feeling inside." He glowered.

"Oh, I can imagine." Jefferson smirked. "And believe me, I'm thrilled to be back."

Luke stood. "If you'll excuse me, there's something I need to take care of inside." He pushed the door open with a vengeance, almost knocking Mitch down. "Sorry, man," he mumbled, walking past his brother-in-law and into the entryway.

He took a deep breath and headed up the stairs.

Summer stood in front of the mirror, twisting her hair into a bun.

"Can we talk?" he asked, sitting down on the bed, admiring the way her skin glowed from a day in the sun.

She turned to face him. "Luke, they're waiting downstairs. I don't think this is the right time."

"When will be the right time then?" He rubbed his jaw.

"I don't know." She turned her attention back to the mirror. "You can't just stop by and expect me to drop everything. I waited days for you to call and didn't hear a word. So the way I see it, our talk can wait a little bit longer."

"I've known you for a long time. I can tell you're upset."

She turned back around, fire in her blue eyes. "You think? My husband moves onto a boat that he purchased with money that I had earmarked for the child that I hoped to have someday." She narrowed her eyes. "The child I *still* plan on having someday. And now you show up like nothing happened and expect me to forget it?"

He shook his head. "It's not like that, and you know it. Besides, *you're* the one who first suggested that I stay on the boat." He sighed. "And you know I don't expect you to forget everything that has happened. But we need to talk about it."

"All those months. All those months I wanted to talk. Begged you to talk." She grabbed her purse from the foot of the bed. "And you acted like I barely existed."

"I know I have a lot to apologize for."

She paused at the doorway. "Luke, I do want to talk to you. We definitely need to. But right at this minute, I don't have it in me. Do you hear me? I am not capable at this point in time to have this conversation with you. It's been a long day. A longer week." She shook her head and sighed. "And at this moment, all I can handle is going to eat some crab cakes and letting Mitch and Jefferson make me laugh. At this moment, I want to forget for a couple of hours that I'll be coming home to an empty house."

"I'm sure Jefferson would be glad to walk you home and check the place out." Luke glowered. "I can't believe you told him that I left. What were you thinking?"

"What was *I* thinking?" She closed the bedroom door and turned to face him. "I don't know—I guess I was thinking that it was the truth. You left. And to top it off, you haven't called. Haven't come by. I haven't heard so much as a peep from you." She narrowed her eyes. "Jefferson happened to see me out for a walk with Milo, and I was upset. I didn't intend to tell him, but I'm not sorry I did."

"He happened to see you out, huh? Don't you think it's a little weird that he shows up all of a sudden, and now he practically lives next door?"

Summer groaned. "Seriously? I thought we'd gotten over the Jefferson hurdle years ago when I married you."

"Is that a hint of regret I hear in your voice?"

She furrowed her brow. "Don't be stupid. Do I need to remind you again that this whole thing—"

"What? Is all my fault?" He shook his head. "Right. And you are totally blameless. Except for the whole walking around like a robot for months, forgetting the simplest things and working sixty-hour weeks at the office. But besides all that, you're perfect." Luke could admit that many of their problems stemmed from him. But it had taken both of them to reach the point where they were now. The breaking point.

"I know I'm not perfect." Her eyes filled with tears. "I know that better than anyone."

Luke took a step toward her, but she held her hands out to stop him.

"Don't." Her whisper carried as much force as any yell.

He sighed. "I didn't come here to argue. I just wanted to see you and Milo."

"Milo is downstairs and needs to be walked. Stay as long as you like. But I'm going to dinner now." She walked out without another word.

Luke buried his head in his hands. Summer had never rattled easily. But he could see that his presence had thrown her. Angered her even. Maybe a surprise visit hadn't been the smartest thing. He should've called her last week and checked in. He should've kept a lid on his anger over Jefferson's presence. He should've done a lot of things.

He got up and watched out the bedroom window as Summer, Mitch, and Jefferson drove away.

So maybe apologizing to Summer and getting things back to normal wouldn't be as easy as he'd expected. He'd keep trying until he won her trust back, even if it took him forever.

Because the idea of not getting back on solid ground with Summer was too painful to even consider. And the fact that his old nemesis had somehow weaseled his way back into her life made him very uneasy.

Chapter 25

Ashley had been replaying that kiss with Justin over and over in her mind ever since Monday. Followed quickly by the reminder that he hadn't reached his thirtieth birthday yet and she was knocking on forty's door. Okay, so maybe she had four years left until forty, but that didn't seem all that comforting right now.

Summer tapped her fingers on Ashley's desk. "I don't think you've heard anything I've said. Are you okay?"

"Huh?" Ashley looked up to see Summer standing in front of her desk, an amused expression on her face.

"I asked you if you're going to go with me to the new bridal boutique over on Calhoun Street. I want to officially introduce myself. Jennifer St. Claire is getting her dress and bridesmaids' dresses there. She's been really pleased."

The St. Claire–Wentworth wedding was coming up in the fall. Ashley had met with Jennifer what seemed like fifty times already. She hadn't seen the dress though. "I'd love to go with you. I wonder if they can show us Jennifer's dress."

"Only one way to find out. Let's go." Summer grabbed her purse and a binder from her desk and led the way out the door. "Are you okay though? You've been quiet all week."

Ashley hadn't been sure what to tell Summer, so she'd opted to keep her mouth shut. But it would be nice to unload it. She quickly filled her in on her outing with Justin and Colton, the cookout, and the kiss. "Why didn't you tell me he wasn't even thirty?" she whined.

"Honestly, I didn't think about it. I guess I always forget that Justin is younger. He was actually one of Bobby's friends first, but he and Luke hit it off." Summer unlocked her SUV and climbed inside.

Ashley got into the passenger seat and buckled her seat belt. "I can't imagine continuing the relationship now."

Summer waited for a car to pass before she pulled out of her parking space. "I think you're silly. Justin is a great guy. Very mature for his age. And you don't look a day over twenty-five."

Ashley laughed. "I know he's a great guy and all of that. But as soon as I found out his age, I felt so self-conscious. I have little laugh lines around my eyes."

"Maybe if you look with a magnifying glass."

"At twenty-nine, that means some of the girls he's gone out with over the past year have probably barely been in their twenties. I can't compete with that."

Summer let out a huge sigh. "I can't believe you're this insecure. You look amazing. You're a smart, interesting *woman*. Twentysomething girls have nothing on you."

Ashley wanted to believe Summer. But after what happened with Brian, she couldn't let go of the fear. "He might be happy with me for a few months until some tanned, flat-bellied girl-woman saunters by and turns his head."

Summer groaned. "What's this really about? Because if that kiss was as good as you say, I can't believe you're going to let a little something like age keep you away from him." She pulled into the parking lot at the boutique.

"Just some stuff I've gone through." Ashley sighed. "I agreed to go out with him again this weekend, but I'm thinking of canceling."

Summer turned off the engine and looked at Ashley. "Does he know how old you are?"

Ashley shook her head. "No. I don't want him to know."

"I can guarantee you that he doesn't care if you're a few years older than him. He might even find you more attractive." Summer grinned. "You never know."

Ashley followed her into the store. She wasn't sure she wanted to know. Because her self-confidence couldn't take it if the opposite was true.

"It's so nice to meet you," Madelyn Ashworth said. "Jennifer has said such wonderful things about Summer Weddings." She smiled.

"Likewise," Summer said. "We wanted to come over and introduce ourselves and take a look around your beautiful shop."

Madelyn beamed. "It's a lifelong dream of mine. I have four daughters, and let me tell you, helping each of them choose a wedding gown is one of my favorite memories." She gestured to the rows of pristine gowns. "Wedding dresses are so personal, aren't they? I try to make sure that each of my clients tries on several different styles. Sometimes a girl comes in here thinking she wants one thing and realizes that something else is better suited for her."

Ashley thumbed through an old issue of *Modern Bride* from a nearby table. "I was one of those girls. I always said 'no way' to a princess-style dress. But wouldn't you know it, I tried on a poufy, lacy thing and fell in love with it." She laughed.

Madelyn turned to Summer. "How about you? Did you wear the dress you'd always dreamed of or were you surprised by what you wound up with?"

Summer grimaced. "Actually, I got married at city hall." She shook her head. "I never even tried on a wedding dress."

Madelyn drew back, her eyes wide with horror.

"Don't worry though. I've been doing this for a long time. Just because I didn't have my own fairy-tale wedding doesn't diminish my ability as a wedding planner." Summer tried to laugh it off, but she could see her credibility had fallen as far as Madelyn was concerned.

Madelyn looked over at Ashley. "Are you thinking what I'm thinking?"

Ashley nodded. "I am."

"Come on." Madelyn pointed at a row of dresses in the back of the store. "This is the new collection for the fall. Try one on. Just for fun."

Summer drew her brows together. "Oh, I shouldn't." She didn't want to appear unprofessional. But she had always wanted to try on a wedding dress. Last year she'd picked up a dress from the cleaners for one of her brides. It had absolutely been Summer's dream gown and in her size, too. It had taken all her self-control not to try it on. She'd held it up in front of herself in the full-length mirror at the back of Summer Weddings and imagined what it would've been like to float down an aisle toward Luke.

"Come on," Ashley said. "Seeing you go all princess will cheer me up."

Summer twisted her mouth into a smile. "I'll try one on. But only if you promise not to cancel your date with Justin."

"If it means you doing something spontaneous and trying on your dream gown. . .I'm in." Ashley smiled and held up her iPhone. "And I'm totally willing to document this little fashion show."

"What style do you have in mind, Summer?" Madelyn asked.

Summer thought for a moment. "My dream gown used to be a ball gown with a full skirt. But now I think I like a straighter, column style. But not strapless." She chuckled. "I get so tired of seeing strapless dresses all the time."

"Maybe a high neck?" Ashley asked, pulling one off the rack and holding it up. "Like this?" The white chiffon had intricate beading at the bodice.

Summer inhaled sharply. "Oh that's beautiful."

"Go try it on," Madelyn said, pointing at a fitting room. "If you need help, let me know."

Summer carried the gown into a lavish dressing room. The A-line chiffon dress had a high halter neck in the front and a deep V in the back. It might not be as traditional as a poufy, strapless dress, but it fit Summer's sophisticated style perfectly.

She slipped it over her head. "Can someone zip me?" she called.

Madelyn opened the door and carefully zipped the dress. "Oh my. It's like it was made for you. Come step up on the platform and look in the mirror."

Summer tentatively walked out of the dressing room and stepped up on the block that was in front of a floor-length mirror.

"It's perfect," Ashley breathed. "Just perfect." She sighed. "You make a beautiful bride."

Summer laughed. "Okay, simmer down. I've already been a bride, remember? Now I'm just an old married lady."

Ashley raised an eyebrow. "Please don't mention the word *old* to me today."

Summer turned to face herself in the mirror. She might be married, but her husband was living on a boat. Without her. So much for the fairy tale. "This is a gorgeous dress."

Madelyn walked over with a tiara and veil. "Try this, too. You want to get the full experience."

Summer bent down, and Madelyn placed the headpiece on top of her head. She stood upright and looked back in the mirror. "I look so—so. . .bridal."

They burst out laughing.

"That's kind of the point," Ashley said. "Here, smile." She held up the phone and snapped a couple of pictures.

Summer turned back to the mirror. She'd never told Luke, but not having a real wedding had always bothered her. She'd dreamed of a church wedding at St. Michael's. Chloe's wedding had taken place in the historic building, and it had been so beautiful. Every time Summer planned a wedding at

St. Michael's, she imagined what her own would've been like. But it was too late now. "This has been fun. I guess now I know how I would've looked as a bride."

Madelyn smiled. "Hon, with your looks and figure, you could model those dresses. Be a bride every day."

Summer stepped down from the platform with a laugh. "This was enough. Besides, if I were dressed like a bride every day, it wouldn't be special anymore."

"Um, I'd take that job," Ashley said. "Any day that includes a tiara sounds like a great day to me."

Summer paused for Madelyn to unzip the dress. "Thanks for this. It was fun." She smiled. "The most fun I've had in a while."

"I'm glad you were a good sport." Madelyn smiled. "I love to see that look on a girl's face when she sees herself in the dress for the first time. You were no different. For a minute, even the toughest girl turns into Cinderella."

Summer closed the fitting room door behind her and glanced in the mirror one last time.

She was nobody's Cinderella. But it had been fun to pretend for a few minutes that everything was perfect.

Chapter 26

Luke sat in his truck in the nursing home parking lot. He hadn't seen his dad since Bobby's funeral almost a year ago. Almost exactly a year ago.

And even then the old man had been feeble. Broken. A lifetime of regret had been etched on his weathered face.

Luke hadn't tried to contact Summer since he'd seen her on Memorial Day. He hadn't known what to say. Her eyes had been so full of anger and hurt. He'd never dealt that well with emotions, so he wasn't sure what he could say or do to take away her pain.

But today he wished he'd called her. He wished he'd asked her to come here with him. She would've known what to say, how to act. Her presence would've put him at ease.

He climbed out of the truck and walked slowly toward the entrance. Rose had warned him that Daddy might not recognize him. She'd given him so many instructions on the phone last night, his phone battery had almost given out. He walked inside the building and glanced around the big hallway.

A few elderly people shuffled past in robes. A teenage girl pushed an older woman in a wheelchair.

He inhaled. He must be near the cafeteria, because there was a distinct food smell in the air. It didn't seem as much like a hospital as he'd expected. It was a little homier with nice décor and wallpapered walls.

He glanced at the sign on the wall. His dad's room should be down the left corridor. He walked to the room and stopped in the doorway.

Roy Nelson sat in a recliner next to his hospital bed, staring straight ahead. His gray hair was longer than the buzz cut he'd worn most of Luke's life.

Luke tapped gently on the door. "Hello," he said.

Daddy looked up, and his face brightened. "Pete," he said with a grin. "It's great to see you."

Pete Nelson had been Daddy's older brother. He'd passed away fifteen years ago while Luke was in Nashville. Everyone in the Nelson family had always thought Luke resembled Pete more than he'd favored his own father. "Hi," Luke said. Rose had warned him, but even so, the situation made him uncomfortable.

"It's been such a long time. How are Lucille and the kids?"

Luke smiled. "Fine. How is your family?" He wondered what year it was in his dad's mind.

Daddy shook his head. "You know how hard it's been since I lost Martha."

Luke nodded. "I know."

"But the kids are doing well. Rose stays with Martha's sister a lot. She's turning into such a good little cook. And so sweet. And Bobby is my athlete." Daddy grinned. "Even though he's just in junior high, I think he might end up playing football someday for the Gamecocks."

Bobby had played for a year until he'd torn his ACL. Luke had been so proud of his little brother and had gone to every home game. "That's great." He leaned forward. "How's Luke?" He steeled himself against his dad's response.

Daddy's face lit up. "Luke's my pride and joy."

Luke's eyes filled with unexpected tears. "Yeah?"

"He's so smart. That boy can be anything he wants. He's in Nashville right now, trying to make it as a musician." The older man chuckled. "But his heart's here. Her name's Summer."

"She's a nice girl?"

Daddy nodded. "She comes from money, but that doesn't matter to Luke. First time I saw them together, I knew. He'd found someone to love like I loved Martha." He sighed. "I've been so hard on him over the years. I've always been so proud of him, but I wanted him to want more than the life I had. Sometimes I wish I'd handled things with him differently."

Luke gripped his daddy's hand and forced back the tears. "It's not too late. I'll bet he'd love to hear from you."

"Oh, I wouldn't do that. I don't want to bother him. He's got his own life to live now."

Luke nodded. "They do grow up quick, don't they?"

Daddy's face grew sad. "Too quick. I blinked, and they were gone. Bobby's the only one at home now, and the next couple years will fly by."

"Make the most of it." Luke couldn't stay in the room any longer. The pain was too much.

"Oh, I will. I'm hoping to have all the kids back in the house for Christmas."

Luke remembered that Christmas. He'd stayed in Nashville instead of coming home. And right now he'd give anything to be able to go back and accept the invitation his father had offered. "That sounds so nice."

Daddy beamed. "Oh, it will be."

"I'd better get going." Luke stood.

"Tell Lucille and the kids hello."

Luke nodded. He turned to go then turned back around and threw his arms around Daddy's neck. "I'll be back soon."

Daddy smiled and patted him on the back. "Okay. Bye, Pete."

Luke rushed out of the room, almost knocking down a nurse. He had to get to the truck. As soon as he hit the exit door, he broke into a run. He climbed into the truck and hunched over the steering wheel, his body racked with sobs.

Luke hadn't cried in years. Not when Bobby died. Not when Summer miscarried. Not even the night last week on the boat when he'd realized he might not be able to put his life back together again.

He'd heard of people hitting rock bottom. But this was the first time he'd experienced it for himself. He'd waited his whole life to hear those words from his dad: *I'm proud of you.* They'd never come. Not once. Not when he'd graduated second in his class and spoken at the ceremony. Daddy had made some comment about how he should've worked harder and been first. When Luke married Summer, Daddy had just warned him not to mess up. And when he'd graduated from college and begun working for the National Park Service, Daddy had only shaken his head and muttered that Luke hadn't reached high enough.

But today, as Daddy thought he was talking to Uncle Pete, his pride had been evident. Maybe it had been there all along and Luke had been so sullen he hadn't noticed it. He thought about all the times Summer had tried to persuade him to visit Daddy. Luke had given her a million reasons why he didn't have time.

And now time had run out. Even if he visited Daddy every day for the rest of his life, it wouldn't matter. He couldn't turn back the clock.

Luke leaned back and rested his head against the seat, his eyes blurry with tears. He glanced over at the passenger seat. He'd tossed Bobby's things there and left them. He reached over and picked up his little brother's Bible. He flipped it open, surprised by how many passages were highlighted and how many pages were dog-eared. He stopped in Ecclesiastes where nearly all the text on one page had been underlined and began to read in chapter 3:

There is a time for everything,
and a season for every activity under the heavens:
a time to be born and a time to die,
a time to plant and a time to uproot,
a time to kill and a time to heal,
a time to tear down and a time to build,
a time to weep and a time to laugh,
a time to mourn and a time to dance.

He looked over the words again. How had he missed it?

He'd looked at everything that had happened in his life over the past year as a personal attack. But that wasn't it at all. It was just life. Unpredictable and unsteady. But God must know what He was doing even if Luke didn't understand.

And even though his pain was fresh, that thought gave him comfort.

Summer flipped through her planner. June was flying by. Maybe it was best that this was one of her busiest months, because she'd barely had time to think about her problems. She'd spent the day being all too aware of the significance of today's date though.

Bobby's accident had happened exactly a year ago.

She'd been expecting Luke to call her all week. After the way he'd stopped by the house on Memorial Day wanting to talk, she'd thought he would seek her out. But maybe he'd expected the same thing from her. Or maybe he was so mad at her for letting Jefferson know about their problems that he didn't want to talk to her.

She leaned back in her chair and sighed. She'd been thinking lately that their relationship problems were a two-way street. He'd alluded to it on Memorial Day. It might be easy for her to blame Luke for pulling away and being distant, but she knew she'd done the same thing. After the miscarriage, she'd felt so lost. Luke didn't want to talk about it, and only Gram and Ashley knew the truth. So she'd tried to handle her feelings herself.

Over the months, she'd been so distracted, so foggy. No wonder Luke hadn't known how to respond to her. He wasn't the only one who'd acted like a different person. She had, too. It had taken some time alone to see her part in their problems more clearly.

"You okay?" Ashley asked.

Summer startled at the sound of her voice. "I'm fine. Just thinking. Today is the anniversary of Bobby's accident."

Ashley furrowed her brow. "I'm so sorry. I know that's got to be tough. Have you talked to Luke?"

Summer shook her head. "No. I think I'm going to call him. Although I doubt he'll tell me how he's really feeling about everything."

"Why are men so much trouble?" Ashley dramatically put the back of her hand to her forehead. "Is it them or us?"

Summer couldn't help but laugh at her friend. "Probably a little of both." She shook her head. "Any news on the website launch?"

Ashley nodded. "Yep. It's finished. Justin says it will be live come Monday."

"Awesome. Thanks again for your work on that."

A shadow crossed Ashley's face. "You're welcome."

Summer tried to read Ashley's tone. Something was off with her. "Everything still okay with Justin? You went out last week, right?"

"I did. But all I could think about was that I clearly remember the year he was born. I was in the first grade for Pete's sake. Then I realized that when he was seven, I was fourteen. Which means I could've been his babysitter."

"I think you're overthinking it."

Ashley sighed. "Maybe. Probably. But I still can't shake that feeling. He is great though."

"You kissed him again, didn't you?"

"I sure did. And man, that boy can kiss. I swear, he makes me feel sixteen when he kisses me."

Summer couldn't hide her smile. "I still think he's a keeper."

Ashley shook her head. "I've made up my mind. We're going out this weekend, and I'm going to tell him I can't see him again." She frowned. "I wish I could handle it, but I can't. I'm too scared he'll start to think of me as old and want to trade me in for a younger model."

Summer could only surmise that had been what happened in Ashley's marriage, but she wasn't certain. "You might be surprised."

"Or I might be heartbroken. I'd rather be alone than have my heart broken by Justin."

"There are no guarantees. On anything." Summer had learned that lesson the hard way.

Ashley raked a strand of blond hair from her face. "I know. But I'd rather be safe than sorry."

Summer stood up from her desk. "I'll be out for the rest of the afternoon. I'm going to the boat to wait for Luke to get home from work. I want to see how he's doing. Maybe he doesn't realize what today is."

"Okay." Ashley turned her attention back to her computer.

Thirty minutes later, Summer pulled up to the marina. Luke should be here soon. She turned off the engine and went to sit on the dock next to the water. It was so peaceful. Water had always calmed her. She glanced over to where the *Summer Girl* sat. Had she been too hard on him for buying it? Maybe they would've had a great time on the boat this summer.

She glanced at her watch. He should be here by now. She picked up her phone and dialed his number.

Voice mail.

Where would he go? She took a deep breath and tried not to worry.

After fifteen minutes, she tried the call again and still got his voice mail. Her heart pounded. What if something had happened to him? It had been her constant thought over the past weeks. That something would happen and no one would know.

Until it was too late.

Summer picked up the phone and tried Rose's number. Maybe Luke had decided he needed to be around his family today.

"Hello," Rose said.

Summer quickly explained why she'd called.

"I haven't seen him, but I'm glad you called me," Rose said. "He told me what was going on. He told me everything. I'm so sorry for your loss."

Summer's eyes widened in surprise. It wasn't like Luke to confide in anyone. "Thank you. I'm surprised he told you though."

Rose chuckled. "Oh, I had to drag it out of him, and he kicked and screamed the whole time. Getting that man to talk is almost impossible."

Tell me about it. "Well, I'm sorry to bother you. I hoped

you might know where he was today."

"Hang on. I think you and I should get together. I've dealt with the loss of a child, too. I'd love to talk to you about it. See if I can help any. I wish I'd known when it happened. I know how lonely the experience can be."

Unexpected emotion washed over Summer. She'd always gotten along with Rose, but Luke had wanted to keep his distance from his family. "Thank you. I'd like that."

"No problem," Rose said. "I'll call you in a week or two, and we'll make plans to meet."

"Okay."

"And Summer? You might try the cemetery. I went out earlier this morning and took some fresh flowers. I have no idea if that's a place Luke would go, but it might be."

Summer ended the call and sat in the SUV for another minute. As far as she knew, Luke hadn't visited the cemetery since the day of Bobby's funeral. Maybe today had been the day he'd finally faced it.

She headed to North Charleston to the cemetery where Bobby had been laid to rest. Her mind reeled with the news that Rose had also lost a child. She and Luke should've known about it. And they would have if they were closer to his side of the family. She resolved to strengthen that bond once she and Luke got things worked out.

If they did.

She drove the SUV through the cemetery gates and spotted Luke's truck in the distance. She quickly parked next to it and set out toward Bobby's grave. It seemed like just yesterday when they'd been out here for the burial. Luke had been stoic, unwavering. At first she'd admired his strength, but soon she had begun to worry that it was unhealthy.

And then she'd miscarried and had been so focused on herself, she hadn't the time to make sure he was dealing with his grief.

"Hey," she said quietly as she approached Bobby's grave.

Luke rose from where he was kneeling and turned to face her. "How'd you find me?"

"Lucky guess." She stood next to him. "You okay?"

He raked his fingers through his hair. He still wore his park service uniform but had left his hat in the truck. "I'm not sure." He reached over and took her hand. "I've made a mess of things, haven't I?"

She squeezed his hand. "Let's focus on remembering Bobby today."

"He's at peace," Luke said quietly. "It took me a long time to realize it."

She glanced over at him. Something seemed different, but she couldn't put her finger on it.

Luke continued. "I think the accident was so violent, I couldn't imagine him being at peace. You know?"

Violent was the only word that could be used. Bobby's car had been unrecognizable as a car. And an open casket hadn't been an option. In a lot of ways, she knew that had only made it more difficult for Luke. "He knew the Lord. Had his life in order. So yes, I believe he's at peace."

Luke nodded. "I'm trying to find my own peace with the situation."

"It's hard. But you know Bobby would want you to let go."

Luke knelt down and brushed a speck of dirt from the headstone. "I'm getting there." He rose and faced her. "I'd like to take you out to dinner. Would you go with me?"

His uncertainty surprised her. After years of dating and marriage, she wouldn't have expected him to be so unsure about asking her. "I'd like that." She smiled. "A lot."

"Saturday? Pick you up at seven?"

She nodded. "Sounds good." She jerked her chin toward her vehicle. "I'm going to go and give you some time alone." She turned to go then walked back to him. "I'm glad to see you." She reached up and cupped his face with her hand. "I miss you."

His lips curved into a smile, and he put his hand on hers. "You, too. See you Saturday."

She walked to her SUV feeling much lighter than she had when she'd arrived. Luke's dinner invitation told her that he was willing to work on their relationship.

And that gave her more hope than she'd felt in a long time.

Chapter 27

Justin paced in front of Samantha's townhouse. She'd called and asked him to stop by, but no one was home. He glanced at the clock on his phone. If he didn't hurry, he'd be late picking up Ashley.

They'd gone out on a date once since the Memorial Day cookout. He'd taken her to dinner at his favorite little hole-in-the-wall restaurant, and they'd finally made it to a movie. The kisses had been fiery, but he'd had a suspicion Ashley was upset about something. She'd been quiet at dinner, but when he'd asked why, she claimed to be tired.

He couldn't help but worry he was going to mess up their budding relationship. Ashley was easily the best girl he'd ever dated. She had every quality he'd been looking for. Hopefully tonight would go better.

Samantha's older model car pulled into the driveway. She climbed out and lifted eight-month-old Allison out of her car seat. "Hey."

"You need some help?" Justin walked over to the car.

She shook her head. "Nah. Allison and the diaper bag are all I've got." She held her keys out to him. "You can unlock the door though."

He quickly unlocked the front door and held it open for Samantha. "Where's Colton?" he asked.

"At Mama's. He's staying the weekend."

Justin narrowed his eyes. Each time he learned that Colton was staying with Samantha's mother, he cringed. The older woman was in no shape to care for an active toddler. Her poor health kept her bedridden much of the time, and she definitely had a hard time keeping up with Colton. "Oh."

Samantha set Allison on a blanket on the floor. "Sorry to call you over here like this, but I didn't want to talk on the phone."

"Do you need money? Because if the kids need something, I'll do what I can."

She smiled. "You might be the nicest guy in the world. Honestly."

He blushed. "I just want to help if I can."

"Actually I just wanted to let you know that I'm moving."

An icy vise gripped his heart. He'd known this day might come, but he hadn't realized how it would impact him. "When? Where?"

Samantha sighed. "As soon as I can get packed. Carl and I want to make a fresh start."

He didn't say anything about the wisdom of making a fresh start with a felon. He believed in second chances as much as the next guy but hated to think of Colton being raised by a less-than-stellar role model. "I see."

"Don't judge. Carl was in the wrong place at the wrong time. He's not a bad guy."

Justin held his tongue. He wasn't so sure about that but

didn't want to get into it now. He was much more concerned with Colton.

"He's got some family near Atlanta. So it looks like we're Georgia-bound." She tucked a strand of platinum blond hair behind her ear. "We're not taking Colton." She glanced at him. "He'd just be more than we can handle, with trying to find jobs and daycare and all."

Justin narrowed his eyes. "Where is he going to live?"

"With Mama," Samantha said. "I wanted you to know because I hope that you'll still be involved in his life. She'll need all the help she can get."

He frowned. He knew he should be relieved that he'd still be able to be part of Colton's life. But he wasn't sure it was the best situation for the child. He didn't want to get into that with Samantha though. "Thanks for letting me know. If you need me to help move his stuff over to her house, I'll be glad to."

She smiled. "Thanks. That would be great."

Justin said his good-byes and climbed into his pickup. His mind whirled with possibilities he wanted to talk through with Ashley. Maybe she could help him figure out how to handle the situation.

Ashley glanced in the mirror one last time. She'd opted for low-key tonight. A simple yellow V-neck top, jeans, and flip-flops were a lot more casual than she normally wore on a date. But she knew tonight was the night she had to end things with Justin.

She went into the living room and peeked out the window.

Justin slammed the truck door and started up the sidewalk to her porch. He looked adorable. As usual.

But she had to be strong. She couldn't get distracted by his surfer-boy blond hair and blue eyes. And she certainly couldn't look at his mouth and wish it were on hers.

Because that would only make things tougher.

She flung the door open, unable to keep a smile from her face. "Hey." She heard the excitement in her voice and hated herself a little bit for being so weak. When she was around him, she could actually feel herself glowing. That didn't bode well for her decision to walk away from him.

Justin beamed back. "Sorry I'm late." He pulled her into a big hug.

She relaxed against him for a second and inhaled his soapy scent. "Don't worry about it." She pulled away and met his gaze. "You ready? I'm starved."

He hesitated. "Actually I wondered if you'd be okay with ordering a pizza. I need to get your opinion on something."

She shrugged. "Of course. Pizza is good." She stepped back and ushered him inside, thankful she'd spent time that morning cleaning.

Justin sank onto the couch and looked up at her. "It's not too soon for a night in is it?"

She adored quiet nights at home. But the knowledge that he was going to be in her personal space unnerved her. A restaurant would've been safe. It's easy to keep distance in public. But a night at home, on the couch, eating and talking?

It would be impossible for her to keep her hands off of him. She felt drawn to him like a magnet. "It's not too soon. Plus I love pizza." Instead of going to sit next to him, she grabbed a phone book from the end table. "Any certain brand?"

He grinned. "I'm a Domino's kind of guy, but we can order whatever you like."

"Domino's it is." After a brief discussion, they settled on a large, thin crust pepperoni. Ashley called for delivery then sat down in the recliner next to the couch.

Justin looked at her with a puzzled expression. "I took a shower before I came over. What gives?"

She shrugged. "Nothing. Sorry. Just habit, I guess." *And the fact that I'm afraid when you find out I could've been your babysitter, you'll run away.*

He twisted his mouth into a smile. "Okay. As long as it's not me." He sighed. "So I've had a weird day. That's part of why I wanted to stay in."

"What happened?"

She listened to his story about Samantha's impending move. "How do you feel about it?" she asked.

"Torn. On the one hand, I'm glad she's not taking Colton. But on the other, I'm worried about him living with his grandmother." He shook his head and sighed. "Samantha's mom means well, but she's in poor health. I can't imagine what kind of life Colton will have growing up there."

Even though she'd only seen Justin and Colton together twice, she still had a pretty good idea of how much Justin cared for the child. And it was clear that Colton was crazy about Justin. "I guess you need to decide how far you're willing to go for Colton. And what kind of sacrifices you're willing to make."

Justin met her eyes. "Am I crazy? Single guy, about to turn thirty, and considering raising a child who isn't even mine?"

"Like I said. It will be a huge lifestyle change. I think you'd better be sure you're ready for that kind of commitment before you start down the path. Because Colton certainly doesn't need to be displaced again."

He leaned his head back against the couch. "Decisions are hard."

She chuckled. "Some decisions are easy. But life-changing decisions take a little more thought. And a little more prayer."

Justin sat up and looked at her. "You're right. I should pray about it. Talk to my parents." He raked his hands through his hair. "Because they would be part of the commitment. Obviously I would need help."

"For what it's worth, from what I saw at the cookout, they're crazy about Colton." She was pretty sure Justin's parents would be completely supportive. She couldn't help but wonder what that kind of family support felt like. Maybe she'd never know.

Justin nodded. "They sure are. They've known him since he was a tiny baby."

"Do you think you're ready for that kind of commitment?" she asked.

He chuckled. "I've never been one of those commitment-phobic guys. I've never been scared of settling down, just scared of settling down with the wrong person. And in my mind, kids were always going to be part of the picture."

"So you think going from a couple of visits a week to being responsible for him full-time is something you want?" Ashley wasn't trying to discourage him. But she wanted him to realize that commitment should mean forever. Not until something better or more fun came along. She'd been on the wrong end of that once and had been devastated.

He nodded. "I do. I think anything worth having is worth making changes for. And Colton makes my life more complete."

"Well then, I think you should talk to your parents to see what they think. And you don't know for sure that Samantha would be on board, right?"

Justin nodded. "True. But over the past year, I've started getting the impression that if I even broached the subject, she'd be ready to give me custody of him on the spot." He reached over and took her hand. "But I need to know what you think."

She regarded him for a long moment. "I think this is something you have to figure out for yourself."

Justin's face fell.

The doorbell rang and saved her from more questions.

She grabbed her purse and took some bills from her wallet.

"Let me get it." Justin walked over to her.

She shook her head. "Nope. It's on me. You might be raising a child soon." She patted him on the arm. "I hear that's expensive. You should save your money." She motioned toward the kitchen. "You can go get us drinks and plates though."

She paid the delivery guy and put the hot pizza on the coffee table. She sat on the floor in front of the coffee table and opened the box.

"That looks great." Justin set down the plates and two bottles of water.

Once they'd filled their plates, Justin said a quick prayer.

Ashley flipped the TV on to a rerun of *Seinfeld*, and they ate in silence.

"That was good stuff." Justin tossed a sliver of pizza on his plate and sat back on the couch.

She nodded. "Good call on the takeout." She took a sip of water and watched Justin out of the corner of her eye.

He leaned forward and caught her gaze. "I'm just going to throw this out there, Ashley. I'm sorry to do this to you at this point, because it's not like we've known each other long enough to think about the future. . .but what do *you* think about the possibility of Colton being a permanent part of my life?"

There it was. The question she'd been hoping he wouldn't ask. Except that there was a tiny part of her that was glad he cared. "I think you'll be a great role model."

Justin narrowed his eyes. "That's not what I mean, and you know it. I don't usually lay all my cards on the table so soon, but I really like you. And I could actually see a future for us."

Her heart pounded. It would be so easy to tell him she saw the same thing. Or at least she would if he were a few years older. Or even better, if she were the same age as him and still had a fully functional biological clock on her side. "Justin. . . I don't know what to say. I mean, we've only been out a few times. I've had fun and all, but I don't think you should take me into consideration at all when you're deciding what to do about Colton."

He flinched.

She wanted to take it all back. She wanted to take his hand

and pull him to her and tell him that he was exactly what she'd been looking for. But she couldn't do it. She couldn't risk her heart on someone who would end up disappointed in her in a few years.

"You're right. I'm sorry. It was too much too soon." He stood. "I shouldn't have put you on the spot like that." He jerked his chin toward the door. "I should probably go."

She stood and followed him to the door. "Bye," she whispered.

Justin reached out and smoothed her hair. "I'll call you soon," he said softly.

Ashley ached to kiss him until it was okay.

Instead, she watched him walk out the door.

Chapter 28

Summer smoothed glossing cream through her hair. She'd decided to wear it down tonight because she knew Luke liked it that way. She'd even gone shopping earlier and bought a new dress to wear to their dinner.

She glanced at herself in the full-length mirror, confident Luke would appreciate the results of an afternoon of pampering. She dabbed on a touch of pink lipstick and put the tube in her purse.

She was ready.

It might seem weird to be so excited about a date with a man she'd known for half of her life. But over the past months, she'd felt like Luke was looking right through her. Ever since the miscarriage, Luke had barely touched her. Tonight she wanted to turn his head, just like when they were teenagers. She wanted to show him that she was still the woman he'd fallen in love with. The woman he used to not be able to keep his hands off of.

The ringing doorbell announced his arrival.

She took a deep breath and walked slowly down the stairs. *Please, Lord, help us get back on the right track.* Summer paused at the door then flung it open.

Jefferson stood on the other side, a grin on his face. He let out a low wolf whistle. "You are smokin' hot." He looked her up and down. "Sorry to be so blunt, but wow."

Her face flamed. "Thanks." She smoothed her dress, suddenly self-conscious. "What are you doing here?"

"Clearly you've got plans. I don't want to keep you." He held up an empty cup. "I know it's cliché, but I actually need to borrow some milk. I'm making mac and cheese and was right in the middle of it when I remembered I'm out."

She raised an eyebrow but didn't say anything. She'd never known Jefferson to do anything domestic. In fact, she had her doubts he could even boil water, but she didn't have time to get into it now. "Wait here." She left him standing on the porch while she went to the fridge. She grabbed the milk and walked back to where he stood. "Just take the whole thing. It's only half a gallon, and I've barely used any."

He took the jug from her. "Are you sure?"

She nodded. "Yep. Enjoy your mac and cheese." She started to shut the door, but Jefferson stopped it with his hand.

"Hang on."

Summer sighed. "What?"

"Where are you off to all dolled up?" He indicated her dress with a jut of his chin.

"Dinner with Luke." She steeled her gaze on him, daring him to say anything.

Jefferson raised his eyebrows. "Well, that's great news. I'm glad you two are trying to work things out."

She nodded. "Me, too." She shooed him off the porch. "Now leave. Seeing you here will only put Luke in a bad mood."

Jefferson wrinkled his nose. "Fine. Have fun." With a wave, he walked through the iron gate that led to the sidewalk.

She swung the door closed and leaned against it. Jefferson wasn't all bad. It was kind of nice to see him again after all these years. But she knew Luke didn't share her opinion.

She glanced at the clock on the end table. He should be here in five minutes. That would give Jefferson plenty of time to get home unnoticed. The last thing she wanted was for Luke to have another run-in with Jefferson.

Milo stretched and jumped down from the couch. He walked over and sat down at her feet.

"You're looking fit, sweet boy." She reached down and scratched him behind the ear. She and Milo had been going on lots of walks lately, and he'd already dropped some of his extra weight. He seemed happy even though she'd taken away his off-leash privileges. After the squirrel incident, she'd decided not to risk it.

The doorbell rang.

Better be Luke this time. Summer paused then opened the door slowly.

Luke stood on the other side. He held a bouquet of roses in his hand, but his expression was strained.

"My favorite," she said, taking the flowers. "Come inside."

She waited for him to comment on how she looked, but he went straight for Milo. "I'll put these in a vase, and then we can go." She walked into the kitchen and tried to chase away her disappointment. Maybe he no longer found her attractive.

She filled a vase with water and put the roses inside. She carried the arrangement into the living room and set it on a table. "Perfect." She smiled at Luke. "Ready?"

He nodded. "Starving." He held the door open for her, and they stepped out onto the porch. "The yard looks pretty good, but it's getting a little high. I'll come over and mow soon."

She glanced at him. He looked good but tired. "If you'd rather me get someone else to do it, I'd be glad to."

His jaw tensed. "Maybe Jefferson would like to take care of it. Except for that whole manual labor thing."

She furrowed her brow but didn't say anything.

"My car or yours?" he asked.

"Yours."

Luke opened the passenger door and helped her inside. "Magnolia's okay?"

"Perfect." She watched as he walked around the truck and climbed into the driver's seat. "So did you stay long at the cemetery after I left the other day?"

He backed slowly out of their driveway. "Not too much longer. I left there and went to see Daddy."

She turned to look at his profile. As far as she knew, Luke hadn't seen his father since Bobby's funeral. "How's he doing?"

Luke shook his head. "Not well. Not well at all. His mind is wandering. He thinks I'm Uncle Pete."

She reached over and rubbed his leg. "I'm sorry. I know that's got to be tough."

"I waited too long." Luke slowed the truck to a stop at a red light. "He doesn't even know it's me." He reached down and covered her hand with his. "It's one of many regrets."

She hated to hear it. She'd always hoped Luke and his daddy would somehow make amends. When she was pregnant, she'd foolishly thought the baby would be the bridge that healed the relationship. But it sounded like that wasn't going to happen.

Luke parked the truck and came around to help her down. He didn't let go of her hand as they walked toward the restaurant.

And even though there was still a distance between them at least a mile wide, Summer held on to his hand for all she was worth.

Luke wasn't sure which was the biggest surprise of the evening so far. The fact that Summer looked more beautiful than he could ever remember her looking or that he'd seen Jefferson leaving the house as he pulled into the driveway.

That dude was really on his nerves. Jefferson had held up a half gallon of milk and pointed to it as Luke drove by. But Luke wasn't stupid. Jefferson had no more needed to borrow milk than Luke needed a hole in the head.

He wasn't going to mention it to Summer though. Sweet Summer. She'd never think Jefferson had an ulterior motive for anything. She'd always believed the best in people. And he could hardly complain about it, as that was one of the things that had drawn him to her in the first place. But it really chapped his hide to see Jefferson with that smirk, sauntering out of the driveway like he'd just won a ticket to paradise.

Luke knew he'd only look like a jealous fool if he said something, and he didn't want a repeat of their Memorial Day argument. So he'd keep his mouth shut. "You look pretty tonight." He tugged on her hand as they walked into the restaurant. "Even prettier than the day we met."

She beamed. "Thanks."

They followed the hostess to a table for two and ordered their standard fare.

"Is it boring that we always order the same thing here?" Summer asked.

He shook his head and admired the way her dark hair fell in waves around her face. "Not at all. It's comforting. Like a warm blanket on a cold night." He grinned.

"So what made you decide to go see your daddy?" she asked.

He filled her in on his visit to see Rose and go through Bobby's things. "I couldn't be the reason Katie Beth and Dale didn't get to go to Disney."

Summer nodded. "I'm glad you stepped in. I actually spoke to Rose on the phone earlier in the week." She locked eyes with him. "I think we've messed up by not being more involved with their lives."

"You mean *I've* messed up." He took a deep breath. "I've had a lot of time to think. A lot of time to consider the wrong decisions I've made. I don't know why I always thought everyone was against me, but I did."

"I've never been against you," Summer said quietly. "You know that."

He reached over and took her hand. "I know. You're the reason I'm not completely screwed up."

Summer gave him a tiny smile. "Glad I could help." She sighed. "What are we going to do here?"

"Eat?"

At her steely glare, he chuckled. "Sorry. I'm trying. But this whole getting in touch with my emotions thing isn't exactly easy for me."

"No. Emotions have never been your strong point."

He sighed. "I've been really focusing on letting go of my anger. I don't know how you stood it for so long." Ever since he'd opened Bobby's Bible, he'd been thinking about where his anger was coming from and how to get rid of it.

"I kept thinking you'd snap out of it. But you never did."

The waitress set their food on the table.

Summer caught his eye. He knew she was waiting on him to pray for their food. But he hadn't quite worked up to talking to God yet. "Dig in," he said with a smile.

"Summer," a petite blond woman said, coming up to their table. "It's nice to see you again."

Summer smiled at the woman. "Thanks, you, too." She glanced at Luke. "This is Madelyn Ashworth. She's just opened up a new bridal shop over on Calhoun Street." She turned to Madelyn. "This is my husband, Luke Nelson."

He stood and shook Madelyn's hand. "Nice to meet you," he said.

"Did you tell him about the dress?" Madelyn trilled.

Summer shook her head.

"What dress?" he asked.

"Your beautiful wife had never tried on a wedding dress before. But you probably know that." Madelyn giggled. "We had her try on her dream gown the other day just for fun. She looked like a princess."

He raised his eyebrows at Summer. "I'll bet."

"You'll have to get your friend to show him the pictures." Madelyn patted Summer on the back. "Well, I don't want to keep you from your dinner." She smiled at him. "Nice to meet you."

"You, too," he said.

Once she was gone, he looked at Summer. "Your dream wedding dress, huh? You're not planning on running off with some other guy are you?" As soon as the words left his mouth, he had a vision of her with Jefferson.

She shook her head. "It was stupid. But Ashley and Madelyn were so persuasive. And the dress was beautiful." She shrugged. "I guess I've always wondered what I'd look like in a fancy bridal gown."

"I already know what you'd look like. I don't need a picture to tell me. You were the most beautiful bride I'd ever seen on the day I married you, even if we were just at City Hall in church clothes."

She gave him a half smile. "Thanks." She sighed.

"Are you upset?"

Summer shrugged. "Just trying to process things here." She chewed on her bottom lip. "I know you're working through things. But I think maybe there's stuff with us that needs to be worked through, too."

"I don't want to lose you. To lose us." He raked his fingers through his hair. "I'll do whatever it takes."

"You mean that?" She looked at him hopefully. "Counseling even?"

He slowly nodded. "Yes. Whatever it takes. You make the arrangements, and I'll be there."

Her lips turned upward in a smile. "It means a lot that you're willing to do that. I think after the year we've had, we could both use some help dealing."

He nodded. "I'm sorry I didn't see it sooner. I kept thinking I could handle everything on my own. Kept thinking that if I didn't talk about things, they'd go away." He shook his head. "I don't want to turn into my daddy."

She reached out and squeezed his hand. "Why do you say that?"

"I get the feeling that he wishes he'd done things differently and not been so distant from us, especially after Mama died. And it hit me the other day that I was doing the same thing. I watched grief eat him up. Watched it turn him into someone I didn't recognize. And then I almost let it do the same thing to me." He shook his head. "I need to learn from his mistakes. At this point, I think it's the only way to be the son I never was."

Summer's blue eyes glistened with tears. "I've been praying that you'd come to that conclusion."

He gripped her hand. "Keep praying for me, Summer. It helps me sleep better at night, knowing you're praying for me."

A tear trickled down her face. "Let's go."

He pulled some cash out of his wallet and put it on the table then stood and held out a hand to her.

They walked slowly to his truck.

He paused before he opened the passenger door. "We'll be okay. Right?"

She nodded. "Hope so."

He pulled her tightly to him and inhaled the sweet scent of her shampoo.

Chapter 29

Ashley listened as Summer filled her in on the events of the weekend. "What do you think changed his mind about counseling?"

Summer shrugged. "I have no idea. Rose. His daddy's condition. Having time to think." She sighed. "Honestly, I don't care who or what the catalyst was. I'm just thankful he wants to give it a try."

Ashley had been surprised when Summer started the day by telling her something personal. Since Luke had moved to the boat, Summer had started to open up more. It was almost as if she'd been letting things build up inside her until she couldn't help but let them out. "Me, too. I know I saw a counselor after my divorce. The thing that helped the most was for me to talk through my feelings. It sounds like that's what y'all need, too."

"Luke's never been much on sharing the way he feels. I think that's one reason why he writes songs. They help him express things he can't say out loud in conversation."

Ashley doodled on a pad in front of her. "He's that way even with you? I mean, I can see that he might not be all touchy-feely with other people, but I figured it was different where you're concerned."

Summer chuckled. "I wish. Just getting him to say, 'I love you,' is a big deal. He usually says 'Me, too,' or something like that." She sighed. "I *know* he loves me. But it would be nice to hear it verbalized every now and then."

"I guess that doesn't come easy to everyone." Ashley couldn't help but think of Justin. He might be the exact opposite of Luke in that regard. Justin wasn't afraid to express himself.

"So how about you? Have you gotten over the age difference with Justin yet?"

Ashley shook her head. "It's more than the age difference. I mean, that's the driving force behind my uncertainty. But then there's that awful feeling of vulnerability that goes along with letting someone into your life."

"And you're not ready for that?"

Ashley didn't know if she'd ever be ready for that again. "I love spending time with Justin. But he seems like he's ready to jump in with both feet, and I barely have a toe in the water. You know?" She sighed.

"So how did it go the other night? Did you tell him that you couldn't see him again?"

Ashley shook her head. "Not exactly. He'd had a tough day." She explained about Samantha and Colton. "And then he wanted to know what I thought he should do. I could tell he was implying that his decision to take on more responsibility for Colton would impact me. It's kind of flattering that he'd even take my feelings into consideration. Except that it adds another dimension to the situation." She sighed. "Because then I would be involved with Colton's life, too. And then if things didn't work out or whatever, that's one more hurt to add to the pile."

Summer frowned. "It still seems like a lot of excuses to me. Are you sure you're not just looking for a reason to write him off in order to protect yourself?"

"No. At least I don't think so." Ashley rifled through some papers on her desk and refused to meet Summer's gaze. Maybe her friend was right. Were the qualms she had about Justin legitimate? Or was she just scared of getting hurt again?

Justin wasn't used to carrying around so much anxiety. But between trying to figure out what to do about Colton and trying to guess what was going on inside Ashley's head, he was a basket case.

He'd spent Sunday afternoon talking to his parents about the situation with Samantha and Colton, and they'd been very supportive. He was supposed to talk to Samantha tonight, and he had no idea what to expect.

"I'm not going to pray for Samantha to agree to Colton living with you," Mom had said. "Instead, I'm going to pray that the situation will work out according to God's will."

Justin liked that outlook. Some people might think it was crazy to have that kind of faith. But he couldn't imagine living any other way.

He pulled up in front of the townhouse and thought about what he wanted to say. He'd decided that either way, he'd make the best out of the situation. And even if Samantha was firm in her decision for Colton to live with her mama,

Justin knew he'd still get to hang out with the little boy often.

He closed the door on his pickup and walked up the sidewalk to the townhouse. He rapped on the door and waited.

The door swung open, and Samantha stood on the other side. She smiled. "Come in. But please excuse the mess." She ushered him inside.

Boxes in various stages of being packed were piled around the living room. He stepped over two boxes labeled KITCHEN and sat down on the couch. "Looks like you've been busy."

She nodded. "Yeah. I'm ready for a fresh start." She knelt on the floor next to a bookshelf and began to stack books in a box.

"Can I ask you something?"

Samantha looked up. "Sure. What's up?" She set down the books and looked at him with tired eyes.

Justin sighed. "I'm here about Colton. Have you told him that you're leaving him behind?" It broke his heart to think of Colton feeling unwanted.

"Look, it wasn't an easy decision." Samantha picked at a loose cuticle. "But I think it's the best one for everyone."

"Do you see this as a permanent arrangement?"

She shrugged. "I don't know. Maybe. I guess it depends on how Mama does with him."

"So you realize that she might not be able to care for him forever?"

Samantha narrowed her eyes. "Of course I do. It's just that. . ." She trailed off. "Carl doesn't like Colton too much. I mean, Allison is his own flesh and blood, so he dotes on her. But Colton gets on his nerves. You know how much energy he has."

Justin had suspected as much. "And this is your chance to get out of here and start over as a family."

"Well, yeah." She buried her face in her hands. "Honestly, sometimes I think it would've been better for all of us if I'd have given Colton up when he was born. I never feel like I give him what he needs anymore. Allison ends up getting my attention, and he has to do his own thing." She wrapped her arms around herself. "And then I start to feel like I must be the worst mother in the world."

Samantha had always been plagued by insecurities about her mothering skills. That was one of the reasons Justin had gotten so involved in the first place. When Colton was newborn, she'd been terrified she'd hurt him somehow. Justin had ended up doing a lot of bottle and diaper duty as a result.

"In light of that, there's something I want you to think about." He took a breath. "I'd like for Colton to live with me." He leveled his gaze on her. "Permanently."

Her eyes widened. "No way. You don't mean that."

He nodded. "I'm serious."

"But he requires a lot of attention. I mean constantly. And soon he'll be in preschool, so there'll be all that stuff to contend with." She narrowed her eyes. "Why would you want to do that? Don't you think it will mess up your life?"

Justin rarely got angry. But with each word she spoke, he felt his blood boil. "I know he needs attention. And I don't mind giving it to him. And contending with stuff like preschool and T-ball and homework wouldn't be an imposition, because I love him and want what's best for him."

Samantha's head dropped. "Sorry. I can't fathom someone

voluntarily choosing that life."

He stood. "I know I don't have a claim to Colton. But I want what's best for him. If you decide that's being raised by your mama, that's fine. But if you think he'd be better off with me, my offer stands." He turned to go.

Samantha walked him to the door. "Would it be just a trial basis?"

"No." He paused in the doorway. "Colton doesn't deserve to be some kind of guinea pig that lets me figure out if I'm ready for the responsibility. If I didn't think I was ready on a permanent basis, I wouldn't have offered." He turned to go.

"Wait," she called, following him down the sidewalk.

He turned to face her. "Yeah?"

"You're right." She gave him a tiny smile. "Colton would be better off with you than he would with anyone else. Even me. You've been there for him when no one else was." She bit her lip. "He'd be lucky to have you."

"No. . . I'd be lucky to have him," Justin said.

She smiled. "Maybe you'd be lucky to have each other."

"Then it's settled?"

Samantha nodded. "I'll talk to Mama about it tonight. I think she'll be relieved. But you'll take him to visit her, right?"

"Of course."

"And I'll want to see him when I come to town to see Mama."

Justin nodded. "I'm glad to hear it."

He waved good-bye and climbed into the truck. He'd tried to tell himself he was going to be okay no matter the outcome of the conversation with Samantha. But the relief that washed over him now told him that only one outcome would have satisfied him.

He didn't know how it would go when Colton moved in. But he knew that with his parents' help and lots of prayers, they'd be fine.

Chapter 30

Summer tossed a rawhide chew onto Milo's dog bed at the shop. He'd seemed depressed this morning, so she'd decided to bring him to the office.

She sat down at her desk and flipped open her planner. As she turned the page to today's date, her heart dropped. The words DUE DATE written in bold jumped out at her. She shut the planner tightly and sat back in her chair.

How had she forgotten?

"Morning," Ashley said. "You're here early."

Summer looked up. "I'm supposed to meet with Jennifer St. Claire tomorrow." She shrugged. "You know how picky she is. I was trying to put together a couple of possible itineraries for her out-of-town guests."

Ashley nodded. "Yes, being overprepared is the best bet where Jennifer is concerned." She smiled. "Otherwise she'll start trying to take over, and everything goes downhill from there."

Summer managed a smile. It was silly to be so upset over a date that didn't mean anything anymore. But telling herself that didn't take away the sorrow.

"You okay?" Ashley asked. "You look pale. Do you think

your blood sugar is low or something?"

Summer shook her head. "I probably just need some sunshine." She turned her computer on. "I might walk down to Marion Square later on and get a little sun." The historic square was a gathering spot for college students, tourists, and businesspeople who worked along nearby King Street. She'd spent countless hours there as a teenager, watching college boys play Frisbee or football. Now that her office was within walking distance, it was a favorite place for an outdoor lunch or quick afternoon break.

"Sounds nice. I'd offer to go, too, except that Justin is supposed to drop by around lunchtime. It's our final meeting about the website." She sank into her office chair. "But if you happen to stop in at Cupcake, I'd be glad for you to bring me a sample." The little bakery across from Marion Square was one of their favorite places to go for an afternoon pick-me-up.

"Of course." Summer glanced up from her computer. "And I hope things go well with Justin."

A shadow crossed Ashley's pretty face. "It's strictly business." She shrugged. "At least mostly."

A little before noon, Summer grabbed her purse. "I'll be out for a little while. But I have my phone if you need me."

Ashley nodded. "Okay."

She headed North on King Street, lost in thought. She considered calling Luke but thought better of it. He was at work. Besides, he probably wouldn't realize today had been her due date anyway.

"Summer," a voice behind her called.

She turned to see Jefferson hurrying toward her. "Hi."

He grinned as he reached her. "Sorry to sneak up on you. I went by your office, and your assistant told me where you were headed." He chuckled. "Of course I had to really turn on the charm to get her to tell me."

"I'll bet. I feel certain that once you found yourself in the presence of a beautiful blond, the charm automatically turned on."

He laughed. "You've got me there."

She rolled her eyes, certain that Jefferson had laid it on thick with Ashley. Thankfully she was too suspicious to fall for any of his lines. "What did you need? You in the market for an event planner?"

"I was going to see if you wanted to grab lunch."

She furrowed her brow. "I'm not hungry. I'm actually on my way to Blue Bicycle Books."

"Oh. Well then, will it annoy you if I tag along?"

She wanted to be alone for a while to sort things out in her head. But if she said that, Jefferson wouldn't leave her alone until she explained why. "I'm going to browse around the bookstore and then maybe pop over to Cupcake for a treat. I doubt that's the way you want to spend your lunch hour."

"You underestimate me. I happen to love books *and* cupcakes. So it's a win-win."

They walked in companionable silence the rest of the way.

"I love this place," she said once they reached the bookstore. "The bicycle outside and the quirky window displays. . .such a great little store."

Jefferson nodded. "I've only been in it a couple of times, but I've been impressed."

She always tried to support local businesses over chains when she could. Whether it be the farmer's market or a bookstore, it always made her feel good to do business with local owners.

Jefferson held the door open for her, and they went inside.

She browsed the new release section while Jefferson went to check out the literature room. She picked up the new Mary Higgins Clark and took it to the checkout counter. Once she paid for her purchase, she poked her head into the back room. "I'm going to get a cupcake."

He followed her outside. "Is everything okay?"

She nodded. "Just having one of those days."

"Tell you what. . .why don't you go find a place to sit in the park. I'll go grab some cupcakes. There's probably a line."

She should say no. The less Jefferson did for her, the better. But for just a moment, it would be nice to let someone take care of her. "Okay. Thanks."

"Chocolate, right?" he asked with a knowing smirk.

She nodded. "You got it. And get an extra one for Ashley."

He hurried off.

Summer found an empty bench in Marion Square and sat down. She tilted her face toward the sunshine and closed her eyes, not even caring if she looked silly. The warm rays bathed her face, and she began to relax.

"You know they say that's bad for you," Jefferson said.

She jerked her head down. "I need to put a bell on you so you'll stop sneaking up on me."

He chuckled. "Sorry." He held up a bag. "Maybe this will make up for it. Prove my usefulness." Jefferson sat down next to her. "We were in luck today. I didn't have to wait in line."

She reached for the bag. "Thanks." She pulled out a chocolate cupcake piled high with icing and bit into it. "So good."

He watched her eat. "How was your dinner the other night?"

She glanced up. "Good. Thanks for asking."

"I'm concerned, that's all."

She took another bite of her cupcake and watched a group of kids toss a football around. On this day in particular, she wished she could be like them. Light and carefree. Lately she'd felt like the weight of all her problems might crush her.

"You sure there's not anything else going on?" Jefferson asked. "Because you don't seem like yourself."

She glanced at him. "You don't even know me anymore. So maybe this *is* me being myself."

"Maybe. But I don't think so."

She finished her cupcake and brushed the crumbs from her skirt. She felt his eyes on her but refused to look at him. She wished she were somewhere else. Preferably the kind of place where no one would pry into her life and ask her what was wrong. Except that she'd learned the hard way that no matter how much you closed yourself off, the memories still managed to hitch a ride. They went wherever she did. No matter what.

Jefferson pulled out a handkerchief and handed it to her. "You'll feel better if you get it off your chest."

Summer took a breath. If she were thinking more clearly, she probably could've bluffed her way out of the situation. But as it stood, she did want to talk about it. Even if it was to Jefferson.

"This was supposed to be a really special day," she began.

Luke wasn't the kind of guy who called in sick to work when he wasn't actually sick. But this morning, he hadn't been able to get out of bed. And while he knew that the thing that plagued him wasn't contagious, he was still thankful for a generous sick leave policy.

Because he couldn't imagine facing the day as if it were just a normal day.

Today was supposed to have been their baby's birthday. He'd typed it into the calendar on his phone months ago and hadn't thought about it again. Until he happened to see it last night.

His fingers had itched to call Summer, but he'd resisted. She had enough grief of her own without dealing with his.

So instead he'd called in sick today and had taken the boat out. It was a beautiful day, but it may as well have been raining to match his mood. Finally, he realized the only thing that might help him was talking to Summer.

He drove by the grocery store and picked up a bouquet of flowers. It had been ages since he'd shown up at her office to surprise her. He smiled to himself as he thought about her reaction.

Traffic snarled as he turned off of Cannon Street to King Street. He should've gone a different way. He tapped on the steering wheel as he waited for the red light to change. He hated traffic. He rolled down his window and tried to relax, despite the bumper-to-bumper cars.

He finally made it to Marion Square. Not too much farther now. He glanced out at the park. When he was in high school, he and some of his buddies used to play pickup football games there. It looked like not a lot had changed.

A familiar figure sitting on a bench caught his eye. He peered closer. Summer sat with Jefferson, engaged in what looked like an intense conversation.

His heart dropped. So this is what it had come to. Having a rendezvous with Jefferson on her lunch break. He fought the urge to park the truck right there and confront them.

Instead he kept driving.

An hour later, he found himself parked in front of Gram's house on Isle of Palms. His mind reeled. He trusted Summer. But he didn't trust Jefferson. And right now he was having a hard time rectifying those things in his mind.

A knock on his window made him jump.

Gram peered at him through her bifocals.

Luke cut the engine off and opened the door. "Hello." He climbed out of his truck and hugged the elderly woman.

"This is a surprise." Gram smiled. "And I can't say it's a bad one." She motioned toward the house. "Come inside and let me pour you a glass of fresh lemonade."

He followed her inside.

Gram's house was as nice as Summer's parents' home but on a much smaller scale. When she'd turned the family home on Legare over to Summer and him, she'd said it was because it was time to downsize.

He walked into the living room where large windows provided a spectacular view of the water. Gram might've moved into a smaller space, but the price tag on the property must've been enormous.

"Here you go," she said, handing him a tall glass of lemonade. "Let's sit out on the deck." She led the way outside.

He sat down in a comfortable chair on the deck opposite Gram.

"What brings you here?" she asked.

He sighed. "I'm not sure."

She smiled. "Oh Luke. I know what's going on. Summer told me you'd moved onto the boat." She reached across the table and patted his hand. "I know how difficult this year has been for y'all."

He nodded. He'd assumed Summer had confided in her grandmother. And in a way he was glad, because that made his visit easier. "I need to know how to fix things."

Gram raised her eyebrows. "I don't think that's anything I can tell you. You'll have to figure it out all by yourself."

He shook his head. "It's so messed up. I have no idea how to make things right." He sighed. "And now she's spending all this time with Jefferson."

Gram met his gaze. "I've noticed."

Luke bristled. He'd hoped she would tell him he was crazy. "You have?"

"At the Memorial Day cookout. I noticed that he seemed to have an eye on her." She shook her head. "I've never cared for Jefferson, you know. He's just like his grandfather. Manipulative and vindictive."

"That's not a good combination." He sighed. "I'm trying hard not to be mad at Summer though. What is she thinking?"

"She's not thinking. I've spoken to her a few times over the past few weeks. You know how she is. Summer likes everything to be on schedule and everything to run smoothly. And when it doesn't. . ." She trailed off.

"When it doesn't, it's hard for her." He nodded in agreement. "But still, that's no excuse."

"I'm going to be blunt here, Luke." Gram raised an eyebrow at him.

He took a deep breath. "Please do."

"I've watched you and Summer drift apart this year. It hasn't been pretty. You went from being the kind of couple who could finish each other's sentences to the kind of couple who has no idea what the other is thinking." She shook her head. "I know there've been tough times. Your brother's accident and then Summer's miscarriage. And I know that sometimes after high stress events like that, relationships can take a hit. But you've got to decide if your marriage is worth fighting for. And if it is, then you're going to have to give it all you've got. And that might mean sacrifices and compromises and asking forgiveness."

He nodded. "I know it's worth fighting for. But what if she doesn't feel the same way?"

Gram furrowed her brow. "She's crazy about you. When she was here on Memorial Day, she looked so defeated and so lonely."

Although that sounded an awful lot like him these days, Luke hated to hear Summer described that way. "So what do I do?"

"Prove to her that you're on her side. What is it that I've heard the two of you say so often? That you're on her team?" Gram smiled. "That's the answer. Make sure she knows that you still want to be on her team. . .no matter what."

He nodded. He could only think of one thing that might prove to Summer that he wanted to stay in it for the long haul.

But he was going to need help to pull it off.

Chapter 31

Justin paused outside of Summer Weddings. Ashley was expecting him, but that didn't squash his nerves. Their last date had left a lot to be desired, and their last couple of phone calls had been awkward.

He opened the door, and Milo jumped up to greet him. "Hey, boy." He scratched the dog behind the ears.

"Hi," Ashley said, coming through the archway that separated the front of the shop from the kitchen. "Perfect timing. I just finished lunch."

He tried to mask his disappointment. He'd thought he'd ask her to have lunch after their meeting. But it looked like that would have to wait until another day.

She motioned at the chair across from her desk. "Have a seat."

He sank into the plush chair. "Well, I have great news."

She raised her eyebrows. "The site is ready?"

"Well that, yes. But I was actually going to tell you that Samantha agreed for Colton to live with me. We're still working out the details, but I guess I'm going to be his legal guardian." He grinned. "I'm a little nervous, but I know a lot of people were praying for the outcome. So I feel really good about the situation."

Ashley smiled. "That's great news. I'm happy for you." She turned her attention to the computer. "So about this website. . ."

He frowned. She wasn't making any effort to hide that she wanted to keep things professional today. "It's live. People can log on and create an account then build their 'dream' wedding out of the choices you've given them. They'll put all those things into their cart and submit it. The information will come to you, along with their contact information," he explained. "The cool thing is that since all the components have a price attached to them, it's possible for them to pay right online."

"So I'll get an e-mail?"

He nodded. "Yes. You'll get an e-mail whenever someone submits an event. It will tell you all of the specifics, and then you can reply either by phone or e-mail and go over everything. But this lets them narrow down and make choices without having to actually come to Charleston and do any legwork."

"I think this is going to be so cool."

"Me, too." He winked. "Whoever thought of it must be a genius."

She blushed. She'd confided in him that the project had been her brainchild. "There's also the possibility that no one will use it and it will be a huge waste of money."

"You might need to work on being a little more optimistic."

She brushed a loose strand of hair from her face. "I know."

He cleared his throat. "So what would you think about having dinner this weekend?"

Uncertainty flitted across her face. "I'm not sure. I've got a wedding on Saturday, and by the time that's over, I'll be exhausted."

He nodded. It had been his experience that people found time for the things they thought were important. So if she couldn't carve out any time over the whole weekend to see him, that spoke volumes. "Maybe some other time then." He liked her a lot. He thought they could actually have a future together. But he wasn't going to beg.

He stood. "If you have any problems or questions with the site, don't hesitate to call me."

Ashley nodded. She walked him to the door.

His instinct was to hug her, but he held back. She seemed to be drawing a line that she didn't want him to cross.

And even though he didn't like it and didn't understand it, he would respect it.

Ashley sat back down at her desk after Justin left. She couldn't remember ever feeling so conflicted. Part of her wanted to throw caution to the wind and see where things with Justin could go. But the more practical part of her knew that wasn't a good idea.

The front door opened, and Summer walked inside, followed by Jefferson. Ashley hadn't been especially charmed by the guy when he'd stopped by earlier to see Summer. There was something about him that she didn't trust. "Hi," she said.

Summer set a bag from Cupcake on her desk. "For you." She grinned. "It's chocolate. I already had mine, and let me tell you, it was worth the calories."

Jefferson laughed like that was the funniest thing he'd ever heard. "I'd better get back to the office," he said. He glanced down at Summer. "Chin up, Sunshine. Things will get better." He turned to Ashley. "And it was nice to meet you." With a wave over his shoulder, he walked out the door.

Summer sat down at her desk and turned her attention to her computer.

Ashley bit her tongue. It probably wasn't her place to tell Summer what she thought about Jefferson, but holding it back didn't feel right either. "So what was that all about?"

Summer looked up with wide eyes. "What was what all about?"

She jerked her head toward the door. "Jefferson. Swooping in and giving you cupcakes and a pep talk."

Summer made a face. "You make it sound like something inappropriate happened. We've been friends since we were in diapers. He moved back at the beginning of the summer. I see him every now and then around town or at my parents' house."

Ashley stood up from her desk and walked over to lean against Summer's file cabinet. "I know you've been through a lot and all that, but do you really think spending time with another man is a good idea?"

"You make it sound like I'm sneaking around and doing something I shouldn't." Summer's normally calm face flamed with anger.

Ashley raised her eyebrows. "I want you to recognize that the path you're on could be dangerous. I've seen it happen too many times. It starts out innocently, but soon you're confiding in someone who isn't your spouse." She met Summer's narrowed eyes. "That's what happened in my marriage. Brian told me later that he'd never intended on being unfaithful. That he'd run into an old friend and they'd caught up. And then that turned into them talking about their problems. And eventually it turned into something more." She sighed. She knew she was jumping to conclusions, but Summer wasn't in a good place right now.

"I'm sorry that happened to you, but just because it happened to you doesn't mean that's what is going on in my life."

Ashley nodded. "There was something odd about the way Jefferson sauntered in here looking for you. I get the feeling that he sees you as some kind of prize. I think you should keep your guard up."

Summer didn't say anything. Finally, she stood. "You're entitled to your opinion. But there's nothing to worry about. In fact, I'm meeting Luke this afternoon at the counselor's office." She slung her bag over her shoulder. "See you tomorrow."

Ashley watched her walk out. Were they good enough friends that they could be totally honest with each other and it not have a negative impact?

Only time would tell.

Chapter 32

Luke carried his bag and guitar into Justin's apartment. "Thanks for letting me stay here. I was going stir crazy on the boat."

"What, it's not a luxury liner?" Justin asked.

Luke set his things down in the living room. "It's nice, but it was starting to get a little cramped. I honestly thought the walls were going to close in sometimes."

"I can't imagine. That's the kind of thing that probably sounds like fun until you actually do it."

Luke nodded. "So when is Colton going to be moving in?" He'd been surprised when Justin had filled him in on what was going on with Samantha. Talk about a lifestyle change. Going from being a single guy to a full-time guardian would be an adjustment.

"Actually, next week. I'm trying to get the spare room turned into some kind of kid's room," Justin said. "My mom has a big plan to paint the walls with pictures of animals playing sports." He chuckled. "I have no idea how that's going to turn out, but I told her to do whatever she wanted."

Luke had to admire his friend for his willingness to step in and do what needed to be done for Colton. "Is Colton excited?"

Justin shrugged. "I'm not sure that he even understands what's going on. I suspect I'm going to be in for a difficult time at first. I'm not the only one whose world is about to change, you know?"

Luke nodded. "Kids are resilient though. He'll probably adjust just fine."

"I hope so."

Luke tapped his watch. "We'd better go."

"I think we're getting better, don't you?" Justin asked. "Last week I actually thought we sounded as good as some groups on the radio."

Luke nodded. "Yeah."

They walked out the door and got into Luke's truck.

"You given any more thought to that songwriting contest I mentioned awhile back?"

Luke bristled. He had given it thought, but it wasn't going to be the answer Justin was hoping for. "I'm not interested. I have too much other stuff going on in my life right now." He merged onto the James Island Connector. "Honestly, I'm starting to regret even signing on to play at the Sand and Suds on a regular basis." He shot a quick glance at Justin to gauge his reaction.

"Fine by me. I was just along for the ride anyway. And now that I'll have Colton, that means either finding a babysitter every Friday night or depending on my parents to keep him. And honestly, if I'm going to have to do that, I'd much rather it be because I'm going out with Ashley."

Luke sighed with relief. He'd been afraid Justin might be upset. Now if Jimmy and Will felt the same, he could tell

Charlie to find a replacement. "How are things with Ashley, anyway?"

"We seem to have hit a brick wall. I'm not sure what happened. One minute I thought we were on this really good track, and the next we veered totally off course." Justin sighed. "It's so frustrating."

Luke was all too familiar with veering off course. When he saw Summer and Jefferson together earlier in the week, he'd felt like someone punched him. And even though Gram tried to assure him that nothing was going on, he'd still been so upset that he'd called and canceled their counseling session. Summer had acted as if she understood, but he had his doubts.

His plan to win her back had already been set into motion though. All he could do now was wait.

Summer walked into the office on Monday resolving to make it a good day. She and Ashley had talked things out on Friday, and there were no hard feelings. Granted, Ashley's accusation that Summer might be getting too close to Jefferson had stung, but she knew her friend's concern was coming from a genuine place.

Still though, the conversation had played heavy on her mind all weekend. Jefferson did have a habit of popping up out of nowhere and saying the right thing. Ashley thought his moves were more calculated than spontaneous.

But Summer couldn't imagine him being that vindictive.

Even so, she'd decided that it might be best to curb their friendship. Because if Ashley thought it was suspicious, others might as well. And Summer never wanted to give anyone the wrong impression.

"Morning." Ashley walked into the office wearing a frown.

Summer held up her coffee cup. "Surely it's nothing a little coffee can't cure."

Ashley flung herself into the chair across from Summer's desk. "I had a date this weekend. And it was *awful.*"

"What happened?"

"You know how I said Justin was way too young? Well, this friend of mine from church called me last week and asked if I was dating anyone. When I said no, she said she had someone she wanted me to meet." She shook her head. "I should've said no. But I thought maybe this would be the guy to make me forget all about Justin."

"But he wasn't Mr. Right?"

"That's an understatement. He wasn't even Mr. Someone I'd Be Friends With."

Summer couldn't help but smile at Ashley's dramatics. "That bad?"

"He's forty. Which I thought was great at first. But that means his children are almost grown, and he made it very clear that he has no interest in having more. And then he proceeded to explain his fitness regimen in detail and ask me how I planned to stay in shape as I age."

"Wow."

Ashley nodded. "I know. The whole night made me sad."

"Because it was such a bad date?"

"No. Because it reinforced how strong my feelings are for Justin." Ashley leaned forward and put her head in her hands.

"I still think you should be totally honest with him. You might end up pleasantly surprised."

Ashley shrugged. "Maybe you're right." She got up and walked to her desk. "But I do have some good news at least."

"Oh yeah?"

"We got our first client through the new website." She smiled broadly. "Cool, huh?"

Summer nodded. "Very. What's the deal?"

"You're not going to like it, but I think we can pull it off."

"Why does the sound of that make me nervous?"

Ashley giggled. "It's a pretty quick turnaround."

"How quick?" Summer raised an eyebrow. She liked to have as much time as possible. In fact, she preferred six months to a year.

"Two weeks from Saturday."

Summer stopped what she was doing and looked up. "You have got to be kidding me."

Ashley shook her head. "Nope. But the place where they want to have the ceremony is available. You know that resort over in Mt. Pleasant? The same place the Jennings wedding was earlier in the spring?"

Summer nodded. "That's a nice place."

"Well, it just so happens that it's available," Ashley said. "And get this—the couple who wants it is giving us free rein to plan the details. As long as we come in within their budget, they don't want any input. Their *generous* budget."

Summer's eyes widened. "Seriously?"

Ashley nodded. "They say they've looked at some of the weddings we've done and can tell we have great taste. So since they're from out of town, they want us to take care of all the details." She grinned. "Can you imagine? All the details. So we get to pick out the flowers, the colors, the food, the cake. . .the whole nine yards."

"Cool."

Ashley stood and brought the information sheet over to Summer. "And I think *you* should be the one to do it. Since you and Luke tied the knot at city hall, this will be like your chance to put your dream wedding together."

Summer took the sheet of paper from her. At least it would take her mind off of things. Like why her husband had really skipped out on their counseling session. And how it was possible that he'd been on the boat for four weeks yet she still missed him as much today as she had on the first day.

Chapter 33

Luke finished his explanation of Civil War artillery pieces and hung around to take questions.

"Thanks for your time," an older man said to him. "That was a great talk. Do you have any idea what time I have to be back on the boat? I think they announced it, but I didn't hear."

"Enjoy the rest of your visit here. You still have fifteen more minutes until the boat departs." The only way to get to Fort Sumter was by boat and they were very strict about departure times.

"Luke," Mr. Young called. "Can you come over here for a second?"

Luke made his way over to where his boss stood. "Yes sir?"

"I wondered if you'd thought about the position we talked about."

He'd been thinking about it a lot. He nodded. "I'd like to accept the responsibility. I think it's something I'm really going to enjoy."

Mr. Young nodded. "I'm very glad to hear that. I know you're going to do a great job."

"Thanks."

Mr. Young walked toward the museum with a wave.

Luke wondered what Summer would say about his new responsibilities when she found out about them. These days he wondered what she'd think about a lot of stuff. She was the one big piece missing from his life now.

Even after Rose and Dave had come back from Disney, Luke had continued to visit Daddy. He'd even had a moment of clarity the other morning and had known Luke was there. It seemed like many of the pieces of his life were starting to fall into place. But the missing piece was Summer.

He'd finally started talking to God again. At first he'd mainly apologized for being such an idiot. But soon he'd started praying specifically for things in his life. And then he'd started to thank God for his blessings and to praise His name.

And even though he didn't expect life to be perfect, Luke knew that he had the tools to deal with the disappointments and the failures that were inevitable parts of life.

He couldn't wait to share the changes in his life with Summer.

And he hoped and prayed that she'd give him the chance.

"Have you seen the weather?" Summer asked as soon as Ashley walked in the door.

Ashley nodded. "Yes. But according to my e-mail, the wedding is still a go in spite of the hurricane watch."

Summer's stomach churned. "Do they realize that our ability to pull off this wedding totally hinges on the weather? Because if this thing hits, we won't be able to have a catered dinner and flowers brought in from a flower shop. We'll be lucky to keep a roof over our heads and maintain electricity."

Ashley shrugged. "It was all very clear on the site, and they sent me an e-mail last night that stated everything was a go."

"Okay." Summer tapped her pencil against her desk. She flipped through her planner and penciled in a couple more items on her to-do list. "You know what? This wedding is the same day as my anniversary." She frowned.

"Do y'all have plans?"

Summer shook her head. "Not exactly. Luke came over yesterday to mow the yard. We ended up talking for a while. I came super close to asking him to move back in the house." She sighed. "But I'm a little scared. I'm afraid if he moves in, we'll never actually deal with any of the problems. I don't want to sweep them under the rug. I want to face them together and then move on."

Ashley smiled. "I think you'll get there."

"I hope so." Summer lifted her hair off her neck. It was so miserably hot outside today. "He moved off the boat and moved in with Justin. And Colton."

"Whoa. I'll bet that's an interesting household."

Summer chuckled. "Luke said Justin and Colton are like two peas in a pod. He says that considering Colton isn't Justin's biological child, it's uncanny how alike they are."

"I hope the situation is working out."

"Seems to be." Summer glanced over at Ashley. "Except that Justin is still really sad. I ran into him at the grocery store a couple of days ago. I can tell he's happy to have Colton with him, but he asked about you right off."

"He did?" Ashley asked. "I figured I'd sabotaged any chance I had because I was so scared."

Summer shrugged. "You'll never know until you try."

Chapter 34

Friday afternoon, Summer looked out the window from her room at the resort. The clouds were rolling so fast they looked like they were from a time-lapse video. If the TV weather guys were right, things didn't bode well for tomorrow's wedding.

"You worried?" Ashley asked. She was perched on the sofa, tapping away on the keys of her laptop.

She let out a breath. "A little bit. It's not a good sign when the Weather Channel has someone stationed at your hotel, is it?"

"I guess not. But they probably have people stationed all over the coast. Just because we're in the cone of uncertainty doesn't mean we're going to get hit."

"My whole life is a cone of uncertainty." Summer managed a smile at Ashley's amused expression. "What? It is."

Ashley rolled her eyes. "Haven't you figured it out yet? Life is uncertain. Thankfully we can be certain of what comes after that."

"Has anyone ever told you that you have a good perspective on things?"

"A time or two." Ashley twisted her mouth into a smile.

"Or maybe it's that wisdom comes with age."

"Speaking of age. . . I meant to tell you that Justin's birthday is coming up in August. His thirtieth birthday." Summer raised her eyebrows. "Does that push him over your mysterious threshold and make it appropriate for you guys to see each other again?"

Ashley sighed. "I don't know."

"If it's honestly that you don't see the possibility of a future with him, that's one thing. But if it's because you're scared of taking a chance, that's another."

"I never thought I'd be in this position, you know?" Ashley tucked a stray hair behind her ear. "Starting over with someone new. Trusting that this time love will work out for me." She sighed. "It's a lot harder than I expected it to be. So yes, I'm scared."

"I wish I could give you a guarantee," Summer said. She sat down on the plush king-sized bed and toyed with her wedding ring. "But obviously I can't. I will say that some things are worth the risk. Worth the hurt."

Ashley nodded. "I know. And I believe that, too. I have to find that courage to take a leap of faith."

Summer smiled. "I used to have trouble with that. You know what a perfectionist I am."

"You, a perfectionist?" Ashley giggled. "No way."

"I'm serious." Summer sighed. "It's hard for me to do things that I might fail at. Whether it's planting a garden or expanding the business. But a few years ago, I realized that in the end I'd rather regret something I did than something I didn't do." She shrugged. "It's that simple. I don't want to look back and have to wish I'd taken a chance or wish I'd told someone how I felt. So I started living that way."

"That's actually really good advice." Ashley looked up from her laptop with wide eyes.

Summer grinned. "Sometimes I do have good ideas."

Ashley closed her laptop and looked seriously at Summer. "Okay then. In light of that, I have something I've wanted to talk to you about for a few months." She took a deep breath.

Ashley willed the words to come out of her mouth. She tried to remember all the points she'd planned to make if she ever got the nerve to make this little speech. But for the most part, they eluded her. "I've put in a lot of hours over the past six months," she said finally.

Summer nodded. "And I'm so appreciative."

"And with the new website launch, we're only going to get busier. I even have some ideas on ways we can expand from weddings to parties and general events." Ashley met Summer's curious gaze. "You know I'm a good employee. I'm dependable and responsible, and I get along well with our clients."

"I know. Finding you has been such a blessing to me and the business."

"Well, I've been thinking lately that I'd like to play a bigger role in the business side of things." Her heart beat faster, but she plunged ahead. "I'd like for you to consider making me a full partner."

Summer's eyes widened. "I guess that should have occurred to me already, huh?" She shook her head. "I'll need to talk to my accountant and to Luke, but I don't see any reason why we can't make that happen."

"Are you sure? Because I don't want you to feel like you have to say yes just because we're friends."

Summer smiled. "I'm positive. I'm sorry you had to ask though. I should've thought of it myself. I know how hard you've worked over the past months, and I know how good you are at what you do." She sighed. "Honestly, I think it will be a relief to share responsibilities with someone. The business is at the point where we're either going to have to expand or start turning down work. There's only so much two of us can do without literally working around the clock."

"Thanks." Ashley couldn't hide her surprise. She'd fully expected Summer to be upset at the very idea of being partners.

"It might be the answer to a prayer actually. I'm hopeful that Luke and I will have things back on track soon. And honestly, I don't want work to be my primary focus all the time. But if we restructure some things and hire some support help, I think you and I can both have real lives outside of work."

Ashley nodded. "That sounds perfect." A real life. She knew that's what she'd have with Justin. The kind of partnership she'd always wanted. Everything she knew about him told her that he'd be committed to her and to their future.

The only thing holding her back now was her own insecurity.

Chapter 35

Luke stopped at the front desk of the resort. "Could you tell me if Summer Nelson from Summer Weddings is on site?"

The receptionist gave him a shaky smile. "I think so. She was in the east ballroom earlier. The flowers didn't get delivered, and she was pretty upset." She glanced around and leaned forward conspiratorially. "To tell you the truth, I feel sorry for her. What kind of people insist on having their wedding during a hurricane? I mean, honestly." She sighed. "I wouldn't be here except that I figure this building is safer than my house, plus I'm making overtime. I don't even normally work the desk here, but everyone else headed out of town. My boyfriend loaded up our dog and is driving west."

He nodded. "I'm sure it will be fine. It's not supposed to hit for several hours, and maybe by then it will have weakened."

"You sound just like my daddy. He refuses to evacuate. I guess I'm a big old chicken."

Luke's daddy had the same philosophy. His only concession to a potential tropical storm had been to put the plastic lawn chairs in the garage. "About Summer. Do you know where she might be now?"

"She has a suite reserved. You want me to ring it?"

He thought for a minute. "Actually, can I make a reservation? But not on the same floor as her."

The girl narrowed her eyes. "You're not some kind of stalker are you? Because I don't want any drama." She smiled. "I'm hoping that if I do a good job, they'll offer me a position at the desk permanently. And if I end up letting a psycho in the building, that'll never happen."

"I'm her husband," he said quietly. "I'm trying to surprise her for our anniversary. That's all." He raised his hands in surrender. "I promise."

She seemed satisfied by his answer. "Well, okay. We do have a lot of rooms available. Just a few guests are riding out the hurricane. And that crew from the Weather Channel." She sighed.

He paid for a two-night stay and went outside to his truck. He needed to call Ashley and see if everything was in place.

And he didn't want to risk running into Summer before it was time.

Justin lifted Colton from his car seat and carried the sleeping child into his parents' house.

"Just put him in your old room," Mom whispered.

He gently put Colton on the bed, and the little boy curled up in a ball. He was such a good sleeper. He smoothed Colton's blond curls, covered him up, and shut the door behind him. He took two steps and turned around. What if Colton got scared and Mom couldn't hear him? He opened the door a crack and made his way to the living room.

"Thanks for letting me bring him by. I appreciate it so much." Justin leaned down and kissed his mom on the cheek.

She looked up with a smile. "Anytime. But I wish you'd stay. They're saying it's only a matter of hours before the storm rolls in." She nodded at the weather coverage on TV. "Your daddy has gone to get gas for the generator in case we need it."

He shook his head. "Thanks. I'm hoping it's going to miss us completely. I'm glad you're going to be with Colton though." He sighed. "Luke has concocted some crazy plan to win Summer back. He won't let go of it. I'm headed down to Folly Beach to help him. I have to go by their house and pick up their dog and take him down there."

"Can't you tell him you don't want to be out in a tropical storm? It could turn into a hurricane, Justin. That's not anything to play around with."

"I know. But I'll get there in plenty of time to hunker down. You know that after the last one came through here, most of the buildings were built to withstand high winds."

"Okay. You need to go on then. I don't want you out when it hits." She stood and gave him a hug. "And don't worry about Colton. He'll be fine."

"Thanks, Mom." He headed out the door and climbed in his truck. The sky looked ominous. Not at all the kind of weather he wanted to be out in.

The only upside to the situation was that Ashley was with Summer at the resort. And even though things hadn't worked out the way Justin wanted them to, he still held out hope that she would have a change of heart.

Chapter 36

A knock at the door startled Summer. She wasn't expecting anyone. After Ashley rushed off to take a phone call, Summer had tried to get some e-mails answered. But she kept a wary eye on the sky.

Even though she'd been a little girl when Hurricane Hugo hit, she still remembered the destruction. It had taken days for them to get power back and years for the area to return to normal.

The pounding continued, and she peeked through the peep hole. *You've got to be kidding me.* She opened the door. "What are you doing here?"

Jefferson stood in the doorway clad in a red polo shirt and khakis. "I came to check on you."

After her talk with Ashley the other day, his appearance made her uncomfortable. "You didn't need to do that. I'm fine. This place is solid. And the wedding I'm working on should go off without a hitch." *If I can find a flower shop willing to deliver during hurricane conditions. And a photographer. And if the bride and groom actually make it.*

"Without a hitch, huh?" He cleared his throat. "I'm actually here because I was worried about you. I thought you might need some help. You know, some muscles to move things or somebody to corral a rogue groomsman." He winked. "Or console a bridesmaid."

She narrowed her eyes. "Thanks for the offer, but I'm sure I'll be fine."

"You just gonna leave me standing here in the hallway, or are you going to invite me inside?"

She frowned. Two weeks ago she wouldn't have thought twice about inviting him inside. But now. . .it seemed inappropriate. "I have a lot of work to do."

Jefferson cocked his head to the side. "Come on, Sunshine. I haven't seen you in over a week. You didn't come out to your parents' the other night for game night. I even knocked on your door a couple days ago, and you didn't answer." He comically furrowed his brow and stuck out his bottom lip in a pout. "Are you avoiding me?"

She shook her head. "Fine. You've got ten minutes. I'm working. And you shouldn't be here." If Ashley came back and saw Jefferson in the suite, she would hit the roof. And probably retract her desire to become business partners. Summer felt like an idiot for not thinking of it herself. She was proud of the business, but there was no denying she could use the help. Relinquishing control would be a challenge, but it would be good for her.

Jefferson plopped down on the plush sofa. "Man, what a spread you've got here." He looked appreciatively around the room. "This looks like a honeymoon suite."

"Don't act like you've never been in a nice place before." She sat down at the desk and shuffled through her itinerary for tomorrow's festivities. "I know good and well that you spare no expense when you travel."

He chuckled. "Okay, you've got me there. But it's only because I want the best."

"Of course."

Jefferson patted the cushion next to him. "Come sit down. Take a break."

She reluctantly stood and made her way over to the sofa. If focusing on him for five minutes would get him to leave, then that's what she'd do. "I can't take much of a break. And you need to be hitting the road. It looks like the bottom is going to drop out any minute." She narrowed her eyes. "I'd hate for you to get stuck here."

"Would you hate that? Really?" he asked. "Because I don't think you would."

She sighed. "What are you getting at?"

Jefferson turned toward her. He reached out and lightly ran his finger down her arm. "We're alike, you and me. We come from the same background. We want the same things out of life."

She got to her feet. "Please don't touch me!"

"These last weeks have been nice. You confiding in me. Me putting a smile on your face." He stood, tipped her chin up so she'd have to look at him. "Luke never deserved you. And he still doesn't."

So Ashley had been right. Summer started to turn away, but Jefferson grabbed her hand. "Don't deny it. You've wondered over the past weeks if you made a mistake in letting me go, haven't you?" He pulled her close until they were face-to-face.

"No one ever has to know. This can be just between us."

Bile rose in her throat. She pushed him away as hard as she could. What a fool she'd been. "That day in the cemetery." She glared at him. "You said you wanted to be friends. I should've said no. But I wanted to believe that you were a good person."

"I am a good person. And I know a good thing when I see it. What was I supposed to do? I come to town and find out you and Luke are having trouble, and I'm supposed to walk away? How could I do that?"

"He's twice the man you are. Without even trying." She walked to the door and flung it open. "It's time for you to go. Whatever you thought was going to happen between us isn't happening. I'm a married woman. And in a moment of weakness I might have confided in you. But that doesn't change the fact that I love my husband. And I will always honor him."

Jefferson shook his head. "Your loss, Sunshine." He shrugged. "But it was worth a try."

A sudden blast of rain pounded against the windows, startling her. It looked like the storm had arrived early. "If you won't leave, I will." She pushed past Jefferson and ran to the stairwell. She didn't want to chance being stuck on an elevator with him.

She pushed the exit door open and sank onto the top step. What was wrong with her? She'd come dangerously close to betraying her husband. Not because she was tempted by Jefferson. But because she never should've allowed herself to confide in him in the first place. No matter what was going on in her life. *Lord, please give me the right words to apologize to Luke. And guard my heart in the future.* She slowly made her way down the stairs.

She reached the first floor and took a deep breath. Had Jefferson had time to leave? She hoped the blinding rain outside didn't mean he'd have to stick around. She pushed the door open and looked both ways. All clear.

She went down the long corridor toward the reception desk. Maybe the girl there could tell her if the wedding party had made it yet. She rounded the corner and stopped in her tracks. Her hands rose to her mouth and muffled the sound of her gasp.

Jefferson and Luke stood facing each other in the grand lobby. And from the look on both of their faces, they might need a referee.

The hurricane-force winds outside had nothing to do with Luke's bad mood. He'd been so excited about the prospect of surprising Summer for their anniversary. He had it all planned out. From the words he was going to say, to the gift he was going to give her.

Yes, it should have been perfect.

But when he walked into the resort lobby carrying a huge bouquet of roses and his suitcase, he ran right into Jefferson.

"Fancy meeting you here, Jeff." Luke forced a smile.

Jefferson looked from the roses to Luke and sneered. "You're a little late." He nodded toward the elevator he'd just stepped from. "Those would've looked great up in Summer's suite. Number 432, in case you didn't know."

Realization hit Luke like a brick. "I don't know what kind of game you're playing, but I feel like you might need to be reminded again that Summer's my wife. She made her choice a long time ago."

"Maybe. Or maybe she finally came to her senses and realized she chose wrong." Jefferson smiled a slow, menacing smile. "She's too good for you. Always has been."

Luke glared. "There might've been a time when you could get to me with those jibes. But not anymore. It isn't worth it. You're not worth it."

"Summer seems to think I'm worth it. In fact, she's spent a lot of time over the past weeks telling me how unhappy she is. Because of you." Jefferson shrugged.

Luke's blood boiled. "Why are you here?"

"Summer and I had some unfinished business." He met Luke's eyes. "She's a feisty one, isn't she?"

Luke flinched. He fought the urge to knock the smirk from Jefferson's face. The idea that Jefferson might have acted inappropriately with Summer made him nauseous. "You'd better not have laid a hand on her."

"Her skin's as soft as it was when she was sixteen."

Luke had worked all summer to let go of his anger. He'd promised Summer. So he had no choice right now but to turn the other cheek. No matter how much it hurt. He calmly rolled his bag to the reception desk and carefully placed the bouquet on top.

Then he turned and walked right out into the storm.

Chapter 37

Justin sat in the lobby and watched as Luke had a very heated conversation with some preppy-looking guy. Luke was normally so laid-back. But whatever the tall guy was saying was causing Luke's whole body to tense up.

Justin had already snuck Milo up to Luke's hotel room and was waiting on his friend to fill him in on what the big surprise was supposed to be. It had better be good to justify all the trouble he'd gone to. Thankfully it had been easy to distract that girl at the desk while he led the big dog onto the elevator.

"Justin?" A familiar voice said from behind him.

He turned to see Ashley with her laptop under her arm. "Hey." Man, he'd missed her.

"It's looking bad out there." She motioned toward the big windows. Rain pounded against them, and the sky outside was dark even though it was daytime.

He gestured toward Luke. "It's looking bad in here, too."

Ashley made a face. "Ugh. I can't stand that guy." She filled him in on Jefferson and his history with Summer and Luke. "He's so smarmy. I don't understand why Summer doesn't see it."

He sighed. "Some things are easier to see from the outside

looking in, I guess."

She sat down next to him. "Yeah. Maybe." She jerked her chin toward the two men. "Do you think we should go over there?"

He shook his head. Whatever was going on, Luke needed to handle it himself. "Nah. It'll be okay." At least he hoped it would. Luke wasn't a fighter. And that preppy guy didn't look like he could throw much of a punch even if he tried. Probably wouldn't want to mess up his manicure.

"I guess you got Milo here okay?" Ashley asked.

Justin raised his eyebrows. "You know about that?" He was always the last to know about stuff.

She giggled. "Yeah. Luke and I have been working together."

Before he could ask her what the big surprise was going to be, he spotted Summer hovering in the hallway watching Luke. He leaned over to Ashley. "There's Summer. She looks really upset."

Ashley halfway stood then sat back down as they watched Luke put his things down and walk out the lobby door.

Summer took off running. She pushed against Jefferson and said something that made him glare, then ran outside after Luke.

Ashley raised her eyebrows at Justin. "Should we be worried that they've both gone out into a huge storm?"

He shrugged. "I'm sure they won't go far. Maybe to the parking lot. They'll be back in a minute."

The lights flickered in the lobby.

"That's not good." Ashley looked around nervously. She stood. "I think there's a TV in the restaurant over there. I'm going to check to see if there's any update on the weather."

He nodded. "Mind if I come with you?" He wanted to talk to her and see if there might still be a chance for them. But he didn't want to come across as a creep who wouldn't leave her alone.

"Yeah. I'd like that." She smiled.

They walked past an empty bar then an empty section of the lobby. No one was in sight.

"It's kind of eerie how deserted it is here."

Ashley nodded. "Most of the guests left yesterday. There are a handful who chose to stay. I met a couple of older ladies this morning who are here from the Gulf Coast." She laughed. "They said they were too old to drive back and fight the evacuation traffic, so they were staying put."

"My family decided to hole up at Mom and Dad's. Colton is there with them." He frowned. "I hated to leave him, but I wasn't sure what to expect here. Luke's been so evasive about everything."

They stopped at the restaurant entrance.

"You think there's anyone there?" he asked.

She nodded. "Yeah. This is the only place to get anything to eat. I think some of the resort employees are staying here tonight with their families." She shrugged. "You know, people who are afraid their homes might not withstand the storm."

"It's good that they have a place to go."

They walked inside, and a harried woman waved to them. "Just sit anywhere. We're short staffed, as you can imagine, so the menu is pretty limited. Soup, salad, or sandwiches."

He held out a chair for Ashley.

"Thanks."

He sat across from her. "Even though this is some kind of crazy situation, I'm glad to see you."

Ashley's eyes filled with tears.

Justin peered at her. "Do you want to tell me about it?" he asked quietly. Though she'd made her lack of feelings for him clear, he still didn't like to see her upset.

"There are things I should have told you. Things that are hard for me to talk about." Ashley angrily wiped a tear away. "You've always been so open and up-front with me. About who you are and about where I stand with you." She gave him a shaky smile. "And I was never able to do the same."

Justin regarded her with serious blue eyes. "I disagree. I'd say you were pretty clear about where I stood."

She shook her head. "Yeah, but not for the reason you think."

"Okay. You can tell me anything. I think you know that."

She took a breath. She'd gone out on a limb by telling Summer she wanted to be business partners, but that was nothing compared to this. "You know I'm divorced."

He nodded.

"My husband left me for another woman. I know. It's the oldest story in the book. But when it happens to you, it feels different." She grimaced. "I was never totally convinced he was 'the one,' but in the town I lived in, there weren't many options. We got along pretty well, and I thought we wanted the same things." She hesitated.

Justin reached over and took her hand. "Go on."

"And soon after we married, he cheated on me. I'm not sure when the affair started or if there was more than one."

"One is enough."

She nodded. "She was several years younger. One of his sister's friends. They reconnected online of all places." She made a face. "I noticed that she'd posted on his Facebook page a couple of times but didn't think anything about it. But apparently there was more to it than that." She looked into his sympathetic eyes. "And then one night he came to me and told me he loved her. There was no discussion. Nothing I could do."

Justin squeezed her hand. "You're better off."

"It was difficult though. I know I'm better off. I know I don't want to be treated disrespectfully. But my family, especially my mom, thought I should look the other way. She actually made a comment about how I wasn't exactly in the prime of youth anymore." She sighed. "And I think that's been part of my problem with you."

Justin furrowed his brow. "What do you mean?"

"I know you're not even thirty yet. And I'm thirty-six."

He looked at her with wide eyes, then his face broke into a smile. "That's what this is about? Our age difference?"

"You knew I was older?"

Justin looked sheepish. "Well yeah. I saw your diploma on the wall. And I figured based on the dates that you must be a few years older. Either that or you were some kind of prodigy."

Ashley swallowed. "And that doesn't bother you? I mean, technically I could've been your babysitter."

He burst out laughing. "I really don't want to lose you over a technicality. Besides, if you'd been my babysitter, I would've had a crush on you and hoped that someday I'd grow up and be able to take you on a date."

She couldn't help but smile. "But don't you think you'd be better off to date someone younger than you?"

Justin laced his fingers through hers. "Ashley. I've dated girls younger than me. And you know what? They aren't serious. They want to go out and have a good time, and that's it. I'm looking for more than that. I thought you knew that."

She nodded. "I know, you say that now. I guess I'm worried that you'll get tired of me and want someone more exciting."

"Are you kidding? Do you know how amazing you are? You're smart and kind and funny. Not to mention beautiful." He squeezed her hand. "I was an idiot who messed up from the beginning and then brought a toddler on a date." He laughed. "If anything, I expected you to tell me that I wasn't even in your league."

She looked at their joined hands. Maybe she shouldn't throw away their obvious connection because she felt insecure. "Thanks. I might have overreacted a bit." She gave him a tiny smile. "But you have to remember that it's been a long time since I've met anyone I could actually see a future with. And things seemed to happen so quickly." She sighed. "I guess in my experience, things that happen fast don't always work out in the end."

"That's my bad. I was so excited to finally meet someone

like you that I jumped the gun. I know I started talking about the future way too soon. Part of that was because of the situation with Colton. And part of me wanted to hear you say you'd want to be a part of both of our lives. But I can see that it was probably too much too soon."

She nodded. "Can we take things slowly? Are you okay with that?"

Justin lifted her hand to his lips and kissed it gently. "If it means I get to have you in my life, I will move as slow as molasses."

She smiled. "Sounds perfect." She raised an eyebrow. "Although I probably wouldn't complain if you kissed me a time or two."

"I'm more than happy to oblige."

Chapter 38

Luke, wait!" Summer ran after him through the parking lot. The pouring rain soaked her clothes and plastered her hair to her face, but she didn't care. "Luke!" He'd almost made it to his truck.

He turned around. "Summer? What are you doing out here? Go back inside."

She could barely see him with the rain coming down so hard. A gust of wind sent a plastic pool float whizzing past her.

Luke grabbed something out of his truck and ran toward her. "Come on. We've got to get inside." He pointed at a building just off of the parking lot.

She ran toward the building, fighting the wind as she went. The hard rain stung her skin, and she tried to shield her face with her arms.

The Weather Channel reporter and a cameraman opened the door just as she got there.

"We're heading to the main building," the reporter said. "But this place is for authorized personnel only."

Luke came up behind her. "It's okay. She's the wedding planner."

The reporter looked at her for a minute then shrugged. "Whatever. Be careful."

The two men ran toward the hotel.

She couldn't stop the laugh from escaping her lips. "It's okay, she's the wedding planner," she mocked. "Like that means anything."

He joined in her laughter. "Use your powers for good and all that, right?" He held the door open for her. "Hurry. It looks like the storm is almost here."

She ran inside the building. "Looks like this is where they keep the beach chairs and supplies."

Luke grabbed a white pool towel from a shelf and tossed it to her. "Here."

"Thanks." She toweled off her soaking hair then wrapped the towel around her wet clothes.

Neither of them spoke for a long minute, and the only sound was of the wind and rain outside.

Finally, Summer turned to Luke. "I'm sorry," she said softly.

"You shouldn't have followed me." Luke attempted to mop up some of the water that fell around him in puddles.

Her mouth quivered. "I didn't want you to leave without hearing me out. Jefferson being here is not what it looks like. I didn't know he was going to show up, I promise."

Luke walked over to her and took the plush towel from her hands. He gently wiped her face, a mix of water and tears. "I wasn't leaving," he whispered. "Just getting a little air."

She met his gaze. "I saw you talking to Jefferson. I need to explain."

Luke lifted a beach chair from a stack and set it on the

floor. He guided her to it and motioned for her to sit. "We might be here for a while. May as well get comfortable." He sat next to her.

She swallowed, hoping the right words would come out and not the mixed-up thoughts that were rolling around in her head. "Why are you here in the first place?" she asked. While Jefferson showing up had been unexpected, Luke being here in the middle of a potential hurricane was totally out of the blue. He was supposed to be at home with Milo, boarding up their windows in case the storm hit.

He shook his head. "I came to see you. I admit, I was surprised to run into him. And I wasn't too happy to hear him insinuate that you might be falling for him again." He frowned.

"He said that?" She closed her eyes. "Ugh. I'm sorry. I can't say it enough. Nothing happened between us. I honestly thought he just wanted to be my friend. And I somehow convinced myself that a friendship would be okay, because at first he seemed genuinely concerned about you and me." She sighed. "I was an idiot not to see him for who he really is."

She'd never thought she might be one of those people who did something that could be construed as inappropriate. She was a firm believer that an emotional affair was as bad and as damaging as a physical one. And even though things hadn't gone that far with Jefferson, she could see how easy it would've been to go down that path.

To her surprise, Luke took her hand.

"You believe the best in people until they give you a reason not to. From where I sit, that's a good quality." He half smiled. "Although I could do without you thinking the best of Jefferson."

"You're not mad?"

Luke shook his head. "I was pretty upset a couple of weeks ago. I saw the two of you together at the park."

"You did?" That explained a lot. "It wasn't planned. At least on my part. Looking back, I wonder if maybe those chance meetings weren't so much chance after all." Summer sighed. "Honestly. I planned to go to Blue Bicycle Books and then over to get a cupcake. I needed a little time to decompress. I'd barely left the office, and then there he was. I sat at Marion Square while he went and got cupcakes. And of course, he insisted on staying with me and walking me back to the office." She hung her head. "He could tell how upset I was."

"I passed by there on my way to your office. I knew it was supposed to have been your due date, and I wanted to see how you were doing. But when I saw you with him, I got mad and left."

"That's why you didn't show up to the counseling appointment later that day?"

He nodded. "I know I gave you a flimsy excuse about work. But I actually went to see your grandmother instead."

She raised her eyebrows in surprise. She'd spoken to Gram on the phone that very day, and Gram hadn't mentioned Luke's visit. "Well, if it makes you feel any better, Ashley tore into me when I got back to the office. She said I was playing with fire and not even realizing it. She had Jefferson pegged all along. I guess everyone did but me."

"As far as I'm concerned, that's all over now."

Summer gripped his hand. "Thanks." She'd never expected to be in this situation. "You have to know that I never would've done anything to jeopardize our marriage. Not with Jefferson or with anyone else. I love you, Luke. And the vows I made to you are sacred."

He nodded. "I believe that. But honestly, I don't even think Jefferson is one of our problems. He doesn't have anything to do with what's been going on between us."

"I know."

"There are a lot of things I wish I'd done differently. I know I shut down on you. Not that I was ever that open to begin with."

"I should've tried harder," she said.

Luke shook his head. "I don't think there was anything you could've done. This lesson was one I had to learn on my own. I'm sorry I hurt you in the process."

"So what did you learn?" Summer knew she'd learned her own lessons over the past months, but she wanted to know what Luke had gleaned from their separation.

"The first time I went to see Daddy in the nursing home, I fell apart. I didn't know where to turn and felt like I was completely alone. Bobby's Bible was in my truck, so I picked it up and flipped through. He'd highlighted a lot of pages, so I started reading to try to calm myself down. The first one I came to was that passage in Ecclesiastes that talks about how there's a time for everything. It helped me to put things into perspective, you know?"

She nodded. Luke had struggled with his faith ever since

Bobby's accident. So for him to finally open his heart again was a big step.

"I was so selfish. I looked at all these things that had happened in my life as being things that had happened just to me," he said, pointing toward himself. "But I started to realize that I'm not the only one who was impacted. It's not all about me." He shook his head. "I might not understand why Bobby was in that accident or why you had a miscarriage. But I can accept those things now without feeling like I'm being singled out."

She squeezed his hand. "I'm glad you can accept things."

"And then I realized that I might have talked the talk, but I didn't walk the walk. I went with you to church. I prayed. I tried to do what was right. But the moment things got tough, I turned my back. I stopped praying. I stopped being the man I know I'm supposed to be." He shook his head. "I see now how foolish I've been."

She hadn't seen that honesty in his brown eyes in a long time. "I haven't been perfect either. Even before Jefferson came back to town, I'd started to pull away from you. I was exhausted. I didn't have it in me to try to fix whatever was going on with us, because I felt like I was broken myself. The miscarriage is the worst thing I've ever gone through, and I felt like you wanted me to get over it and move on. And I wasn't ready to do that." She sighed. "So I felt stuck, you know? I wasn't able to handle it the way you wanted me to, so I did nothing. I turned into this scattered, foggy version of myself."

Luke put an arm around her and pulled her close.

She sat like that for a long minute, relishing the nearness

of her husband and shutting out the storm that had been raging in their marriage. And the storm that was raging outside the door.

Luke had missed her even more than he'd realized. But he hated to hear that he'd hurt her. "I'm sorry," he murmured against her hair. "I wanted both of us to move past losing the baby because it was so painful." He pulled back from her so he could see her face. "But there hasn't been a day when I haven't grieved."

"Why didn't you share that grief with me? I felt like it was mine alone."

He rubbed his jaw. "I wanted to be strong for you. I saw how hurt you were, and I didn't want to add to that by making you watch my own pain." He shook his head. "But I guess I didn't realize how it would come across."

"Like it didn't matter."

The words stabbed him. "I think about our little boy all the time. What his laugh would've sounded like. How proud I would've been watching his first step. What he would want to be when he grew up."

"You say it like you were certain it was a boy." She looked at him curiously.

He laced his fingers through hers. "I'm pretty certain."

"How?"

He smiled. "I read this article right after we found out you were pregnant. It told how to figure out if you were having a boy or a girl. It said that when a woman is carrying a girl, she's sharing her beauty, so she's not as attractive as when she's carrying a boy. And I knew right then that you must be having a boy, because you were more beautiful than I'd ever seen or even imagined."

Tears filled her eyes. "You really thought that?"

He reached out and tenderly wiped a tear away. "I sure did. Sometimes you would literally take my breath away." His mouth turned up in a smile. "And you still do."

"Thanks," she said softly.

The wind howled outside the building.

"It's getting nasty out there," he said.

She smiled. "Good thing we're warm and dry in here."

The power flickered and went out, leaving them in total darkness.

He put his arm around her. "Are you scared?" he whispered.

She turned her face toward his. "A little. But it has nothing to do with the weather."

He pulled her to him, and his lips found hers in the darkness.

Chapter 39

Ashley paced inside the ballroom. It was the interior room and supposedly the safest. But she wasn't crazy about being there. She felt trapped.

"You okay?" Justin asked. He'd brought Milo down, and the big dog was curled up in a ball next to him.

"It's the waiting I hate. Will it hit, will it not hit? If it hits, what category will it be. . . ?" She trailed off and sighed. "The uncertainty is a pain."

"If it makes you feel any better, I talked to the weather guy a few minutes ago. He thinks we're going to dodge a bullet." He patted the floor next to him. "Sit down. Milo and I will keep you safe."

She had to admit, having him here was a comfort. She sank down onto the floor. "Thanks." A loud cackling laugh came from the other side of the wall. "Those ladies I was telling you about found a Monopoly game in the library. I guess the game is going well."

"You want to go join them?" Justin asked.

She nodded. "I think that might help take my mind off the storm. This is my first tropical storm, so I guess I'm extra nervous."

He stood up and shook his legs out. "Come on, Miles." He tugged on the dog's leash, and Milo slowly rose from his spot on the floor.

She led them into the next ballroom.

Two elderly women sat hunched over a table, a Monopoly game between them. They were glowering at each other.

"Hi, ladies," Ashley said.

One of the women stood up. She had to be close to six feet tall. Her bright orange hair, while not a color found in nature, somehow suited her. She grinned at Justin like a schoolgirl. "I'm Mavis Bunch," she said. She stuck out a manicured hand as if she were royalty.

Justin never missed a beat. He took her hand and lifted it to his lips. "Charmed to meet you, Miss Bunch. I'm Justin Sanders."

She giggled. "If I didn't love Alabama so much, I would move to Charleston just for the Southern gentlemen."

The other woman stood up and smacked her on the arm. "We have Southern gentlemen in lower Alabama." As if remembering her manners, she batted her eyes at Justin. "I'm Mary Bunch. Her sister." She motioned her head toward Mavis. "Although sometimes I think there may have been a mix-up at the hospital."

"She's my *older* sister," Mavis said with a wink.

Justin shook Mary's hand.

"Ashley from Alabama, how's the wedding planning going?" Mavis asked. They'd met yesterday as Ashley was attempting to carry an arch through the double doors. Once they found out they shared a home state, the two women had wanted to talk to her until they found someone they knew in common.

"Pretty good." She sighed. "Of course the storm might be a problem."

Mary shook her head. "Here we thought we were so smart. That Jim Cantore keeps saying that the Gulf Coast might get hit hard by the tropics this year. So we decided to come to Charleston. And now here we are right in the middle of a hurricane."

"So we have y'all to blame for this, I guess," Justin said.

Mavis giggled. "Our daddy used to say we went through the house like tornadoes. So maybe there's some truth to that."

"That's not what he said. He said we went through the house like whirlwinds," Mary chided her sister.

Mavis shrugged. "Same thing."

Justin met Ashley's eyes. She could tell he was as amused by them as she'd been yesterday.

"I've got to sit down. I've had a bad knee ever since we hiked the Grand Canyon a couple of years ago." Mary sat down, clutching her knee.

"Y'all hiked the Grand Canyon?" Justin asked.

"We sure did." Mavis wiggled her hips. "We stay in shape. I'm the oldest certified Zumba teacher in the country."

Mary groaned. "Don't encourage her. She'll have us up doing the rumba or something, and I tell you, my knee can't take it." She patted the chair next to her. "Y'all sit down. You're makin' me nervous."

Ashley, Justin, and Mavis sat down in the empty seats.

Milo collapsed into a heap on the floor.

"That is one big dog," Mavis observed. "Yours?" she asked Justin.

He shook his head. "I'm watching him for a friend."

At the mention of Luke, Ashley furrowed her brow. "Do you think they're okay?" she murmured.

"They're fine. That reporter told me they went into the pool house."

Mavis and Mary looked at them with identical quizzical expressions.

"Our friends went out into the storm earlier and haven't come back," Justin explained. "But we got word that they're safely holed up in the pool house."

Mary raised her eyebrows. "Why did they go out in the storm? That seems like a dumb thing to do."

Justin burst out laughing. "I like you. You tell it like it is, don't you?"

"Once I hit eighty, I decided it was time to stop holding back." Mary motioned at her sister. "Now Mavis has never held back. She was born telling her opinion about everything. I used to hold my tongue because I didn't want to ruffle any feathers." She shrugged. "Until I realized that holding it in was only hurting me. I used to worry and fret about things. Now I just get it off my chest and feel all kinds of better." She winked. "Of course, the trick is to speak your mind with tact."

Mavis sighed. "I have tact, too. I just forget to use it sometimes." She winked. "So, Justin and Ashley from Alabama. . . How long have the two of you been an item?"

"Don't pry into their personal business," Mary chided.

Mavis shrugged. "I'm just trying to pass the time."

"Actually, we aren't technically a couple, I don't guess," Justin said. He glanced at Ashley. "Or are we?"

She cringed. There was nothing like being put on the spot, especially in front of people she barely knew. She smiled at the women. "We haven't really had that conversation just yet."

Justin enjoyed watching Ashley squirm as she tried to explain to Mary and Mavis exactly what their relationship was.

"Do you like her?" Mary asked.

He nodded. "Very much."

Mavis turned to Ashley. "And do you like him?"

"I do." She blushed.

"Well, at least you're on the same page about that," Mary said. "Now let me give you two some advice."

"We need all the advice we can get," Ashley said.

Mary chuckled. "Well, we love to give advice. Now, the most important thing is to remember that your relationship isn't a competition. If one of you is always trying to win, it will never work."

Justin nodded. That made good sense.

Mavis patted her hands on the table. "And you can take it from me, because I was married for fifty-one years. You have to believe that you're equal partners. And don't hold back anything, even when you fight. If you're going to be partners, then be partners in every sense. Which means the good, the bad, and the ugly." She chuckled. "But try not to go too heavy on the ugly."

He glanced at Ashley across the table. He knew he didn't want to leave the resort without knowing exactly where they stood. "Ladies, it's been a pleasure," he said. "But I've got to go feed Milo and check on my family." He stood.

Ashley rose from her seat. She bent down and hugged first Mary and then Mavis.

He waved to the women and grabbed Ashley's hand as they made their way out of the ballroom.

"Do you really have to feed Milo?" she asked once they were alone in the deserted lobby.

He grinned. "Soon. But first I wanted to do this." He pulled her to him and kissed her gently.

Ashley smiled against his lips.

"Does this mean that from this day forward if someone asks us how long we've been an item, we can pinpoint now?"

She nodded. "Yes. I think that sounds like a good story. It happened in the middle of a hurricane."

"Kind of romantic." He kissed her forehead.

"Definitely." She furrowed her brow. "Do you think Luke and Summer are okay?"

Justin took her hand and led her to the couch. "Yes. I do. I hope that being forced together like this is exactly what they needed."

"Me, too," Ashley said softly.

He settled onto the couch and held her hand. The rain pounded on the roof, and the wind continued to howl, but he felt as peaceful and calm as he could remember feeling.

Chapter 40

Summer had just dozed off when she felt Luke's breath against her face.

"Summer," he whispered. "Are you sleeping?"

She lifted her head from his shoulder. "I was resting my eyes." They'd been in the dark for at least an hour, but the lights had finally come back on. The resort must have some kind of backup generator or something.

"Why are you so tired?" he asked.

"I've been working on a wedding that's kind of been thrown together at the last minute. And you know how I like stuff like that."

He laughed. "I know."

"Plus it's not really coming together because of the storm. The florist didn't deliver, the photographer canceled, and the last time I checked, the bride and groom weren't even here." She sighed. "So maybe I've been working for nothing."

He shifted on the lounger. "I think I need to tell you something."

She looked at him. "What's wrong?"

"Nothing's wrong. . . . It's just that I have a confession to make."

Her stomach tightened. Things were finally starting to smooth out between them. She wasn't sure she wanted to hear a confession.

He stood and got the large white box he'd gotten out of his truck earlier. He brought it over and set it in front of her. Then he got down on one knee.

She cocked her head to the side. "What are you doing?"

"Do you know what tomorrow is?"

She laughed. "Saturday?"

He took her hand. "Seriously. Tomorrow?"

"It's our anniversary."

He smiled broadly. "The wedding you've been planning these past weeks. The one where you had free rein to plan however you wanted? That was for us."

Her jaw dropped. "No way." She'd never suspected a thing. She smiled at him. "You wanted to renew our vows?"

"I did."

She bit her lip. "But now you don't? I don't understand."

Luke handed her the box. "First I want you to open this. It's an anniversary gift. A little more personal than a boat." He smiled.

Summer lifted the lid off of the box. The wedding gown she'd tried on at Madelyn's boutique, her *dream* gown, lay inside ensconced in white tissue paper. "Luke," she breathed. "I can't believe you did this."

"You like it?"

She felt tears spring into her eyes. He'd put so much thought into this surprise. "I love it."

"I wanted to renew our vows on our anniversary. . .but I

think I'd rather wait."

She furrowed her brow. "Why?"

Luke sat down next to her. "Summer, I meant my vows when I said them seven years ago. Till death do us part. I still feel that way today." He smiled. "So I know we don't need to have another ceremony for any reason other than symbolically. But I don't think we should renew our vows here at some resort with only a couple of friends present," he said. "And Milo."

"Milo's here?" She couldn't believe the length he'd gone to in order to make her happy.

He chuckled. "Probably giving Justin fits as we speak." He took her hand. "This time around, I want it to be different. I want our families around us. And I want to say those vows in a church."

Summer couldn't stop the tears of joy that trickled down her face. "You do?"

He nodded. "This year has taught me that we need God at the center of our marriage. And I don't want to leave Him out of the ceremony."

Just hearing Luke say those words gave her such comfort. They'd been married for seven years, most of those good years. But she couldn't help but believe that the future was going to be even better.

Luke smiled as her face lit up. "What do you say?"

"I'm speechless. You surprise me so much sometimes. I

don't guess I ever told you that my dream had always been for us to get married at St. Michael's. Did I?"

He shook his head. "No. But I started thinking about it on my way here today. I realized I'd planned the perfect surprise, but it didn't feel right. Even if the florist and the photographer had made it, I still would've asked you to wait until we can invite our families and make arrangements at a church." He reached out and stroked her smooth cheek.

Her mouth quirked into a smile. "I think it sounds amazing." She gripped his hand. "I think we're back on the right path, don't you?"

He nodded. There was one more thing he knew he had to talk to her about, and he had no idea what she would think. "I do. I know we're both committed to this marriage. And that makes all the difference." He pushed a strand of hair from her face. "But I think we need to talk about having a family."

She frowned. "Is this where you tell me that you don't think we should keep trying?"

He shook his head. "I know that's what I said before. But I didn't mean it. If you want to meet with the doctor again and see what he thinks our best bet is, then I'm on board."

"Really?" she asked.

He nodded. "You know I've always wanted a family. That hasn't changed."

"But you said. . ."

If he could go back in time and erase any conversation, it would be that one—the night he told Summer he wasn't sure if they were cut out to be parents. His own words had haunted him almost since the night he'd said them. "I know. I was so scared we would go through losing a child again. And at that point, I knew I couldn't handle it. Do you know that the reason I took the things from the nursery to the landfill instead of giving them away was because I couldn't stand the thought of another child using the stuff that had been meant for our baby?" He shook his head. "But I've had a lot of time to think about things."

"And what have you decided?"

"Our life is full of kids. Chloe's baby will be here before we know it. Katie Beth and Dale adore us. Even Colton has become part of our world. And watching Justin step in and be like a dad for Colton has made me realize that there are a ton of kids out there who need someone to care about them." He rubbed his jaw. "So yes, I want to have a baby of our own. But I'm prepared to find another way to be parents if that doesn't work out."

"Like adoption?"

He nodded. "Sure. We have that big house and plenty of money. And a lot of love to give."

Her face lit up in a smile. "That sounds amazing."

"Besides. . .I've made a decision about my music. A decision that will give me more time to devote to a family."

Her blue eyes narrowed. "What do you mean? Are you finally going to pursue music full-time?"

He chuckled. "Actually, just the opposite. The band is breaking up." He'd weighed his decision carefully and prayerfully, and in the end, he knew he was making the right choice.

"I don't understand. You love to play."

Luke nodded. "I do. I love the music. I love to write

songs." He shrugged. "But over these past few weeks I started to question why I felt the need to halfheartedly pursue music." Summer had told him more than once that she'd be behind him if he wanted to give his music another shot. But he'd always found an excuse why it wasn't a good time.

"Yeah?"

"I wanted to make something of myself. I guess I always had this idea that if I made it in Nashville as a musician or if I actually had some of my songs recorded, that would mean I was really somebody." He shrugged. "But you know what? I'm *already* somebody. And I have a great life with you. My career with the park service has gradually morphed into something I love. This fall I'll be handling all the school groups that come through, which is something I'm really excited about."

Summer beamed. "Really? That's awesome. I know you'll be great at it." She paused. "But won't you miss playing?"

"I'll still play. At home. Or we'll do a show every now and then." He shook his head. "But weekly practices and shows aren't for me. Not anymore." He raked his fingers through his hair. "Music will always be part of me. I'll always tinker with my guitar and write songs. Maybe I'll record them and put them on YouTube or something."

"So I'll still get to hear you sing, but I won't have to share you with screaming groupies?" She chuckled.

"Something like that, yes."

She glanced at the tiny window above their heads. "I think the storm has stopped, at least for now."

"Should we make a run for it and check on Milo? It's getting kind of late."

Summer leaned forward and kissed him square on the mouth. "How about we stay here for a little while longer? Just us."

He pulled her to him. "Just us," he whispered. "That sounds wonderful."

Chapter 41

Three months later

Summer took one last look at herself in the mirror. The Mori Lee wedding gown looked like it had been designed with her in mind. Madelyn had made a couple of alterations, and it was the most perfect article of clothing Summer had ever worn. She glanced at the clock on the wall. It was almost time.

It was hard to believe three months had passed since she and Luke had celebrated their anniversary. Thankfully, the hurricane had spared them. By the time the storm reached land, it had been downgraded to a tropical storm. There was a lot of wind and a lot of rain but none of the devastation that easily could have happened. They'd spent their actual anniversary at home with a low-key celebration for two.

Since the storm hit, they'd made a lot of good progress as a couple. The counselor stood behind Luke's idea to renew their vows, and Summer had gone into full wedding-planner mode. And loved every minute of it. And now, on the third Saturday in October, it was time for their vow renewal ceremony.

"You ready?" Ashley stuck her head in the door. She stopped in her tracks. "Wow. You look incredible."

Summer took in Ashley's red Grecian-style, floor-length gown. "Likewise. Justin's eyes are going to pop out when he sees you in that."

Ashley beamed. "Thanks." She walked over and stood in front of the mirror next to Summer. "Thanks for having me as your bridesmaid." She chuckled. "A few months ago, the idea of being a thirty-six-year-old bridesmaid would've had me drowning my sorrows in a bucket of Ben and Jerry's. But honestly, I'm honored to stand beside you as you renew your vows."

"It doesn't hurt that you're totally in love with the guy who'll be standing opposite you either." Summer grinned.

"That's just a bonus." Ashley returned her smile. "But do you think Britney can handle things out there?"

She thought for a second. They'd hired Britney, fresh out of college, to work as an associate at Summer Weddings. She was energetic, overly enthusiastic, and sometimes made Summer feel about eighty. But she also came with great references and so far had been an asset. "It's time for her to sink or swim, I guess." She sighed. "I officially relinquished control yesterday. Today I'm just the bride. I'm not solving any problems. Not putting out any fires with a florist or a musician. I'm focused on Luke and our vows."

"Good girl."

"Summer?" Britney whispered from the door. "Are you ready?"

"I sure am."

Britney walked in and closed the door behind her. "Everything is going smoothly so far. The church is filling up, and the music is perfect." She glanced at her watch. "In five minutes, it will be time for y'all to take your places."

"Did Luke's dad get here?" Summer asked.

Britney scrunched her face up in thought. "Is he the one in the wheelchair?"

Summer nodded.

"Yeah. I saw Luke talking to him a few minutes ago." She smiled. "By the way, I think it's very cool that y'all scheduled this so he could come."

They'd talked to Luke's daddy's doctor and had all agreed that if the ceremony was held in the morning, his daddy might be able to come. Summer was relieved to hear that Mr. Nelson was out there. She knew it meant a lot to Luke. Even if his daddy didn't remember the occasion tomorrow, Luke would remember it forever. "I'm just glad it worked out."

"And a postwedding brunch is such a fun idea," Ashley said. "You might start a trend."

Summer nodded. "Gram is excited because brunch is her favorite meal of the day. And my mom is determined to have a write-up about it in the society column."

Before she knew it, it was time. Her dad waited for her in the foyer. "Darling, you look amazing." He kissed her on the cheek. "I know you're technically already married, but it's always been a dream of mine to walk you down the aisle. I'm thankful to get this opportunity."

One of the biggest surprises of all had been how close Luke and her dad had grown. It seemed like the two of them had put their old differences aside and had become something that looked a lot like friends. And Summer had even gone on a shopping trip to Atlanta with Mom and Chloe. She'd come away realizing that even though she didn't have a ton in common with them, they could still enjoy spending time together. "Thanks, Daddy. I'm glad you're here."

Katie Beth, Dale, and Colton stood with Britney by the door. Katie Beth wore a white dress with a red ribbon tied around her waist. The little boys were in matching tuxes.

Summer knelt down to their level. "Everyone know what to do?"

"I do." Katie Beth smiled proudly. "We're going to walk down the aisle all the way to the front where Uncle Luke is standing. If we get tired, we can sit down on the front row."

"That's right, Katie Beth."

Summer walked back and took her dad's arm.

"Think they'll be okay?"

She nodded. "Katie Beth is a girl after my own heart. She's got it all under control." She chuckled. "Plus Colton and Dale know that Rose and Mrs. Sanders are on the front pew with prizes for them if they cooperate."

She watched as Britney opened the door for Ashley.

Ashley glanced back with a wink and then proceeded down the aisle.

"She's a good friend, isn't she?" Dad asked.

"Yes."

Britney knelt down and gave the little ones last-minute instructions then sent them on their way, pulling the door closed behind them.

Summer gripped Dad's arm. "I've planned what seems like hundreds of these and always chide the bride for feeling jittery.

But this is kind of nerve-racking."

He smiled. "But when you see Luke waiting at the end of the aisle, it will be worth it."

"It's time," Britney whispered. She opened the door as the "Wedding March" began.

Summer and Dad paused in the doorway. Seeing the familiar faces of family and friends made the moment so special.

Then her eyes found Luke's, and everyone else faded away. As the music swelled around her, she walked toward him. She knew this was one of those moments she'd remember forever, surrounded by her friends and family and proclaiming her love for Luke. The past year had been tough, but they'd come through stronger than ever.

And as Summer took her place next to Luke at the front of the church, she knew the next leg of their journey together would be even better than the last.

Luke could count on one hand the number of times he'd been overcome by emotion. Watching Summer walk down the aisle toward him today would go on that list. She took his breath away.

It was more than her physical beauty though. He'd known her for so long that he was well aware that she possessed much more than just looks. The way she treated people, the way she cared, the way her first instinct in any situation was to pray— those things made her so much more than just a pretty face.

He took her hand as they faced the minister.

"Luke and Summer have written their own vows," the minister said with a smile. He nodded at Luke. "Whenever you're ready."

Luke turned to face Summer and took both her hands in his.

She smiled.

He took a deep breath. "Summer, I told you a long time ago that you were the best thing that ever happened to me. And that is even truer today. Seven years ago, I pledged to love, honor, and cherish you. I promised to stand by your side through the good and the bad." He sighed. "And I know we've dealt with some difficulties over the past year. There've been things that have almost pulled us apart. But I stand here before you today promising that my love for you has never been stronger." He gave her a tiny grin. "I know I might not say it enough. But Summer, I love you. I love you more than anything."

Her lip trembled, but she returned his smile.

"A few months ago, we were trapped in the middle of a storm. Literally. And we held on to one another and made it through. I know that in our life together, other storms will come. During those times, we will need to cling to each other and to God." He paused. "From this day forward, I promise to put God at the center of our relationship. Summer, you make me want to be a better man. The kind of man you respect and the kind of man who will make our children proud. I come here today and pledge to you my love, affection, and honor as long as we both shall live." He squeezed her hands.

"Summer," the minister said with a nod to her.

She smiled. "Luke, I've known you for half of my life. In some ways, that seems like a really long time, but then there are moments when I feel like we're still seventeen and meeting up at the bandstand at the Battery." She took a breath. "The past year has tested us. There were times when I didn't know what would happen. But there was never a time when I doubted my love for you. I've always told people that I'm blessed because I'm married to my best friend. You're the first person I want to share news with, both good and bad. You're who I want to talk to about big decisions. You're the one who can make me smile even through my tears." She paused and looked deeper into his eyes. "We've both made mistakes. We've both put other things in front of our relationship. But I know in my heart that we've learned from those mistakes." A tear trickled down her face. "Over the years, I've joked that you're on my team. And I still feel that way. I choose you. Always. You are the one I want to go with on this wonderful, crazy journey called life." She smiled. "I promise to love you, honor you, and cherish you until the end of time."

The rest of the ceremony passed quickly. The minister finally said the words Luke had been waiting to hear. "Luke, you may kiss your bride."

Luke pulled her to him and gently kissed her lips.

They turned and faced the crowd and were met with applause as they walked down the aisle, arm in arm. A horse-drawn carriage waited for them out front.

He helped her into the carriage and whispered, "I love you."

She smiled. "I love you, too."

He leaned over and kissed her as the carriage began to move slowly through the streets of downtown Charleston.

"I feel like a princess." She grinned. "Thanks for letting me plan my dream wedding. It would've been just as easy for us to renew our vows right back at city hall."

He took her hand. "Nope. I wanted the world to know how we felt. No hiding this time. There's no reason to be scared someone won't approve of us."

She nodded and then glanced around. "Do you mind if we make a stop before we get to the brunch?"

"Sure."

"Thanks," she said. She leaned up to the driver. "Can you go to King Street, please?"

Luke wondered what she had in store but didn't question the detour. As long as they were together, he'd sit back and enjoy the ride.

Chapter 42

Summer took Luke's outstretched hand and let him help her out of the carriage. She turned to the driver. "This will only take a second."

"What's this about?" Luke asked.

She led him through the gates that led to the Unitarian Church Cemetery. "There's someone I need to visit."

A few moments later, they arrived at the stone bench next to the unknown child's grave. Summer glanced at Luke. "I come here sometimes to remember. Not just our baby, but all of those whose lives were cut short." She sat down on the bench.

He sat beside her. "It's a beautiful cemetery. I don't guess I've been here for years. Not since some long-ago elementary school history trip."

She slipped her hand in his. "I wandered in one day while I was on my lunch break. I found this spot and felt drawn to it." She motioned toward the headstone. "I guess it gave me a tangible place to come to in order to think about our child and to pray for healing."

"Thanks for bringing me here."

She stood. "I think it's time for me to say good-bye." She

knelt down and placed her bouquet of roses at the foot of the grave. "We can go now."

Hand in hand, they walked down the pathway that led to the cemetery gates.

"Your carriage awaits," Luke said with a wave of his hand. "I've always wanted to say that and mean it."

Summer climbed back inside the carriage, thankful for the peace she'd finally found.

"Please welcome Mr. and Mrs. Luke Nelson," Justin said from the stage.

Ashley turned from her spot at a table near the front of the room to watch a beaming Summer and Luke walk inside, holding hands. They made their way into the large banquet room and were surrounded by well-wishers. She shifted Colton in her lap.

"Do you want me to take him?" Mrs. Sanders asked, gesturing to Colton.

She smiled. "No, he's fine." She leaned forward so she could see his face. "Aren't you, sweetie?"

Colton nodded and banged his toy truck on the table.

"We're going to eat some pancakes in a minute, okay?"

"Okay."

"Is this seat taken?" Summer asked, coming over to the table and pointing at a chair.

Ashley smiled. "Please sit." She gestured around the room. "This is awesome, by the way."

"I can give you my wedding planner's card if you'd like." Summer laughed.

Ashley joined in her laughter then noticed movement on the stage. "What's he doing?" she asked.

Luke stood center stage and took the microphone from the stand.

"I have no idea," Summer confessed.

"Ladies and gentlemen, we'd like to thank you for coming today to celebrate the renewal of our vows," Luke said. "Everyone in this room is special to us, and we appreciate your prayers and support. But it wouldn't be right if we made this day totally about us." He motioned for Justin to join him. "And now I want to turn the floor over to my best man, Justin Sanders."

Ashley shot Summer a questioning look.

Summer shrugged.

"Everyone loves a wedding, don't they?" Justin asked with a smile. "But a wedding is more than a nice ceremony and pretty flowers. It's about the joining of two lives. It's about two people who are going to stand together through thick and thin." He took a breath. "And I have to confess, I've always wondered if I'd ever find someone of my own. Someone who would be my partner and my companion. Someone who would love me no matter what."

He gripped the microphone and stepped down from the stage.

Ashley watched, mesmerized, as he walked right toward her. Her heart pounded, and she clung to Colton like he was a lifeline.

Justin stopped once he reached her and dropped to one knee. "Ashley, I know it hasn't been that long since we met. But I also know that my whole life has changed for the better because of you. The moments that we spend together are the best I've ever had."

She wiped away a tear.

"I've fallen in love with you, and I can't imagine my life without you in it." He smiled. "Ashley Watson, will you marry me?"

"Yes," she whispered. "Of course." She stood and hoisted Colton to her hip.

Justin pulled both of them into his arms, and the crowd cheered.

He kissed her lightly on the lips. "I'm going to make you so happy," he whispered.

"You already have." She smiled.

He headed back to the stage and put the microphone back on the stand.

Summer walked over, a huge smile on her face. "Congratulations."

"Did you know?"

Summer shrugged. "I suspected. Luke told me that there would be a couple of surprises."

"A couple? I wonder what the other one is."

Summer nodded toward the stage. "I'm thinking this might be it."

Justin, Luke, Jimmy, and Will were on the stage gearing up to play.

"I didn't know they were playing." Ashley was surprised

Justin hadn't mentioned it.

"Me neither."

Luke tapped the microphone. "There's one more thing I need to do today." He smiled broadly. "I started writing this song when I was seventeen but didn't finish it until recently," he explained as he strummed his guitar. "This one is dedicated to my beautiful Summer Girl."

Summer gasped. "I don't believe it."

The opening chords of an unfamiliar song filled the room.

Ashley glanced over at Summer. Tears flowed down her face as she listened to the song written just for her. She hugged Colton and glanced down at the beautiful ring Justin had slipped on her finger.

There was a time when she would've been wary because everything was going too well. She would've been expecting something to happen to mess it up.

But today, all she felt was joy. She'd been given a second chance at happiness, and even though life wouldn't always be perfect, she was surrounded by people who cared about her and who would always stand by her.

The Lord had blessed her with a beautiful life, and she wasn't going to miss another minute of it worrying.

Annalisa Daughety, a graduate of Freed-Hardeman University, writes contemporary fiction set in historic locations. *A Wedding to Remember in Charleston, South Carolina*, is her seventh novel. Annalisa lives in Arkansas with two spoiled dogs and is hard at work on her next book. She loves to connect with her readers through social media sites like Facebook and Twitter. More information about Annalisa can be found at her website, www.annalisadaughety.com.